ESCAPE TO THE STARS

An Adventure of Christian Drake and the Unintentional Space Pirates

ESCAPE TO THE STARS

An Adventure of Christian Drake and the Unintentional Space Pirates

By Mark T. Sneed

ISBN: 9781736669846

Table Of content

DEDICATION

To my mother, family and friends who continue to inspire, encourage and challenge me to be a better person.

THANK YOU

To the various dreamers that look to the stars and continue to dream despite those which seem to live to kill dreams. Hold onto to those dreams. Aim for the sky, because even if you fail you will have at least seen the stars. Know that the lack of resources, equipment and education does not limit your dreams.

We carry our future in the hurts and injustices which have brought us thus far. Our scars and imperfections are marks of experience and dignity.

ESCAPE TO THE STARS

An Adventure of Christian Drake and the Unintentional Space Pirates

By Mark T. Sneed

Chapter 1

The USS *Indomitable* (A-1947) was the workhorse spaceship of the Galactic Force. It was a hearty ship which cut the travel time from one end of the galaxy to the other by nearly seventy percent. This space carrier was one of the largest at 950 feet long, 160 feet wide and nearly 200 feet high. The A-1947 possessed eight patent-pending Boeing/Lockheed Martin antimatter-powered motors, which were twelve feet tall and nearly thirty feet long, moving the gargantuan beast of a space carrier through space at near lightspeed.

The unique combination of highly accelerated antimatter-powered propulsion was the standard means of locomotion in the Milky Way and had saved the initial 144,000 people who had escaped to the stars as Earth imploded. The acceleration of antimatter had been science fiction until Trevor Nelson, a high school science teacher, and the Cal Tech team proved it was feasible. The propulsion system was created at Boeing and the rest is history, as they say.

Prior to the antimatter-powered propulsion travel to the mammoth planets from Earth would have taken three years. With the antimatter-powered propulsion the same trip from Earth to Saturn was now three months. On an interstellar jump from one end of the galaxy to the other there were always two captains and two space teams assigned.

There were other forms of accelerated space travel used but the quick antimatter-powered propulsion engine was what most spacecrafts used throughout the galaxy, thanks to the innovations of a team of NASA scientists and public and private high school science teachers. The innovation had shrunk the Milky Way and exponentially enlarged the knowledge of the once vast galaxy.

The three-story USS *Indomitable* was equipped with a state-of-the-art AI and manned by a talented crew of Galactic Force pilots and engineers. The AI was the brains of the A-1947. The crew were the human fail-safes. Both were tasked with patrolling the galaxy.

Four pilots were always awake on galactic trips from Venus, past the ruins of Earth to the promising red planet, and through the asteroid belt, past Jupiter—where the 50,000 residents of *The*

Wanderer orbited—past *The Arc*, the large satellite housing nearly 74,000 of Earth's refugees. Past Jupiter and twenty miles above Saturn also orbited the Galactic Force HQ, *Sentinel*. A month away from Saturn was Uranus where Russian satellites orbited. The JAXA satellites were there as well and Neptune found it home to the satellites of China and India. The one-time planetary body was the furthest reaches of the Milky Way or had been until Rigo-C had been found in the Kuiper Belt. Pluto sat alone, unimportant in space. Yet few ventured to the outer edges of the Milky Way.

Captain Alfred Page, twenty-three, studied the star map and the planet projection on the two screens just above his eyeline. In the corner of the screens were two clocks. One clock was running a countdown until the scheduled shift change. The second clock read the number of hours Page and his crew had been on duty. There was a regulated twelve hours on, and twelve hours off which the military physicians enforced. Pilots were expected to control the spacecraft they were on for sixty solar hours before they were given twenty-four hours to rest and recover. Page, tall and angular, sat in the middle of the bridge of the *Indomitable* and studied the two pilots at the helm of the A-1947. Page smiled mirthlessly at the back of his pear-shaped pilot, who was typing in something on her console.

Lisa Milton, seventeen, with natural curly, brown hair combed into a brown bloom above her rounded shoulders, studied the observation deck's expanded porthole of the bridge and the four screens above her eyesight like a chess player. "We are just ninety minutes from falling into flat and stable orbit, Captain," Milton stated.

Next to Milton sat the clean-shaven, blonde-haired, pompadour wearing, eighteen-year-old Charlie Markham, the navigator. He was a long-faced teen with bushy eyebrows and a sour expression. He turned stiffly to the captain and spoke. "Bringing the teams online now, Captain," Markham announced.

Alfred Page acknowledged Milton and Markham's announcements. According to his recollection the landing team would drop to Rigo-C in about four or five hours after his shift. Page hoped to be sleeping by then.

5

"Okay, team, we should be seeing our replacements in a minute or two. We will be resting while the fireworks take place on Rigo-C." Page smiled despite the reality of their on and off schedule.

The crew at the helm of the A Class-1947 buoyed at the news. They had been on duty, on and off, for three hundred and sixty hours to arrive at Rigo-C from *Sentinel*.

The freshly assigned second team of Eddy King, average build and with a steely gaze, and Rhonda Anderson, the girl who looked like she should be still studying high school English, appeared on the bridge dressed in flight grays. Captains Page and King saluted one another. They were both in their early thirties.

"Good to see you, Eddy."

"As you, Al. Anything I need to know?"

"No. Always like sleepwalking, jumping from one point to another." Alfred Page smiled, and added, "Your timing is impeccable. Should be swinging into orbit in less than ninety and the first fireteam has been awakened," Alfred Page said with a shake of his round head.

Eddy King, who had logged nearly 25,000 hours on the A Class-1947 interstellar transport, took command of the *Indomitable*. He nodded.

Page hovered. "Martin is monitoring," he added.

Rhonda Anderson saluted the captain as well. As the two captains exchanged key documents and binders and saluted, Rhonda Anderson walked to her contemporary's station and stood at ease.

Lisa Milton, upon seeing Rhonda Anderson, climbed out of her seat and gave it up to the wunderkind. Milton was a full foot taller than the younger co-pilot. The two co-pilots exchanged a cold and icy stare.

"We are in retro descent to a smooth and steady orbit above the planet," Milton explained to Anderson. Rhonda Anderson smiled mirthlessly and nodded, silently noting all the computations the co-pilot she was relieving had done. The younger co-pilot stood smiling but not moving into the empty seat or talking.

"Any questions?"

"No, I think I'm fine," Rhonda Anderson replied.

Milton narrowed her eyes at the girl who was two years younger than her and turned on her heels to leave. Anderson watched Milton leave.

The third member of the replacement team, the designated navigator, was Jack Whittaker. The handsome nineteen-year-old navigator appeared on the bridge dressed like the others from his team. He was a square-faced, with a head full of brown curls and aquiline nose and thin lips. He looked like he should be a cartoon hero more than the navigator of an A Class spacecraft.

Whittaker slipped past the captain and nearly ran down Milton as he bounded to his empty navigator's seat. Milton smiled at the near accident and continued toward the bridge elevator where her team was waiting.

Whittaker sat down and did a cursory check of the instruments to make sure they were on course. After the senior officer was far enough away Anderson removed sanitary wipes and wiped down the seat Milton had been sitting in. Whittaker watched Anderson out of the corner of his eye with a slight smirk. Anderson satisfied with her cleaning took her seat. For the next ninety seconds Anderson did a strict and detailed cleaning of the navigation center she would occupy.

"Why are you such a freak, Anderson?" Whittaker joked, sitting in his seat and studying his video monitors for any anomalies.

"I'm not a freak. I just believe in an extreme prophylactic cleaning of surfaces others have encountered that I will be touching as well."

Whittaker just smiled and shook his head.

"Everyone has peculiarities," Anderson spelled out to Whittaker, never looking at him directly.

"Freak," Whittaker said under his breath.

Markham and Milton left the command center.

Yvette Murray, the science officer, appeared on deck. Murray was a petite beauty who looked like a human elf, minus the pointy ears. She had almond-shaped green eyes, a straight nose, full lips and perfectly symmetrical features. Though she was only five foot three inches tall she did not appear incredibly small.

"Yvette, take care of my ship while I'm gone," Captain Page smiled coyly at the attractive science officer.

Murray smiled broadly, revealing a dimple on her left cheek. She did not speak. There was nothing to say to the retreating Page. Murray smiled at the request, watching Page climb into the ship's elevator and disappear.

The elvish Murray turned back to the bridge and took in the skeleton crew who oversaw the *Indomitable*. She bit her lower lip and looked back at the planet coming into view. At any time, Murray calculated, there were just half of the crew awake. For its grand scale, the *Indomitable* was run by no more than half a dozen personnel. Only the most essential were online.

The science officer was online one hundred and forty-four hours a week while the *Indomitable* traveled from one side of the galaxy to the other. Murray looked up and noted the half dozen new readings on her monitor. There were fireteams coming online.

Murray typed in a request to Athena. The message was simple and clear: *Monitor all vitals and keep me informed of any anomalies. Reference based on base standards.*

Athena wrote back: *Roger.* It, Athena, was on every screen on the bridge as a solid green light in the lower right corner of each monitor. It monitored every computer, system and processor on the ship and yet was programmed to give a modicum of privacy when crew members were having personal encounters.

Murray took a deep breath and stood. Before she could convince herself otherwise, she left her station and walked the short distance to the captain's chair. She stopped and found she had no idea of what to do with her hands.

The science officer looked left and right to see who was watching her. The skeleton crew were busy at their consoles. The only person watching her was the senior security officer, Ballmer. Ballmer was a stocky, no neck, thick-biceped character dressed in dark blue security gear. On his hip was a stun gun. Hanging from his belt were plastic restraints.

Murray smiled uneasily at the man tasked to protect the bridge. She turned and looked around the bridge. Ballmer took a step toward Murray. The ten-year veteran, Eddy King, sat and studied the screens overhead. King looked at the science officer.

Murray was caught in the sheer expanse afforded her from the curved bridge view. All around them was darkness. In the furthest reaches were pinpricks of light. Just beneath the panoramic view was the hint of Rigo-C. The view was phenomenal.

"Murray, what can I do for you?"

Murray blinked and found the captain of the *Indomitable* looking at her curiously. In the background, she noted Ballmer moving toward them with a determined look on his face.

"Captain, if you don't mind, may I make a request to go down to Rigo-C with the marines? I have never been on a planet's surface and think that it would be such a great opportunity to see this newest planet even if we cannot maintain it."

King studied Murray for a long moment. He looked back in the direction Murray was looking and saw Ballmer. King gestured and Ballmer stopped. King gestured again and the security officer returned to his post on the other side of the bridge, steadily watching for any trouble.

"Murray, we don't usually send essential personnel to the surface," King said, turning and studying the petite brunette science officer dressed in her grays. "You know the enlisted can be an unsavory lot."

Whittaker, hearing the conversation leaned in, with a smirk. "You want to go down there? This is the wrong place to go for a field trip," Whittaker said. "Scientists are missing. Scientists have been attacked. This is no rock collecting mission."

King looked at Whittaker and the navigator fell silent.

"The landing party is a hard bunch, Murray." The captain pinched his thin lips together. "They can be a hard bunch. They won't hold your hand."

Murray smirked. The science officer knew the enlisted were a dark and sometimes dangerous mix of nationalities she had seen from a distance, but never feared. The landing party would be fine under the control of lieutenant Shepherd, Murray reassured herself. He was a tough and fair man. He had been in the Galactic Force for nearly half a decade.

9

"There's Shepherd and the Sarge," Murray pointed out.

"Just want you to know, you get down there and we aren't going to send a shuttle until the mission is over. You understand that Murray?"

"Well, I figured as much."

King seemed amused at the idea. "I'm not thinking we will have any scientific questions until the teams come back. So, I think that if you can convince Shepherd then you can hitch a ride." King paused and looked at the elvish girl skeptically. "You aren't going to be armed, are you?"

Murray giggled in response.

King nodded. That was all the conversation Murray needed. She was already thinking what she might need to survive for seven days on Rigo-C.

"Captain, we should be entering orbit soon," Anderson pointed out. "As we are planning on a ten-day orbit, I have calculated our optimal orbit and fuel burn. Based on the op specs and our present position we will be in optimal position in fifty minutes, give or take," Rhonda Anderson mentioned from her station.

King nodded to Anderson. "Pass that information onto Shepherd," the captain mentioned. "Whittaker, how are fuel and supplies?"

"All systems are in the green," Whitaker frowned. "The fuel looks good. No alerts, Captain. As far as supplies, based on the reports I am reading we have more than enough to orbit and get us back to base with everyone happy."

Captain King nodded. He was a taciturn individual. He always seemed to be reflecting on something weighty.

"All right. Now that we have that out of the way, we are going to be down a science officer," King looked to Murray who was exiting the bridge. "We have three hundred and sixty hours scheduled on this op. Whittaker you will fill in for Murray. Also, I have recruited Brewster and March to take the shuttle down to the planet. Oh, Murray, check in with Brewster too. It's just a slingshot drop and return to the *Indomitable*. Shouldn't be an issue." The Captain said.

"While the fireteams are on the surface, we are just maintaining orbit. We sit and spin for two hundred and forty hours before Brewster and March return and scoop the teams and we return to the *Sentinel*. So, just be icy and do everything by the books," Captain King announced to his team from the bridge. The captain looked around for Murray, but she had vanished.

Chapter 2

One floor below the bridge, the hyper sleep chambers were monitored by Athena and kept at industry standard. The Alpha squad were alerted and slowly brought out of hyper sleep. Alpha squad was the first of four fireteams to be awakened. The four team members opened their eyes five hours from shuttle drop to Rigo-C. The members climbed out of their hyper sleep chambers.

"Alpha fireteam one hundred percent reactivated," blinked in front of the thin and serious First Lieutenant.

The First Lieutenant, Jason Shepherd, was dressed in MARPAT desert camouflage. Over his heart was his name patch. He was tall and thin and serious. On his hip was a gun belt. From the holster there was the blued crosshatched handle of his service revolver.

Beside the unmoving First Lieutenant stood Corporal Michael Payne. Payne was eighteen, thin, lanky and titchy faced. Payne was dressed and in the standard desert MARPAT utilities as the three marines stirred and awoke. He wore a thick gun belt, and on his hip hung a black-handled pistol. He wore his peaked cap low above his dark eyes.

The only non-military person in the hyper sleep chamber was the *Indomitable's* doctor, Martin. The diamond-faced man with short, cropped brown hair and dark oval eyes stood dressed in black pants, black comfortable boots and a white top with a big red cross on the front and back. He was a quiet observer.

"Payne, you have this," Shepherd said.

Payne nodded.

The First Lieutenant nodded and walked out of the hyper sleep chamber. "We muster at 0900," the man said as he left. "Cargo hold."

The sarge, Wyatt Brin, was a gruff, hard as nails, by the book block of scarred stone. He watched the LT leave the hyper sleep chamber, leaving Sarge with Payne.

"What you thinking, Payne? How long we on the rock before they decide we ain't babysitters?"

12

He was a blockish man with thin eyebrows and thin brown eyes. Sarge was old compared to most in the Galactic Force at twenty-five, bald and muscular. He looked like an old school TV wrestler and someone comfortable with hand-to-hand fighting. Sarge had a thin knife-like scar running through his right eyebrow an inch up to his flat, wrinkled forehead. On Sarge's hip was his service pistol.

"Can't say," Payne said. "You know the quickest way to being wrong is trying to outguess the force."

Brin nodded. He watched the hyper sleep chambers for his men. Brin, though tough, cared about his men.

The first person the fireteam saw was their mustached Sarge dressed in MARPAT desert camouflage utilities and peaked utilities cap, scowling at them as they climbed out of their pods. Sarge stood with his arms akimbo. On his camouflage shoulders were the distinctive three stripes that denoted his rank and nickname.

The first marine out of the hyper sleep chamber was the slender and slightly handsome, brown-skinned Christian Drake. He had skinny arms, a bit of a muffin top and long legs. He was wearing a lightweight white union suit which harkened back to an age when men wore bathing suits that looked like loose fitting wrestling unitards. Drake moved languidly, still shaking off the three-month sleep. He looked as if he could have been a track or soccer athlete if he weren't hurtling across the galaxy.

The second marine out of the sleeping chamber was Benjamin Young, the medic. He donned his combat glasses and tried to allow his body to adjust to the steady movement of the spacecraft. Young reached out and held onto the side of the hyper sleep chamber for stability.

The last marine of the fireteam to climb out of the hyper sleep chamber was the shortest and stockiest member of Alpha squad, Carter Foley. Foley was a round-headed individual of sixteen dressed like the others in their skivvies. He had big cheeks and a round face. Foley stood only to sit on the edge of the hyper sleep chamber for a moment. His brown eyes studied the chamber he and his squad had entered four thousand three hundred and twenty hours ago. They had been in hyperdrive for four thousand, two

13

hundred and seventy-two hours to slingshot them from the *Sentinel* to the far side of the Milky Way Galaxy.

"Man, I hate hyper sleep," Foley said, rubbing at his eyes. Young massaged the back of his neck and nodded to Foley.

"Where are we Sarge?" Drake asked as he moved on wobbly legs toward the motionless sarge.

"Two minutes from nowhere and just a mercury jump from no one cares or gives a whiff," Sarge snarled in his gravelly bass voice.

Drake, the company mechanic nodded, continuing to rub the back of his neck, dressed in his Galactic Force skivvies. In the hyper sleep chambers, the LT was the first to awake. Then it would be Payne. The sarge was third, Drake remembered Payne telling him the order of the first op they had been on. The LT was probably somewhere getting mission details, Drake imagined.

"We got a job to do, boys. We shuttle and drop in five hours. Get up and muster. The rest of the, Lions of Apedemak will be online in the next half hour," Sarge added, pointing toward the exit of the hyper sleep chamber.

The three marines moved toward the corporal and the exit.

"Morning, Alpha squad," Payne announced. "Hit the head, shower and muster in the mess for an informal op sit. We will meet in the cargo hold with our top at 0900," the corporal announced.

Young leaned against one of the hyper sleep control banks. The three marines just tried to stabilize. Corporal Payne frowned. Martin, the doctor, stepped toward Payne.

"They should be fine in a few minutes," Martin said.

"Get out of my hyper sleep chamber," Sarge snapped. "Get some water on those offensive bodies, quick, fast and in a hurry," Sarge sneered. "Get moving. Get cleaned up and get some food in you. We're meeting up at 0900 hours. We are face to face with the top at 0900 hours. Cargo hold. Move it. Move it. Move it. That's two hours." With his grumbling the three were suddenly moving faster in the direction of the exit.

Foley and Drake bumped into each other in their groggy state as they attempted to exit. Foley moaned and Drake ricocheted off the other marine and bounced off Young before stopping near the doorway. Young pushed Drake out of the way. The medic was the first

14

to leave the hyper sleep chamber. Foley and Drake blinked and attempted to focus. Foley rubbed at his eyes. Drake looked left and right and fell in line behind Foley.

As Galactic marines they knew the layout of every A Class spaceship was the same. The three marines moved as if sleepwalking. They walked down the hall from the hyper sleep chamber to the locker room. The hyper sleep chamber was central to the design of the ship. On one side of the hyper sleep chamber were the locker rooms and a short walk from the locker rooms were the bunks.

The three groggy marines found the locker room where the rest of the fireteams would assemble. The locker room was sizeable. A dozen men could dress comfortably in the locker area. The marines opened their lockers and found their uniforms and personals they had stored before hyper sleep.

"Do we get paid for hyper sleep?" Foley asked pulling his toiletry bag out of his locker.

"You better believe it," said Drake. "They tried to say that we didn't deserve to be paid if we were not conscious or something. The Marine Parents jumped all over that."

"Yeah, they cannot mess with a Marine Parent," Young said with a shake of his head.

Each marine had a toiletry kit which included toothbrush, toothpaste, shaving materials and all other essentials. Foley and Young gathered their toiletry kits and headed back through the locker rooms and to the showers, grabbing towels from the benches on their way.

Young was well defined, tall, bronze, muscled, almost chiseled for an eighteen-year-old medic. Stripped down to his birthday suit Young did not have any tattoos or scars. He was a brooding and far too serious medic who took his job of saving lives seriously. Young was the first to head for the showers. He walked naked from the locker room carrying his toiletry kit and wearing shower clogs.

"You good?"

"Yeah, I'll be there in a minute," Drake answered looking at his wrist monitor. Foley nodded and exited.

15

Foley stripped off his skivvies and followed a few seconds behind Young. He had his towel, toiletry bag and shower clogs. Foley was near the exit of the bunk room when he stopped. He looked back at Drake, curious.

"You sure?"

"Yeah, I'm right behind you," Drake said.

Foley nodded and walked toward the showers.

The company mechanic studied his wrist monitor. On the screen was the announcement of hundred plus messages. He grinned from ear to ear at the notification. In a fourth of a year, he had only hundred plus messages. Of the hundred plus messages, Drake wondered, how many were personal? At eighteen, Drake did not have many friends. He had joined the military right out of the education facility matriculation at fifteen. In three years, he had become an E-2. Foley was an E-1. Young was an E-3.

Drake grabbed his toiletry kit and his ditty bag and walked into the bunk room. There he looked at the ten bunk beds screwed to the floor. He looked around the empty room and threw his ditty bag on one of the bunk beds. Drake paused and looked to the rear of the bunk room. At the end was an office where Sarge would sleep.

Three years in the Galactic Force had seen him travel to all nine planets in the galaxy. Drake and the Lions of Apedemak were a division of the Galactic Force called: Retrieve and Reclaim. When they were called, they were retrieving something important to the Galactic Force, or reclaiming it. Drake and Foley liked to call themselves the marine repo men.

In three years, and over twenty-six thousand hours, he had been a marine and gone from one end of the Milky Way to the other. Retrieval and Reclaim had navigated the asteroid belt between Mars and Jupiter searching for lost A Class, B and C Class spaceships.

In that asteroid belt, the marines got a look at the newest threat in space, space pirates. Space pirates were amateur treasure hunters. They were opportunistic thieves. They were highway men in space stripping abandoned spaceships and dismantling satellites if the opportunity presented itself. Unlike the space marines, space pirates were without training and ethics. They were motivated mainly on quick financial gains. For the Galactic Force, they did not consider the space pirates a threat any more than a gnat is a threat to a lion.

All the marines read the rising number of millionaires who labelled themselves as space pirates but no one in the Galactic Force imagined it anything to be concerned about. Most in space were millionaires, generally and there was a belief those millionaires wanted to be seen as bad boys for whatever reason.

The billionaire space pirates, the upper echelon of wealth, were few and far between. Billionaires did not generally risk their riches. They were safe and protected by the Interstellar Committee.

Yet, there was one billionaire who had risked it all and become one of the biggest space pirate treasure hunters. Drake knew of Gregory Scott, an international criminal on Earth who financed a startup company and somehow found himself in space. Scott had climbed into space on the backs of his tech startup. Once there, Scott had brought together a crew of criminals who rivaled the pirates of history.

His first billion came from the discovery of an asteroid which was worth three trillion dollars to the Interstellar Committee for its rare minerals. The criminal Scott became a billionaire treasure hunting hero.

All the pirates were criminals. They flew in stolen or auctioned declassified and unsanctioned C Class or lower spacecrafts. Yet, there were rumors of some pirates liberating B Class spacecraft.

Drake knew all the pirate rumors, but he did not put much stock in the claims. In the three years he had been a Galactic Force marine, he had never to come face-to-face with a space pirate. He figured most of the stories were told to keep people in line.

The belief was that in the four sectors of the Milky Way, the Galactic Force was meant for bigger issues. The smaller issues, in those sectors, good or bad, were given to local law enforcement. The Galactic Force only got involved when it was important to the Interstellar Committee or the Galactic Force itself. Every other incident was given a wide berth.

Yet, it was a discovery in the Edgeworth-Kuiper Belt which reinvigorated deep space exploration. The Kuiper Belt sat on the other side of Neptune had been thought to be populated with asteroids, comets and other small bodies made mostly of ice. But unexpectedly, Carlisle Rigo came across an undiscovered anomaly, Rigo-C, which had been hidden in the shadows of the debris field. Sitting in the Kuiper Belt, Rigo-C was touted as the first new planet in the Milky Way galaxy in over 300 years.

Of course, every space explorer wanted to find and land on Rigo-C. Space was the newest land grab, Drake learned. The discovery of Rigo-C had put the Galactic Force into motion. They sent a scouting team out to determine Rigo-C's habitability. Several probes landed there, and the atmosphere seemed suitable for human life. There were seasons. There were life forms.

The next phase of the exploration was a manned probe. Scientists volunteered and landed. They did their experiments. They built a small settlement. Then things went bad. The dozen scientists had not reported in. Their communications went silent. There was little to be done from Saturn.

Drake and the Lions of Apedemak were now being sent to retrieve the equipment and locate the missing scientists.

Drake sat on his bunk and looked around before fishing out something inside his toilet kit. He removed a folded 3x5 picture. The old, printed picture was of Drake's family, captured on a holiday. His mother, smiled broadly and wearing a bright green dress, stood in the middle of the picture. On either side of Drake's mother were her four children. To the left was Daphne, six, and Michelle, eight. On the right of his mother, stood his brother, Thomas, eleven. He was closest to Drake and his father. Drake flipped over the picture and noted he was nine in the picture. His father, a banana skinned man with a handlebar moustache and dark eyes was dressed in a collared red shirt poking out of a green V-neck sweater. In the background there was a table set for dinner with candles on it.

"Miss you family," Drake intoned. Drake twisted his lips on his brown face. He reached up and kissed his pointer and middle fingers and transferred the kiss to the picture. He refolded the Polaroid and slipped it back into the toiletry kit.

He stood up and studied his wrist monitor. Drake tapped the screen and scrolled through the data he had not seen in nearly a fourth of a year. Surprisingly, there were not as many messages as he expected. Of the messages, there were sixty-five messages from the military about deployment, volunteerism, testing, potential financial opportunities and general missives about esprit de corps. There were thirty messages Drake considered personal. Of those thirty only a handful mattered.

Thomas, his older brother, who was living on *The Arc* sent a short video. "I am so proud of you little brother. I would have done the same mission had I not been disqualified because of my low oxygen capacity. Take names and kick ass. [A thirty second pause.] Listen to some killer music and do those alien [censored] to hell and back."

His older sister, Michelle, sent two videos and wrote one messages. "Just wanted to send this to you to keep your spirits up. We know you are on a long mission to the far side of the galaxy. They say when you return the world will have changed. You need to know we love you and know that what you are doing is important. Thank you for your service."

The second video featured Nyiesha, his niece. "Hey uncle Chris, just wanted to say I love you. Stay safe. Come back soon. Hope to see you for my birthday." Michelle smiled and shook her head at her daughter. "Chris, you be careful," Michelle said, ever the older sister. "Don't do anything stupid. Follow instructions. Keep your head down. Don't be a hero." She paused. "Be a hero if you have to. Know you want to do something important with your life. Love you, bro."

There was also a message from Nyiesha. It was handwritten and had an image of her, her mother, her father and Drake. "Uncle Chris, I love you" was scrawled in her childlike handwriting on top of her message.

Daphne, his younger sister, had sent three videos. Daphne's first two messages were short and emotionless, about her family's support of his mission. "The Galactic office contacted us today to tell us as much as they could about the current mission, you're on. We were informed that you are heading to rescue scientists. The office also asked us to send you a video message of encouragement. I will be uploading a video soon."

The third message from Daphne was a warning: "Chris, be careful. I know that you are a fighter. You have always liked to fight.

19

So, don't let fighting getting you in trouble. Some fights are not worth the effort. Be careful, little brother. Things are not always what we believe or see.

"I've been reading this book, about these kids that learn the world they live in is a lie. A friend of mine picked it. I think you might remember her, Bella? She has always been so smart.

"I asked her why she picked the book. She just said that she heard something about it. She loves to read.

"Anyway, next time I think about it I'll send it to you. Don't know how much time you have to read? Nyiesha is calling. I love that little girl. She sometimes sits and looks out of the window and in those still moments she reminds me of you.

"Do you remember when we would sneak to mom's room and listen to her old MP3s? We would sit and listen to all those old songs and laugh. Those were good memories. Remember the first time you and I heard Michael Jackson? Or Marvin Gaye? Or GAP Band? Do you remember my favorite song? I used to play it all the time. I think I played it for a week straight after hearing it. Well, if you think about it and remember it, think about me back here listening to it and waiting for you to come home safely. There are all these things that come to mind as you head to the far end of the galaxy.

"I'm stupid. I mean here I am on *The Arc* and worried about you. I got enough to worry about. If you get a chance and you find that song listen to it. It may give you peace. When you hear it think of us." Daphne leaned into the camera and raised a peace symbol and made a duck face and signed off.

Drake smiled at the video. He turned off the monitor and got to his feet. He wracked his brain for the song his sister mentioned. He could not recall which song they listened to that mattered enough for Daphne to talk about. The last message flummoxed Drake.

From his toiletry kit he retrieved one of his ear buds. Drake placed it in his right ear and tapped it. Instantly, music oozed from the ear bud into Drake's ear. He listened to the first five minutes of three hours of music compiled for his personal soundtrack. The sound of Boogie Down Production played in his ear. Drake beamed at the saxophone and the KRS-One delivery. It was so amazing that Drake could go back in time when the music played in his ears.

20

He listened to KRS-One and could not help but smile. The marine stripped off his skivvies and headed to the showers. Walking through the locker room Drake absently counted the twenty-four lockers and noted there were only four lockers in use. The other fireteams had yet to be awakened, Drake assumed. He paused and smiled at the idea of more marines on the mission.

The showers were a dozen stalls, each equipped with multifunctional shower heads and soap dispensers. Drake stepped into the shower, and turned on the water, to let the water heat up.

"What's the op?" Foley asked from the sink, towel around his waist. He was of average build and height for a sixteen-year-old. From the shower, Drake noted the wicked scar on Foley's shoulder.

"Retrieve and reclaim," said Drake answering Foley's question and beginning to scrub himself from head to toe. He was methodical. The stream of water from the shower head felt good on his body. He looked down and watched the soap slough off his shiny, mouse-brown body.

He stepped out of the shower buck naked. He was a tall, ropy and long limbed. Drake the boy had been transformed from a scared whelp to a battle scarred marine. He stood in front of the mirror and noted the scars he had picked up during his three years in the Galactic Force.

Christian Drake had been sixteen and a grunt when he began his first tour. He had a cut on his chin from misjudging a step down out of a carrier. Under his right eye there was small scar in the shape of a smile. He had been unfocused and was hit under his eye by a pen thrown to him by Williams, one of the R&R team. There was a scar on his left shoulder from carrying his rifle incorrectly. On his right ear he had a cut from allowing Young to cut his hair. It was also the reason his head was shaven as well. In the center of his forehead there was a small depression where he had been hit in the head with a soup can while waiting for dust off.

As he dried, he walked in front of a thick, expanded porthole which looked out into the dark and vastness of space. Stars blinked as if on a curtain beneath the wide porthole of the transport the crew was on. Drake paused and rubbed the back of his shaved head and admired his hairless face.

He was less than one hundred hours away from his nineteenth birthday on the current mission. He smirked at his reflection in the circular porthole, unable to see anything but space and stars. He had signed up just three years ago, when he was still on *The Arc*. In one tour, Drake had logged nearly twenty-seven thousand hours of service. He had less than nine thousand hours to consider his next step.

In fifteen-hundred-and-sixty-hours Drake would be given a mandatory seven-hundred-and-twenty-hour rest before deciding on doing a fourth tour.

The closest Earth settlement was six hundred hours away from the ass end of the Milky Way where he was presently. The Kuiper Belt was at the farthest reaches of the Milky Way.

He rounded the sinks and stopped at the far side of them and looked in the mirror at his only tattoo. On his right shoulder was the squad insignia for the fearless Nubian Lightning Squad of the Lions of Apedemak. The lion roared and bared its fangs as it lifted one paw to destroy the enemies in front of it. In the background the lion was emerging from a circle of fire. A triangle sat in the midst of the geometric shape.

"I know we're going to Rigo-C," Foley chirped with a slight hesitation. He added, tentatively, "But is that all? Is that the mission?"

Drake did not speak. Young only rolled his eyes. Foley looked at Young and Drake.

"Well, the only thing I figure is that there's some dick measuring going on by one of the programs," Foley smiled mischievously. "That's why they're sending us in." He was brushing his teeth meticulously. Foley had a Lions of Apedemak tattoo on his shoulder as well.

"Ain't that always why they send us?" Drake said at the sink.

"You're wrong. From what I can surmise, we are heading there to retrieve the power plant, but we need to take it offline and then bring it back," Young announced. Young adjusted his prescription space goggles. He had his towel wrapped around his small waist. He was picking his hair into his mushroom of black curls.

"That's why we're going there?" Foley looked surprised. "Don't have no other real reason?"

Drake was drying his back with his towel. Absently, he thought about the sixty plus messages he had scrolled over on his monitor. The Galactic Force was always talking about space pirates, international and interstellar land grabs and attempts by nations to claim sovereignty of planets even though it was against the international Space Committee treaty. He thought back and recalled that the name Rigo-C held significance. Rigo-C was supposed to be the first known planet that holds alien life. The Galactic Force marine imagined they were going to Rigo-C for what Young said, but there was always another reason. The big wigs were always three or four steps ahead of everyone else. Drake smirked at the idea of the Galactic Force commissars and their ulterior motives.

"I thought we were going because they discovered aliens?" Foley joked.

"If there's aliens on the planet I ain't heard that. They got others to deal with aliens. We just retrieve and reclaim," Young said.

"I didn't sign up to be a part of a zoo collection detail," Drake complained.

"We going to this rock to pick up a power plant," Young said.

"It ain't like we get a choice," Foley snorted. "We go where we're told." He added, "We get what they ask for. We get things done."

"Well, from what I got from Martin after the wake-up, was there were some scientists who went to Rigo-C after some probes and thought they could settle it when things went bad. There was a dust up, to say the least, and one of the scientists was killed and a dozen disappeared."

"Damn," Drake lipped. "E.T. done took Elliott?"

"To say the least," Foley smiled mockingly.

"Hero mode," Drake laughed. He shook his head.

"We are decreasing speed," Young announced. Young, as the medic, had explained some people could feel the slight changes in speed on spacecrafts. It was one of the millions of odd data points which made space travel interesting. Most marines had learned to

23

travel at thousands of miles an hour in a spacecraft and not lose their minds.

"We need to get moving," Foley said.

The three left the shower area and as soon as they were on the tiled floor of the locker room heard the chatter and laughter of other voices. Young and Foley looked at each other with smiles on their faces. Drake scowled.

Fireteam Nitro was heading to the showers as Drake and his team turned to enter the bunk room. The four members of the Nitro team were moving away from the bunk room in various stages of undress as they pushed past the trio.

They were led by Corporal Adam Butcher. Butcher was, hands down, the toughest corporal of the Lions of Apedemak. Butcher, at twenty-one, was a coffee brown blunt tool. He had been a space marine longer than anyone in the Lions of Apedemak other than the always serious First Lieutenant. Butcher, at twenty-one, was a dim-witted, mean, chiseled brown man who relished punishing others, Drake judged.

Jamal Everett was a dun brown, buck-toothed, square-headed soldier with bushy eyebrows and a hooked nose. Everett was extremely ordinary. He spent most of his life trying to be interesting. The brown boy only distinctive thing about him was his lineage. He liked to tell people he had ancestors who came from Albuquerque, New Mexico.

"My grams once told me they met an actor from Albuquerque that had done movies and TV and the like a long time ago," Everett liked to remind people. It was as if telling the story of his grandmother meeting a celebrity gave Everett uniqueness.

Everett was a mechanic, like Drake, and but unlike Drake, Everett had a right arm sleeve of tattoos. Drake liked Everett because he was reliable. He was not puffed up or a braggard like Williams or a bully like Butcher. Tolerable but not interesting.

Aricka King, at first glance, looked like a fawn-colored country girl with Afro puffs from *The Arc*. King was the fit and tone tattooed tough who refused to be tied down to one person. She was an attractive girl in her teens who spent a lot of time trying not to be seen only as a plaything. The radio operator for the Lions of

Apedemak, Evan Valentine, was sullen by nature, loved hip hop music and the Twentieth Century which had created it. He was a bit of a memorialist. Drake didn't like the term and would never admit to his fascination with the Twentieth Century.

"Hey, Valentine, how's it hanging?" Asked Young as they fought against the stream of Butcher, Everett, King and Valentine. Valentine gave a crooked grin to Young as he passed in the hall.

When Alpha squad walked into the bunk room the Beta fireteam exchanged greetings. The twelve had been together for eight ops. They had gotten to know each other well in those operations.

According to Springer, the squad chaplain, they were protected by God. Most laughed when the chaplain said it out loud, but secretly, most in the squad believed it.

Foley walked around the bunk room and greeted people he had not seen in nearly three months of hyper sleep. Of the assembled, Drake had to say Foley and Tyler were his closest friends.

Drake greeted everyone and gravitated to Tyler and Williams.

"Where's Payne?"

"Too good to be seen with us when Shepherd needs him," Wiliams said. "He's probably brown nosing with Shepherd for all I know."

Drake looked at Williams and smirked. He looked back and saw the Sarge talking with Butcher before the corporal stepped away to the shower.

Jenkins checked her monitor and snapped the first order of many.

"Beta, shower up and meet up in the mess room. We have a face-to-face with the First Lieutenant at 0900 hours. Move out," Jenkins grumbled before exiting the bunk room.

Williams smiled at Drake. "You know Jenkins is a little upset I was wakened earlier than her," Williams said. "I think it was a glitch." He paused then added, "Perhaps, the big wigs are trying to tell me something."

Drake smiled. "You know that was just a computer error?"

"They don't make errors, Drake," Williams said.

"Heard she's prepping for officer school," Williams said.

Drake looked back at Jenkins and nodded to Williams. Young was suddenly beside him. Drake grinned awkwardly at the medic, awkwardly.

"You okay, Young?"

"Yeah, I'm fine. Just thinking," Young announced. "This is the farthest I've been in the two years I've been a Galactic marine."

Drake smirked. "This is the farthest all of us have ever been."

"Don't get all homesick on me, Young," Williams chided. "I ain't built for compassion or sympathy. I'm just a bad boy with an itchy trigger finger ready to reshape humanity."

Chapter 3

"**W**hat up, stranger?" Raheem Springer smiled, the chaplain of the squad. He was a Mohawk-haired teen from the Midwest Region. Springer had a gold tooth and several tattoos. He was thinly built and wore a cross on a chain around his neck. Raheem looked nothing like a chaplain. At least, no chaplain Drake had read of in his history books.

Fireteam Beta were in various states of dress and undress when Young, Drake and Foley walked into the bunk room.

Sarge stood next to the leader of Beta squad who was dressed in her utilities. Corporal Holly Jenkins was a tall, thin, mahogany ball buster who had a scar across her cheek which looked like a barbed fishhook from the edge of her full lip to her left ear. She had thick, full lips and wide hips and an ample chest, short legs, broad nose and beady eyes. Unlike all the standard gun belts which hung on the hips, Jenkins had a pair of pistols under her armpits. She was a hard ass and a bit of a hellraiser. Jenkins was the unofficial science officer and nerd of the Lions of Apedemak.

Winston Tyler was the behemoth of the Beta Fireteam and the Lions of Apedemak. He was nearly seventy-two inches tall and weighed nearly two hundred and ten pounds. Tyler, like Springer was a teen. Tyler was not seventeen yet but looked like a full-grown man already.

The most abrasive and unfortunately the cockiest member of Beta was the dark-eyed sniper, Lance Williams. Williams was a tattooed bad boy. He was foul-mouthed and fearless. Williams was a street tough who charted his line back to New York City before New York City imploded.

"Yo, Drake, you ready to get paid for wrecking stuff?" Williams asked with a sneer.

Drake only nodded.

Dressed and ready to go, Drake and some of the Beta and Nitro fireteams headed to the mess room. They were dressed in their utilities and combat boots. The mechanics wore the double under armpit holsters. Drake's prized pearl-handled pistols hung beneath his armpits.

Out of the wide circular portholes on the side of the *Indomitable*'s middle deck was the vast blackness of space. Through the expanded portholes that were on the starboard side of the spacecraft was the best view of Rigo-C anyone could get. The two moons rose over the flat side of the rhombus planet.

On the second story of the *Indomitable* where the bunk room, shower and hyper sleep chamber were situated, there was also the main meeting place for the crew members: the mess room. The mess room sat under the bridge of the spacecraft. In the room were ten rows of tables lined up six tables deep. At the end of the room were six tables set apart from the rest. There sat the First Lieutenant and the Sarge and eventually the three corporals.

The twelve members of the Lions of Apedemak fireteams, dressed in utilities and combat boots filed into the cavernous mess room in ones and twos. The galley was a wall of packaged foodstuffs. There were easily twenty choices offered at every meal offered. The packaged food would be selected, heated or thawed and when ready, unlocked and accessible to those that had selected it. Each marine had a tray with packaged meals in cellophane on them.

The marines sat at tables and ate and talked. As they ate, they could not help but look out the six-foot-high portholes on the edge of the galaxy which only a handful of people to date had been able to say they had seen in person. Drake considered all he knew about Rigo-C, as he sat in the mess hall awaiting instruction and watching the unusual planet out of the spacecraft's portholes.

"I thought I had seen pretty much everything this galaxy had to offer," Tyler confirmed. "But I have to admit this is my first time seeing something like this."

"Yeah, that's something you don't see every day," Springer assured.

At 0900 the fireteams found their seats at the tables at the rear of the mess. They could not help but look through the wide porthole and out to the space around them. The unsmiling First Lieutenant sat at the head of the mess table with the Sarge and three corporals. The burly First Lieutenant, of the Lions of Apedemak was twenty-six years old, bearded and thick shouldered. He looked as if he might have been a farmer in another life. His history was limited.

Most Lions of Apedemak were from the Incorporated States of Sovereignty. It was a badge of honor for most to identify their hometown but the usually silent First Lieutenant's history and hometown of his family origin was a mystery.

The First Lieutenant stood and tapped his glass. The Sarge studied the assembled. The corporals did the same.

"All right, Lions, this is a quick update on our new op. We are heading to Rigo-C. Our mission is to just recover the essentials left by the Galactic Force explorers. Now, Rigo-C is home to an alien race that we only recently discovered. Our information on the race is spotty at best. Our op isn't aimed at the alien race. We are on the rivet to arrive at Rigo-C and locate our ISS scientists and return them to the *Sentinel*. We need to retrieve the scientists and return the equipment to Galactic storage. Easy peasy." He forced a thin and uncomfortable smile. "We will deploy at 1400 hours. It is now 0900 hours," the frowning First Lieutenant announced looking at his wrist monitor.

Shepherd looked to the Sarge and corporals. He seemed uncertain of what else to say, but continued, "The Sarge and corporals will address any questions or concerns. Muster at 1300 hours. Get your gear sorted. Get prepped. We are in the transports and locked and loaded in four hours."

The marine leader turned on his heels and headed to the far end of the mess hall. The corporals then stood up and headed toward the far end of the mess hall where the scowling First Lieutenant waited. The four conferred.

"All right comedians, we only have six hours, by my monitor, to get ready for the drop. I want all ordinance up and inventoried. Drake, Tyler and Everett need you to do the one hundred and twenty-five pre-drop check on each transport. Foley, Springer and King pack ordinance for twelve sols. We are going light. Based on the intel, we should be in desert utilities." Sarge paused, looking at the fireteams in front of him. "None of this work is going to get done from here."

The fireteams looked left and right and were suddenly in motion. The marines were moving in unison. Williams, the bad boy, yawned and climbed to his feet. The mechanics of the fireteams; Drake, Tyler and Everett moved toward the exit. The three marines tasked with gathering duffel bags headed to the bunk room. Seven sols, seven Earth days measured in twenty-four periods, was a long op.

The two who still sat scratched their heads. Young stood and walked toward the corporals. Williams and Valentine looked in their direction.

"What do we do?" Valentine asked.

Sarge looked and noted that Williams and Valentine were still in the cargo hold.

"Williams, Valentine go to the mess room and get us thirty MREs for each transport," Sarge yelled. The two marines grinned and slowly stood up. "You are not moving. Move. Move," Sarge shouted.

Valentine, the radio operator, was the first to reach to his feet. Williams stood as well.

"Valentine, you are in charge of the MREs," Sarge noted.

"Hate being voluntold," Williams allowed as the pair of marines headed to the mess room.

"Hell, man, how you hate being voluntold and a part of the Galactic Force? All we ever do is be voluntold to do this and do that. That's the Galactic Force life."

Williams and Valentine moved to the mess room.

"That was supposed to be a pep talk?" Tyler asked, with a shake of his head.

"Yeah, he ain't Phil Jackson," Drake said.

"Who's that?" Tyler asked.

"Phil Jackson? The zen coach of Michael Jordan and the unstoppable Bulls during the 1991 through 1998 seasons," Drake said.

"Who's Michael Jordan?" King asked.

"Who's the unstoppable Bulls?" Foley asked, confused.

Drake shook his head.

The Sarge stood up.

"All right, you heard the man. Finish up here. I want everyone out of this mess in 30 clicks. I need Young, Williams, Tyler and Valentine meet me in the cargo bay at 0930 hours," Sarge barked. There was immediate action. People wolfed down their remaining food.

Drake headed to the cargo hold with Foley and Tyler.

"How do you guys not know who Michael Jordan is?"

"Why should we?" Foley said, as the trio walked to the third floor of the *Indomitable*.

Drake started to answer and chose against trying to explain the significance of basketball to people uninterested in any pre-Earth kind of sports.

Drake and the mechanics gravitated to the cargo hold. In the cargo hold Drake and the mechanics were handed checklists. They each took a vehicle to check.

The cargo hold began just beneath the mess hall and ran two hundred feet to the rear of the spacecraft. It was designed to open like an alligator's mouth and allow the shuttle inside to be removed and returned with minimal crew. The shuttle, a B Class sleek designed transport, sat in the twenty feet tall. It rested in the cargo hold like an angry and anxious black, blue and gray fat falcon. The shuttle looked small in the spacious cargo hold which was nearly the size of two soccer fields. Also, inside of the cargo hold sat five landships. Huge tanks, nearly ten feet tall, on magna-track treads. On the right or left side of the landships were .50 caliber caseless machine guns. On the top of each landship was a gun turret where the gunner sat protected behind an "Ak Ak" gun.

The three landships closest to the drop area were painted in desert camouflage. There were decals on them to distinguish them from one another. The landships were lined up in a row. The first was the Alpha fireteam landship. On the four sides of the landship was the distinct symbol of a lion.

There was no one visible in the cargo hold, but male voices could be heard mixed in with the sound of throwback hip-hop music and metal against metal was distinct.

Corporal Jenkins entered the cargo hold and instead of crossing to the landships looked around and found a place to sit. Sitting near an open toolbox Holly Jenkins reached out and picked up a wrench and twirled it in her hand. She listened to the snippets of mechanics conversation and smiled coyly.

"Rigo-C had been seen out in the Kuiper Belt less than twenty years ago. The Kuiper Belt was thought to be nothing more than an

31

asteroid belt like the one between Venus and Mars. The origin of the asteroid belt was named after astronomer Kuiper was unique in that it was believed to be the first evidence of a dwarf sun exploding. The Kuiper Belt and the asteroids floating in it were supposed to be the remnants of a long dead and gone planet," Everett said from somewhere in the bowels of the hold.

"For years telescopes studied the Kuiper Belt and found nothing other than the dust of asteroids," he continued. "NASA and JAXA had never sent satellites to the Kuiper Belt believing there was nothing significant to discover. It was Indicosmos which sent a satellite to Saturn; it veered off course and before its destruction recorded the asteroid belt."

"What are you reading?" Tyler asked from somewhere in the cargo hold.

Everett popped up near his landship. He beamed and showed off his gold tooth. He disappeared again behind his transport. "This all comes from Wikipedia," Everett decided.

"You know that nobody believes in the articles in Wikipedia. It's open source," Drake said.

"No one trusts Wikipedia," Tyler added. "Learned that in grade school."

"No one cares who found this rock. All we need to do is complete the mission and return home."

"No!" Everett exclaimed. "We need to know where we're headed."

Drake slid out from beneath the landship and found Jenkins sitting on the bench with a wrench in her hand. He did not say anything but looked, curious.

"Hey, can you kill the music for a minute, Drake," said Jenkins, pointing to her ear.

Drake looked at the corporal and frowned. He nodded. He tapped his right ear, and the music went silent.

Everett rose up from behind his landship and looked at Drake. Seeing Jenkins, Everett looked away as if he had seen a ghost. He took a deep breath and looked at Drake. Everett reached into his coveralls and pulled out a handkerchief and wiped the sweat from his brow.

"Hey, why did you turn off the music?" Tyler shouted from within the cargo hold and nowhere to be seen. "Drake, turn the music back on?"

"We got a guest," Drake said.

"How long you been here?"

Holly Jenkins did not answer but smiled as an answer.

Drake looked at Everett and back to Jenkins, twirling the wrench. Drake only shrugged his shoulders.

Tyler popped up from behind his landship. He was for some reason wearing a Rock 'Em Sock 'Em robot T-shirt. The giant looked at the corporal and Everett and Drake. He grinned mischievously.

"What's going on, Jenkins?"

"Jenkins has something important to say," Drake smiled with a shake of his head.

Jenkins cleared her throat. "We need to make sure that all landships are ready to go for the drop," Jenkins said. "We are on a tight deadline." She looked around the cargo hold. There were five landships. Two were still locked down and in reserve. "Anyone need an extra hand?" Jenkins asked.

Tyler disappeared behind his landship. Everett as well went back to his checklist.

Drake looked at Jenkins and back to his own checklist. Drake tipped his chin to Jenkins.

"I ain't turning down help," Drake said.

Jenkins smiled and moved to Drake's landship. Drake tapped his ear and the cargo hold was once again bathed in hip hop music from the Twentieth Century.

"Once a wrench, always a wrench," Drake jested.

Jenkins smiled.

"You might want to help Everett, he has some big words that he can't decipher in some Wikipedia article about Rigo-C," Drake joked.

Jenkins smiled coyly.

Everett studied Jenkins and Drake and flipped Drake off. He went back to his work looking at Drake and Jenkins curiously and awkwardly.

"What can I help you with?" Jenkins asked with a smile.

33

"Well, you could change the air filters on this beast," Drake suggested.

"Right away," Jenkins agreed and scampered to the supply closet to find a filter for the landship.

While Jenkins was at the supply closet, Drake and Tyler rolled from beneath his landship, beside Everett when Jenkins went to get the air filters.

"What gives, Drake?" Tyler asked, suddenly serious.

"What's your problem?"

"Everyone stays in their own lane," Tyler advised from beneath his landship.

"That's bull and you know it," Drake bristled.

Everett was about to say something, but Jenkins began making her way back from the supply closet. Everett tapped Tyler and headed back to his landship. Tyler looked at Jenkins and Everett and retreated to his landship with a head shake.

Jenkins returned and immediately noticed a bit of tension between the retreating mechanics and Drake.

"Is everything okay?" Jenkins asked.

"Everything's fine," Drake responded unconvincingly.

"I was just offering a hand," Jenkins began and stopped. She took a beat and said, "I sort of miss the simplicity of machines and engines and turbines is all. I wasn't trying to overstep."

"It's not like that," Drake said, unsure how to explain what had happened.

Everett had retreated into the interior of the landship. Tyler, working on the third landship in the line, stepped around the front of the vehicle and disappeared. Drake watched Tyler as he grabbed a wrench and bent down to study the housing of the .50 caliber caseless machine gun. Drake sneered as Tyler moved from the machine gun to the magna track. He studied the wheel and was wrenching something on his checklist.

"Maybe I should go," Jenkins said.

"No, don't," Drake said, feeling silly. "Wrenchers gotta stick together. Ain't nobody else gonna care if the torque ain't right but us and I need the help."

Jenkins grinned thinly.

Drake gestured to replace his landship's air filters. There were four air filters on the Galactic Force all terrain magna-track landship. Jenkins began the work and expertly removed and replaced all of them.

While Everett and Jenkins were busy, Tyler tried to get Drake's attention. Drake, under the landship, happened to look in the direction of Tyler and find the giant under his landship as well. Tyler was mouthing something. Drake tried to decipher what the giant was silently mouthing, registering the words after the third time.

"I think that Everett and Jenkins had a little something something between them."

Drake looked in the direction of Everett who was busy wrenching on his landship. He looked back at Jenkins. Drake looked back at Tyler and shook his head.

Tyler again, silently mouthed: "The heart wants what the heart wants."

Drake exhaled with that revelation. The heart wants what the heart wants? What did that mean? Why did it matter? What did the heart have to do with the mission? What Everett and Jenkins did was up to them.

Drake shook his head. He continued working on his transport. He let the angry growl of the most prolific rapper flood his senses. The rapper talked about a world where being black was a crime. The rapper painted this picture of a world where the police shot blacks because they were scared and saw being black as a weapon.

Everett stepped out of his landship with his notebook computer. Drake and Everett stared at each other.

"How you doing?"

"Good. Chopping down the tree," Everett said.

Drake nodded. He smiled.

Tyler was sitting on the roof of his landship looking at the notebook computer. He was rubbing his eyes and scrolling through the pages.

"You good?"

Tyler rolled his eyes. He did not speak. Instead, he continued working on his landship.

Drake rolled his eyes at Tyler's focus. Drake went back to his landship 125-point checklist before the launch.

"How many you got left?"

"Just ten more," Drake smiled triumphantly. "How about you, Tyler," Drake asked innocently.

"About a dozen," the mechanic of Beta fireteam grumbled.

"I've fallen behind," Everett said. "Hey, Jenkins, if you got time, you can help me." Everett smiled broadly.

"Sure thing," Jenkins remarked, leaning on Drake's landship and waiting for instruction.

"Could you check the linkage for the magna tracks? After that, maybe you could top off all fluids?"

"Sure. Love to," Jenkins announced and went to the rear of the landship and to the magna-track engine.

Tyler and Drake grinned evilly at Everett who looked like he wanted to kill them both. Drake placed a hand in his coveralls above his heart and lifted it up and down like a heartbeat and silently gestured to Jenkins. Tyler smiled broadly but did not dare laugh out loud. Everett quietly fumed.

The four mechanics finished their checklists and were happy to sign off their checklists with time to spare. Drake was the first to finish. Tyler was the second. Everett, with the help of Jenkins, finished nearly half an hour after Tyler.

"Thanks, Jenkins," Everett smiled.

"No problem," Jenkins commented wiping her hands with a shop towel in her hand. "Thanks for the opportunity to get some time under the hood."

Tyler and Drake smiled broadly at the uncomfortableness that they were able to create toward their fellow marine.

"You guys are annoying," Everett said.

The three mechanics went to the showers and cleaned up, then dressed in their desert MARPAT utilities. The two armpit holsters remained. They were signature weapon ware for mechanics.

"Where did you get pearl handled pistols from, Patton?" Everett laughed, pointing to Drake.

Drake smiled proudly. Tyler shook his head, laughing.

Foley appeared from the bunk room and nearly ran into Tyler, the goliath, leaving the bunk room.

"Yo, little guy, watch yourself," Tyler complained.

"Sorry, Tyler, I'm late for the meeting," Foley apologized. The mechanics all frowned at the news Foley offered. The trio looked at each other and back at the retreating Foley, who was heading to the cargo hold.

"Let's get there," Everett announced. The three mechanics jogged to the cargo hold. They arrived and found their fireteams. They separated and sat.

Chapter 4

"**O**kay, here's the Cliff Notes on Rigo-C," Holly Jenkins began dressed in her MARPAT utilities, the pair of pistols under her armpits. The tall ball buster with a wicked scar from the edge of her lip to her ear was also the unofficial science officer of the Lions of Apedemak. Jenkins had a computer notebook that she read from to the assembled soldiers "We are expected to land on Rigo-C at the entry to Gargantuan mountain range. We are hoping to hit the ground running. Rigo-C, at this time of the rotation, will be arid, almost desert-like. We will drop in three all-terrain tanks. Once on the ground, we will head toward the outer Rigo-C settlement based up against the intersection of Rigo B. The settlement is approximately the size of old Earth Connecticut. The settlement area we are securing is denoted by our ISS flags distinctive colors." Jenkins paused. The unofficial science officer lifted a distinctive ISS red, white and blue, stars and stripes with an eagle flag. The corporal concluded, "Our simplified mission is to reclaim the settlement, retrieve the scientists, and hold the four points of the settlement while our mechanics take the power plant offline and prepare it for return."

The First Lieutenant smiled awkwardly and rubbed at his stubbled cheek. "Thank you, Jenkins. This is a delicate operation. Well, it is as delicate as delicate gets when they send in the Lions of Apedemak. But we need to keep it tight. No loose cannons. No hot dogs. We get in, find the scientists, and camp out while the wrenches dismantle the power plant. Simple, like Zero G. Just a babysitting job, really, and then reinforcements arrive, and we head back to the *Sentinel* space station for a much, needed rest." The grim First Lieutenant paused before adding. "We have a couple of short videos of the aliens we may encounter."

The first video was reminiscent of a black and white home video and was only about a minute and a half long. The camera was pointed toward the barren frontier. There was an outcropping of rocks. The scientists were exploring an area and taking samples when one of the scientists tapped another and pointed back to the outcropping of rocks. On top of the outcropping sat four teddy bear-like creatures, with a long snout and big star like fingers on the end of their protruding snout standing about two feet tall. They had six appendages, four arms and two feet. At the end of their arms were webbed fingers— if they were fingers— with sharp claws. The feet that the aliens stood on were thicker than their hands, and as the aliens stood, they seemed to sway like a toddler might before he learns to stand on his own and without assistance.

The mole-like creatures turned their heads left and right. One of the four kept its head focused straight forward. He chirped. The chirp was like the sound of an eaglet. It was shrill and high. The three others chirped in reply.

The scientists, dressed in space suits, moved slowly toward the nameless creatures. The four curious creatures watched the scientists as they approached. The first scientist reached out and as he lifted his hand toward the star like fingers on the end of their protruding snout and the fingers spread and the creature jumped back to use the rocks as a barrier between itself and the scientists. The three scientists jogged forward in their spacesuits and only found the other side of the rocks. The aliens were gone.

"Tell me you got that on film," one of the scientists stepped forward, turning and looking back at the camera.

The video ended.

"What the firetruck?" Valentine whispered dressed in his utilities to King, sitting next to Drake.   "Are we popping those cute mole-headed teddy bears?"

"That's cold," Springer agreed leaning over Williams and grabbing Everett.

"Yeah, that can't be the enemy," Foley decided.

The First Lieutenant looked at the now blank screen, then turned back to his soldiers. "ISS decided to send a team of scientists to create a post to study the aliens. The scientists arrived on Rigo-C and upon putting up their biodomes learned the aliens were unfriendly. The aliens, these aliens, were different than the original docile aliens. These were bipedal, fast, strong, and motivated. They have taken hostages. They have destroyed ISS property."

The second video began. It was less than two minutes. Unlike the first video the second video was taken from the tripod that was posted on the exterior of the settlement. Like the first video the camera was pointed out toward the barren frontier. Far out on the horizon there was movement. Dark shapes appeared and disappeared on the camera in the distance. The distance and speed that the dark shapes traversed was impressive. When the dark shapes jumped over the rock formations, they were not the two-foot-tall, cute teddy bear creatures that looked like a cross between a mole and an otter. These creatures were seventy or eighty inches tall and they were darker in color with rounder snouts and the same star-like fingers on the end of their protruding snout. The creatures were incredibly strong. One of the huge blue-black mole-headed grizzly bears in the video, in silhouette, was seen lifting one of the MOXIE oxygen instruments, over its mole-like head, which weighed conservatively two hundred and fifty pounds. The mole-headed bear-like creatures tore the settlement apart as if the biodomes were made of paper.

In the video, there was a scientist who tried to protect himself and used a strut from one of the destroyed biodomes. For the first time there was a clear picture of the extra-large four-armed creatures mouth full of sharp and dangerous teeth. Their mouth was beneath the bloom of finger like protrusions and was incredibly frightening. There were two rows of teeth on top and the bottom. The front fangs were at least an inch long.

The video ended.

"Any questions?"

"Those are the aliens?"

"Well, sort of," Holly Jenkins began. "We have been informed by the various interstellar explorers familiar with the various types of aliens that there are not just two types of aliens but many."

Glowering the First Lieutenant stepped forward and took control of the meeting.

"They are distinguished by their various colors. On Rigo-C we are only focused on these three types of creatures recorded on the video. There is the small, Teddy bear-like, two-foot creatures. They seem to be more docile. We have unceremoniously named them: "s'moles," like small moles. Then there are the gigantic aliens that we have deemed: titans. The third type is not as big as the titans and more human-sized, we're calling them Rigos. They all have four-arms.

The titans and the Rigos have a mean mouth and double rows of sharp teeth," the First Lieutenant explained. "On Rigo-C there are another dozen type of aliens. All of them are distinctive based on their skin color. But we are not worrying about the other aliens. For now, we are focused on the hostiles that attacked the settlement."

There was silence until King spoke.

"Do they bleed?" She asked.

The First Lieutenant chuckled. "The best I can tell you is that the scientists did not come to the planet thinking that they would have to defend themselves. So, they were not armed. They had tools but nothing lethal. So, in the last seventy-two hours, since the settlement went dark, we have no news on killing aliens," he stated.

"Wait, what?" Williams, the sniper, questioned. "No one thought to bring firepower to an alien planet?"

"There was no indication that there were hostiles or more importantly intelligent hostiles on the planet," Butcher noted his permanent scowl plastered to his face. First Lieutenant stepped back up and waited for further questions.

"So, didn't the scientists have flamethrowers?" Everett asked.

"Everything burns," King grinned.

"Again, this was a *scientific* exploration," the First Lieutenant explained.

"Are we supposed to capture the aliens?"

"Not that I am aware of," the First Lieutenant answered. "The aliens, what we are calling s'moles, titans and Rigos, are incredibly quick and strong and have some stealth ability." The First Lieutenant paused, then warned, "Do not underestimate them."

With no more questions the lieutenant turned on his heels and walked out of the cargo hold.

The Sarge and corporals gathered in front of the fireteams. While the leaders gathered the fireteams talked in whispers.

"So, let me get this straight," Tyler said with a smile addressing a few marines. "The scientists find this undiscovered planet filled with diamonds and tanzanite and instead of sending in the marines to check, they send probes."

"Strike one," Drake said, with a shake of his head.

41

"Scientists don't find anything and give the ISS an all clear," Valentine said.

"Strike two," Everett said with disgust.

"Scientists try to win some science award or something for discovering ET," Valentine continued.

"Stupid scientists come in contact with s'moles and think that they are cute and harmless," Tyler said.

"S'moles are not willing to allow scientists to capture them or make them a part of their experiments," Williams says with a shake of his head.

"Or piss on their lawns," Foley said with a smile.

"The said "s'moles" go back and get the titans and wreck the settlement and...," King said.

"They call us in," Drake finished with a smirk.

"Now, we have to find the captured scientists," Valentine scoffed.

"Sound about right?"

"We're the clean-up crew," Drake said.

"No, we're the retrieve and reclaim team," Williams smirked.

"Find 'em and kick some mole-otter ass," said the tattooed Aricka King.

"Don't forget we have to be watchmen too," Young said.

"Yeah, I forgot about that," King said.

There was a lull in the conversation.

"What are the odds?" Foley asked, mischievously.

"For us, we are one hundred percent. Mission complete. For the scientists," Williams paused and shrugged. "They are fish paste" he smiled. "Maybe."

The marines laughed at Williams calculations.

"Well, it's definitely not the life they promised in that brochure they gave out at recruitment," Drake joked.

"You got a brochure?" Everett questioned.

"You *didn't* get a brochure?" Drake joked.

"They had me with the catchy ad. See planets. Visit planets. Travel. Explore," Williams joked.

"That *is* catchy," Valentine affirmed.

"I thought so, too," Williams stated.

On the far side of the cargo hold the Sarge stepped forward and caught up with the First Lieutenant. Ben Shepherd turned and stared at Sarge.

"Yes, Sarge?" Shepherd prompted.

At that moment, one of the two elevator doors opened and into the *Indomitable* cargo hold walked the two pilots for the Galactic Force mission: Cyrus Brewster and Regina March. The old man, twenty-six, and the hotshot, seventeen, entered the cargo hold dominated by five landships, but the pair seemed very comfortable. Cyrus Brewster, a caramel skinned, sculpted, thick eyebrowed, rugged handsome man, who looked like a model from the Galactic Force posters, led the way toward the Sarge and the First Lieutenant.

Cyrus Brewster was a broad-shouldered individual who had clocked nearly ten thousand hours on the B Class transport they would be using for deployment. Brewster was a ruggedly handsome man, just thirty sols from turning twenty-seven. He wore twists on the top of his oval head.

Beside Brewster, was his diminutive co-pilot, Regina March. March had her hair parted down the center of her head, and had it tied back into two distinctive braids made of hundreds of finger thin braids. Her baby face, with apple cheeks and a single, solitary dimple on her right cheek, was dominated by her hazel eyes. Regina March was a little chunky and big chested and heavy hipped. At seventeen, she looked like the girl who should be playing soccer or doing her homework rather than manning a B-916 shuttle.

The pair were dressed in the Galactic Force Flight Academy leather bomber jackets with the Lions of Apedemak emblem across the back. There was a Galactic Force Flight patch on the right shoulder. Above the breast were their stitched names.

"Brewster and March, reporting for duty," Cyrus Brewster announced, saluting the First Lieutenant. Regina March saluted as well. The Sarge stood listening.

The stern First Lieutenant returned the salute reluctantly. The two pilots stood at attention.

"At ease," First Lieutenant nodded; the pilots followed his command.

The two pilots stood at ease.

"What's the sit rep?"

"Well, we should be launching in a hundred and ten clicks and are hoping for a smooth flight. We deploy from *Indomitable* and will enter Rigo-C in ten or fifteen minutes after deployment. After entry we will navigate to the mountain range and drop the teams off. Our goal is to get the teams on the edge of the mountain valley entrance. Right now, Rigo-C has rotated toward the sun and when they land, they will be in the drier season there. According to our reports we have a window of three hundred and thirty-six hours plus or minus before the next seasonal rotation."

"We are aware of seasonal changes," the First Lieutenant scowled.

"We have noted some tremors on the surface. Projections of 3.0 to 4.3 magnitude earthquakes regularly," Brewster advised.

"Just get us on the surface. We'll get to the settlement."

Brewster nodded. March, who had not spoken looked to Brewster and then back to the First Lieutenant.

"Simple mission. Simple request," the First Lieutenant said watching Brewster and March. "Get us to the surface safely. Once we make it to the settlement and retrieve the scientists and take the power plant offline you just need to return to get us back to the *Indomitable*." He paused, dramatically.

"Roger that," Brewster smiled, cockily. The pilot checked his wrist monitor for a message. March checked her monitor a few seconds later.

"We'll launch in less than one hundred clicks and we'll give you as long as you need on the surface. We will yoyo into the atmosphere and then after your landing return to the *Indomitable*," Brewster said. He looked like he should be doing commercials for something. He had the perfect smile and unblemished skin. His hair was combed into a twisted fade. "Unfortunately, there is no real place for the shuttle to land and launch again. To protect all concerned, we will circle the high altitudes once and slingshot back to the *Indomitable*. Standard operating procedure," he clarified.

"So, if we need any air support?" First Lieutenant asked, knowing the answer.

Brewster chuckled.

"Roger that," the First Lieutenant nodded.

At that moment, Yvette Murray appeared carrying a small duffle bag. She walked boldly to the three people who were gathered by the elevator in the cargo hold. She immediately noted the First Lieutenant, who oversaw the operation. Murray had a working relationship with Brewster and had talked with Regina March maybe a dozen times since her deployment.

The First Lieutenant watched the pale elvish girl dressed in the blue top and black trousers of the *Indomitable* crew uniform. Brewster turned and saw Yvette Murray and smirked, studying her.

"Captain," Yvette Murray smiled simply, saluting Brewster. The captain of the shuttle returned the salute. The First Lieutenant stood, waiting.

"Lieutenant," the brown-haired Murray smiled brightly and saluted.

The First Lieutenant returned the salute with a stern look.

"If neither of you mind," Murray explained. "I was hoping to tag along and get a chance to observe this new discovery up close and personal."

The First Lieutenant inhaled. He seemed to chew his words.

"Of course, we got room. It's up to LT if you can tag along or not on the mission," Brewster smiled easily.

"Exactly," Murray smiled mischievously and turned to the First Lieutenant.

The First Lieutenant seemed to be wrestling with his decision.

"I am a science officer," Murray pointed out. She quickly added, "A *real* science officer."

The First Lieutenant rubbed the side of his thin face, uncertain.

"She has some solid credentials, LT," Brewster offered.

The First Lieutenant looked at Brewster out of the corner of his eye but remained silent.

March lowered her eyes and tried to find something to do with her hands as she waited out the awkwardness.

Murray smiled broadly and waited.

"Hm," the First Lieutenant sounded.

Brewster allowed a slight smile. March chuckled and turned away. Murray continued to smile broadly.

"Fine," the First Lieutenant said through gritted teeth. He eyed the petite girl who looked like she should be anywhere other than talking about going to a newly discovered planet with a bunch of space marines.

The First Lieutenant raised a single finger. "You can embed with Nitro team. Find Butcher. He'll get you situated. I'll inform him."

Murray smiled broader.

Brewster sniggered.

The First Lieutenant scowled.

"That will be all."

Brewster and March saluted and the two pilots walked through the cargo hold and to the shuttle.

"Thank you, First Lieutenant," Murray gushed, still beaming.

The First Lieutenant nodded, and the science officer took a step forward, as if about to hug the marine. The First Lieutenant froze Murray with an unfriendly look. The science officer stopped herself, saluted and retreated toward the exit.

The First Lieutenant shrugged his thin shoulders and stood there for a long second. He placed a hand on the butt of his service weapon and looked left and right.

The First Lieutenant tapped his ear bud and spoke.

"Butcher, Murray, the *Indomitable* science officer, will be embedding with your fireteam," the First Lieutenant intoned. "Send."

The First Lieutenant took a few steps and stopped. He tapped his ear bud again. "Sarge, have the teams in the shuttle in ninety."

Tapping his wrist monitor, the First Lieutenant saw the first few lines of the message.

"For your eyes only."

Chapter 5.

Ben Shepherd was a quiet man. He had joined the Galactic Force at eighteen and once in never looked back. His first years were devoted to a relentless pursuit for advancement. He had enlisted and told his recruiter he wanted to become an officer.

"It's possible," the recruiter said. "But it's a lot of hard work."

Shepherd liked the challenge. As a private, he distinguished himself in boot camp and before his first mission he was already a Lance Corporal because of his leadership skills. Shepherd was always someone who could find the bully and use the bully's desire for violence against everyone else. In the Galactic Force, he had repeatedly pit one bully against the other and became seen as a leader.

His second year in the force found Shepherd recognized by the Staff Seargent and receiving a promotion to Corporal. For a full year Shepherd studied for officer training. When the testing was offered, he applied and was accepted.

The year before this mission, Shepherd found himself facing a real decision. He was Second Lieutenant, and the entry into officer training presented bigger and better responsibilities. Yet, he had forsaken missions in his pursuit of advancement. In three years in the Galactic Force, he had only pulled the trigger of his assault rifle at the range, when he had to qualify for certification. The same was true with his sidearm. Shepherd was a strategist, not a warrior. He had applied for and been given the First Lieutenant advancement and pay increase but never imagined being in combat.

Shepherd's idea of combat was him sitting in front of screens and delegating his squads to effect the necessary physical tasks he did not want to undertake. That was Shepherd's belief, even as he prepared for dropping to Rigo-C. In his mind, all he planned on doing was hunkering down in the landship and directing the Lions of Apedemak. It seemed the best use of his talents.

In four years, Shepherd had made O-3. Four years had gotten him to First Lieutenant. His goal, if he had a goal in the Galactic Force, was to one day become a general. Of course, the idea was more a dream. To be a general in the Galactic Force took greater skills and backbone than Shepherd had.

The First Lieutenant thought all this as he returned to his cabin and prepared to video conference with his superiors.

It was not unusual to receive a message from the four or to be told it was for his eyes only. They did not like to broadcast plans through conventional means. Everything was hush hush, encrypted and secret.

Shepherd went to his cabin and plugged in his monitor and waited for it to scan the connection and his monitor for any spyware. A green fist icon would appear in the right corner of the monitor indicating that it was safe to broadcast and receive messages from command. The First Lieutenant waited for the icon to appear and for one of the four to tell him the next operation the Lions of Apedemak were heading to after Rigo-C. It was always that way. His commanders were always one step ahead of everyone, including himself.

The dark eyes of the Captain Dianne Hill and Major Samuel Billings blinked in front of the First Lieutenant and Shepherd saluted his commanding officers. They returned the salute and Billings chuckled, just a little as he started the short meeting. Shepherd bristled with Billings' chuckle. He knew the major delighted in making things hard for him.

Shepherd studied the Major. Billings had dark eyebrows which accented his slightly beady blue eyes and upturned nose. The Major stroked his blonde mustache and well-trimmed beard. He was in his early thirties, Sheperd recalled. Billings was a snake who had been in the Galactic Force for nearly a decade and gunning for general. For some reason Billings did not like Shepherd.

The First Lieutenant had a good working relationship with Captain Hill, but the higher-ranking Billings felt a need to make things tough for the First Lieutenant. Shepherd let the video conference play out. He rarely groused about any of the operations the Lions of Apedemak were given. The missions were puzzles Shepherd had to figure out. Hill and Billings never had a bad word for Shepherd of the Lions as a result of the First Lieutenant's success in motivating his squad to retrieve and reclaim anything the Galactic Force needed.

48

The way Shepherd saw it they were all working for others. They were all marines. They did the hard work to keep the Galactic Force running. Yet, Billings seemed to enjoy creating obstacles for Shepherd and the Lions. There was no pleasing the prickly Major. Seeing Billings' smug face looking at him, Shepherd braced for trouble.

"So, how long until you and the Lions are on surface?"

"We are descending in less than forty clicks," the First Lieutenant said.

Billings nodded and smirked while stroking his beard.

"Remember, Ben, we need a win here. It is crucial for the squad to succeed at this mission," the Captain stated via a secure video feed.

"Roger that, sir," the First Lieutenant said in agreement on the video call.

"It is not enough to secure the settlement, Ben. We need to retrieve those scientists and let the aliens know we were there. It's neither here nor there if we terraform Rigo-C, but the higher ups do not want us cowering from anyone in the galaxy."

Shepherd listened, not sure where Billings was going with his conversation.

"We are not leaving a soul behind," Billings hissed. "Get those scientists back. Priority one. Once the scientists are retrieved get your team to take the power plant offline and get it ready for removal. We are sending another team to reclaim it. The Indomitable doesn't have a rad container. So, we'll leave that for Victorious, the retrieval team."

Shepherd nodded. He had figured as much. Taking a nuclear power plant offline was one thing. Reclaiming it was another.

"Hold the settlement until the reinforcements arrive. Once they are on the ground your mission is complete and you and the scientists are beelining it back to the *Sentinel*."

"Roger that," Shepherd said.

"I need to reiterate, Ben, again, from the higher ups, they want a show of force on the aliens once the scientists are recovered. It can be as simple as burning down a portion of their forest. But they

49

need to know that they cannot threaten us or our assets. We expect a strong response," Billings said with an icy stare.

"If I may, Major," Hill interjected. "This is a dog and pony show, Ben. We need to go hard and forceful to find those scientists. Priority one. When you find them, you can take the gloves off. The only thing we care about after the retrieval of the scientists is taking the power plant offline." Hill paused. She was a diamond-faced woman with a small chin, thin lips, a straight nose, angular cheekbones and brown expressive eyes framed by brown hair pulled back and into a bun. "This is our first encounter with any intelligent alien race, and we cannot be seen as the pussies who allowed the ETs to steal from us. At the same time, we can't be the a-holes who finally met and killed the only aliens in the galaxy."

Billings nodded. "So, find a balance."

The First Lieutenant did not speak.

"Nothing difficult here," Hill assured.

"I need you to take a hands-on approach on this one, Ben. No one pulls a trigger unless you say so." The Major smiled. "You read me?"

"I read you, sir," Shepherd said.

"This is important, Ben. We trust you," said Hill. "We all trust your judgment. You know what's at stake."

The First Lieutenant furrowed his brow. He knew if things went badly the command was making him the fall guy. Standard operating procedure on delicate situations, Ben Shepherd reluctantly understood. He could, but there was no point. He was a soldier. His lot in life was like the men and women he commanded: do or die.

"Yes sir," the First Lieutenant said.

"I need your eyes on this one. More importantly, I need your calm hand on the rudder in these delicate affairs," Hill said.

The First Lieutenant nodded.

"Good, keep me informed," the beady eyed commander said. "You do good on this one and you may find yourself promoted. Of course, I'll expect regular reports at least every twelve hours for the next hundred and sixty hours. Nothing too explicit. Just sit reps." Billings chuckled and looked away. "Stay away from the MREs, they'll kill you. I just survive on the gels."

"I'll buy you a drink when you return to the *Sentinel*," Hill smiled.

Billings and Hill signed off.

Ben Shepherd sat in front of the monitor and pinched his lips to stop from screaming. Billings and Hill had just made the success of the mission exponentially harder to succeed. How was he supposed to find a balance? Don't waste the aliens. Don't let the scientists die. Pretty simple. Yeah, right.

The First Lieutenant sat at his desk and checked his wrist monitor. He had thirty clicks before deployment. In that time, he had to consider what his commanders had told him and how it would effect the mission.

He took a deep breath and steeled himself to the task ahead. He would be in the field. He would decide when to nuke anyone.

The First Lieutenant quickly packed his duffel. He was going to Rigo-C. He was going to be up close and personal. Sarge would appreciate that one. Boots on the ground. Getting to be a general was not done with paperwork, Shepherd thought as he finished packing.

The stern lieutenant, dressed in his desert camouflage utilities, placed his cover on his head and stepped into the hall. On his hip was a service weapon. On his face were safety goggles.

The First Lieutenant took the long walk to the cargo hold. On either side of him there was activity. None paid him any attention to him. They were focused and hellbent to finish their work before deployment.

The first to see the First Lieutenant was Valentine.

"Officer on deck," Valentine crowed, snapping to attention and saluting the First Lieutenant. Everyone in the cargo hold who had heard the announcement snapped to attention and looked in the direction of Valentine, saluting as they had been taught in basic training.

"At ease," stated the First Lieutenant.

Valentine and everyone who was eyeing him returned the salute and stood at ease.

"Back to work," the First Lieutenant scowled. "Where's the Sarge?"

Valentine pointed in the general direction of the landships.

"What up, LT?" Corporal Payne said from near the stack of duffel bags piled behind him.

"Looking for the Sarge," First Lieutenant snarled, The First Lieutenant had his duffel in hand. He had his game face on. There was no humor in his demeanor.

Payne scanned the gigantic cargo hold and pointed.

The Sarge was walking toward the ranking officer, his smile broadening as he closed the distance between them.

"LT? You tagging along?" Questioned Sarge.

The First Lieutenant did not speak. He nodded. The Sarge raised an eyebrow, curious. The First Lieutenant simply tossed his duffel into the first landship and studied the fireteams in pre-flight preparation.

"Sit rep?"

"We are locking things down," Sarge pointed out. "We should be ready to go in twenty."

The First Lieutenant nodded. He adjusted his safety goggles. Around his neck was a gaiter, just in case there was a sandstorm. The First Lieutenant walked around the shuttle and smiled at the name of it. He shook his head and checked his wrist monitor.

With ten minutes to departure, Shepherd found Brewster and March in the cockpit of the shuttle.

"First Lieutenant," smiled Brewster behind the instrument panel which monitored all the mechanics of the B-916. He was pressing buttons and checking gauges, pre-flight.

"What's the atmosphere?" First Lieutenant asked.

"We have a hydrogen and oxygen mix that is tolerable. It might be a little rich and might remind some of high altitudes," March noted.

"Time until we deploy?"

"Less than ten clicks," March asserted from the cockpit. "Everyone needs to be in who's going on this trip."

Shepherd nodded. He retreated to the cargo hold where Sarge and the Lions were standing and waiting to climb into the shuttle.

The three fireteams stood in front of the First Lieutenant.

"Load 'em up," First Lieutenant announced.

With those words the corporals ushered the fireteams into the transports. In the interior of the cramped transport were the duffel bags of each member of the fireteams. Every member of the was armed with assault rifles, helmeted and outfitted with mics up and cameras.

"Lock those weapons up," Sarge roared angrily.

The rifles were locked into the open storage bin in preparation for deployment. Closing the landships, the cargo hold was sealed as well. The airlock opened and the air was drawn out of the cargo hold of the *Indomitable*. The landships' sensors alerted everyone inside there was no oxygen outside.

"We are in prep," the First Lieutenant announced to the corporals in their ears. The message was relayed to every landship and fireteam.

The fireteams prepared in different ways. Jenkins, the hard ass, seemed to have the most serene team. The Beta fireteam had a distinctive patch, a black boot with a star in the center. The corporal checked her fireteam and seeing nothing out of the ordinary, closed her dark eyes and listened to something inaudible to everyone around her. The chaplain, Springer, sat and quietly prayed for the safe deployment of the squad. The titan of the squad, Tyler, leaned against Williams and napped. Williams, the New York bad ass, shook his head at the goliath leaning on him.

In the Nitro fireteam landship the five marines prepared differently, thanks to Butcher. They were lighter and more at ease. The outsider, Murray, sat next to the tall radio operator, Valentine.

"So, what did you do to get stuck with us?" Everett asked Murray.

"I asked to go down with you," Murray said with an expectant smile.

King shook her head at the response.

"Greenie," Everett said. The team nodded in agreement.

"I just figured that it's not every day that someone gets to set foot on an alien planet and see alien life," Murray said.

"It is for us," said King with a smirk.

Murray looked at King, silently.

"How long are we scheduled to be on the surface?" Valentine asked Butcher.

"Not sure," Butcher said. "I know first priority is finding the missing scientists. Beyond that, it's need to know."

"Yeah, we don't need to know, and they don't need to tell us," King said. "Just cogs in the machine."

"Just cogs," Everett repeated.

"This is going to be a real dumpster fire of mission, you ask me," Valentine stated.

"Nobody asked you," said King.

"We get to save the scientists," Everett said with a smile.

"Yeah, this is going to be some real cowboy riding in and saving the day kind of melodrama," King laughed.

"We just have to get there first," Butcher noted.

"What's the real deal with the aliens?" Everett asked, concerned. King leaned in and whispered.

"Well, from what I hear that mole thing is their disguise and the real deal is completely different. They are bipedal, hot as sin and look like your mama," King laughed.

"Kick rocks, King," Everett said, pushing the tattooed girl away from him. Valentine and Butcher laughed. King just grinned her best Cheshire Cat grin. Everett scowled.

"Doc, you ever seen any aliens?"

"No one has," Murray said. She grinned coquettishly. She was the smallest person in the landship.

"Well, what say you? Are they friendly or hostile?"

"Well, again, that's hard to say," Murray began. "I mean, we could be seen as the aliens to them, right?"

"What?"

"Look at it from their perspective," she readjusted her position in her seat. "We show up and suddenly we are planting flags and trying to take over." She smiled sheepishly. "Perhaps, the question shouldn't be are they friendly? But maybe, can we convince them that we are friendly?"

"Bull," Aricka King, the tattooed cowgirl, scowled. "Those freaks know we are the superior species. They have to. If anyone shows up with superior tech and military on a planet, then by definition they are in charge." King clicked her tongue.

Everett, the mechanic, sat and unconsciously drew and holstered his pair of pistols under his arms like an Old West cowboy. "Hey, Everett, we're not in the wild flipping west and you ain't Billy the finger popping Kidd. Put those BB guns away before you pull the trigger and shoot someone in the foot," grumbled Butcher sitting behind King, the landship driver.

Everett holstered his service weapons and kicked out against the pole closest to him. He crossed his arms over his chest and pouted, like a bratty kid.

"So, baddies? Is that what you're thinking, doc?" King asked, looking back at the small science officer.

Murray did not respond.

"So, friendlies, then?" Everett asked. The mechanic found a crescent wrench in the landship and was absently twirling it like a cheerleader might a baton.

"Well, when we land, I think the aliens will look at you and your lot compared to me and...," Murray shrugged. "I think we need to be a little less aggressive," Murray finished.

A claxon sounded.

"Okay, here we go," Butcher said. "They are closing the airlock."

A few moments later the flashing lights were the only things visible. The cargo hold had gone dark. Or the shuttle had slowly begun to inch into space.

There was an audible hiss as the shuttle uncoupled from the spacecraft and slowly nosed toward Rigo-C. The descent was slow and methodic.

In the Alpha fireteam landship Payne was listening to something as the shuttle quieted. On his forearm was a mission plan protected beneath clear plastic. Foley was the navigator and going over the maps and looking for landmarks. Next to Foley was the reliable assault rifle which spit out caseless rounds at three different speeds. Young, the medic, had a med packs strapped to his chest and back. Unlike everyone else in the fireteam Young only had a sidearm.

Drake had a small, mechanic's bag attached to the bottom of his backpack.

"We should land near the entrance to the Winchester Valley. If we do, we should be about twenty miles from the settlement," Foley said to Shepherd.

"How come we aren't landing closer?"

"Above my pay grade," Foley said. "I'm just the navigator."

"Payne, why aren't we landing closer to the settlement?" Drake asked, reaching out and tapping the corporal. Payne tapped his ear and looked at Drake, annoyed.

"What up?"

"I want to know why we aren't landing closer to the settlement?" Drake asked with a smile.

"We are still trying to locate where the aliens are based. So, we are doing a recon at the same time as we joyride to the settlement." Payne nodded. "Now, sit back and stop trying to be a backseat driver."

Drake chuckled at Payne and Payne tapped his ear again. He sat back, smiling at whatever he was listening to.

"Wonder what he's listening to," Drake said to Foley. Foley shook his head. Young did not say anything.

"I think he told me that he likes country bebop music," Young mentioned. "He told me that a few operations ago, when we had some downtime."

"Country bebop?" Drake questioned. "He doesn't look like someone that would like country. I had him for a techno or punk band fan."

Young smirked.

"Listen up," the country bebop music loving corporal began, and the banter quieted. "We should deploy in a few moments, then take a few minutes to break the atmosphere. The flight down to ten thousand feet should take us another five or ten minutes. We'll launch from there. By the books." When he had finished, he sat behind the steering console of the landship, a complicated bunch of dials and pedals.

The deployment alert blinked.

There was a slight tremor and the B-916 shuttle's ion drive engine slowly reversed from the A Class spacecraft. Drake and Foley watched as the interior of the spacecraft's guts slowly receded and dropped away and was replaced by the vastness of space below.

From the B-916 shuttle the craft picked up speed. Most did not feel the acceleration except for Jenkins and King felt the slight increase in speed. The light and agile shuttle descended from the USS *Indomitable* and suddenly it was entering the atmosphere of Rigo-C.

"We are entering the atmosphere of Rigo-C," March announced as the shuttle shuttered just a little on entry. "We might have a little chop as we try to get through the high clouds, so, hang on."

The B-916 bounced over the air turbulence like a transport over rough roads. The marines bounced along with the transport. They were all buckled in. Tyler continued to nap.

After a couple of moments, the shuttle leveled out and March came back on the PA. "We are making our descent. We are opening and launching at ten thousand feet. We will announce at twenty thousand feet."

"LT?" Sarge questioned. First Lieutenant shook his head. He gestured to Sarge.

"It's on you," the First Lieutenant said. "I'm just a fly on the wall."

Payne and Sarge looked from the First Lieutenant back to each other. Payne studied the Sarge. The Sarge smirked. He focused and scowled.

"Okay, Alpha team. Get ready," barked Sarge. "When we break the atmosphere and open that door, we will be the best of the Galactic Force marines." Sarge added, "We got a drop, rock and roll and rescue. So, get ready. Get focused. And get your mind right for this op."

Alpha fireteam all had sidearms on their hips. Drake had three pistols: one on his hip and two under his arms in the two-pistol rig typical of marine mechanics.

On the Alpha fireteam's right shoulders were distinctive patches that had a lightning bolt embroidered through the center with a screaming eagle dominating the round Lions of Apedemak patch.

Sarge unbuckled and grabbed the hand hold above his head. He put a booted foot on the seat he had been sitting in.

"All right sweethearts, we are going to hit the ground running. Alpha should be the first on the ground. Secure the location. Corporal Payne, by the time Nitro lands, if it is okay by you LT, I want you rooster tailing to the settlement," Sarge snapped.

The Lieutenant nodded. "Twenty miles should get us to the outskirts in an hour. We will stop on the outskirts of the settlement and wait for instructions," he announced.

Sarge climbed to his feet. He scanned his forearm. The First Lieutenant stayed seated. There was limited room for movement. Alpha fireteam prepared for the transport launch.

"Twenty thousand feet," March announced.

"We're up," Sarge announced.

The magna-track landship was the vehicle of choice for the Galactic Force ground troops. They were low profile, fast transports which harkened back to the Mark I tank from World War I. The landships had two machine gun turrets on either side of the main compartment. Above the magna-tracks was another machine gun turret. The landships were manned by a fireteam. Sarge entered the screaming eagle stenciled landship through the armored door in its rear.

"Twelve thousand feet," March announced.

There was a loud claxon sounding.

"We are thirty seconds from the drop," Payne announced. From the landship's interior monitor the countdown was visible.

Alpha fireteam prepared for the deployment. Foley tightened his strap on his helmet. He unholstered his service weapon and checked the gun's magazine. He returned the magazine after inspection and holstered his service weapon. Young, the medic, tightened his med packs. Drake, the mechanic, checked his pistols and tried to breathe.

Payne, the corporal and driver, sat in the navigator's seat. In front of him were four levers, but no steering wheel. Payne rested his hand on the console which monitored the landship. He tapped a few buttons and the console lit up like a Christmas tree. Various dials illuminated.

"All right, we know how this goes." Payne buckled up for the parachute drop to the surface of Rigo-C. "Foley, you are in the crow's nest. As soon as we land pop the top and give us longitude and latitude."

"Got it," Foley said.

"Here we go!" Called Sarge.

"Welcome to Rigo-C," crowed Drake, with a crooked smile.

"Welcome to the express elevator to...," Foley began and suddenly they were plummeting.

Chapter 6.

The sand shower plume bloomed up into the sky nearly two hundred feet as the first landship slammed to the surface of Rigo-C. The grit showered down in every direction for easily one hundred seconds, according to Drake's calculations. Inside of the landship, the silt sounded like raindrops. It was surprising, the familiarity of the sound overhead, from inside of the landship.

"We're in it now boys," Payne announced. "We're on Rigo-C."

The landship settled and Corporal Payne, the driver for Alpha fireteam, checked the dozen things necessary to engage the magna-track landship's engine. Several switches were toggled. Buttons were depressed and the powerful mercury engine began to whir. The magna-track treads churned and found purchase on the dunes.

"We good, Payne?"

Payne nodded. He checked the four monitors which gave him general information about the landship. He tapped the monitor which connected to the two other landships. The screen was split in three. Two-thirds of the screen was radar. One third held two screens, currently black, that would hold the Beta and Nitro pilots' information.

"How long until we are moving?" Asked the always serious First Lieutenant Shepherd.

"Based on deployment, we have about ten to fifteen minutes before the other landships land and about ten minutes after that before we start to travel," Payne noted.

"Can we get out and stretch our legs, LT?"

Foley and Young looked to the First Lieutenant.

The First Lieutenant calculated. The Sarge nodded.

"I don't see why not," the First Lieutenant stated.

Drake tapped the button which opened the clamshell rear door of the landship. It was an emergency exit which was used for easy access to the interior.

Sarge stood up and rushed to the exit button and double tapped it. The clamshell had only opened just enough to let in the first natural light of Rigo-C. The Sarge pushed the button again and closed the clamshell.

"What gives Sarge?"

"If we are exiting," Sarge announced, "Then we exit out the top. One at a time."

"Roger that," Drake said, slinging his assault rifle and heading to the turret.

The first to climb out of the landship was Foley, followed by Drake, both clad in goggles on and helmets.

When Foley opened the armored rooftop door to the landship he was hit by the first oppressive wave of heat. The heat of Rigo-C was oppressive. It was more like walking into an oven than out of the landship. Foley stumbled onto the top of the vehicle. Drake pushed through the heatwave and climbed onto the landship roof and stood watching as the silt fell from the sky. Drake looked up and narrowed his dark eyes as the silt shifted and floated downward to the surface below. He reached out his hand and watched as the dust settled in his palm. Drake smiled blithely at the idea of the powder falling like snowflakes.

"Ninth man on Rigo-C," Foley laughed.

Behind Drake came Young. Foley paused, before climbing fully onto the roof, and shaking his head at the heat.

"Tenth man on Rigo-C," Drake yelled as he exited the landship.

"All mighty is it blazing," complained Foley.

"Eleventh man on Rigo-C," Young smiled sheepishly and shook his head. Sarge and the lieutenant were the last to exit the landship. Sarge held his assault rifle horizontally. The First Lieutenant climbed out of the landship briefly and stood looking at the computer notebook scrolling through military information.

Drake unslung his assault rifle and put the long gun to his shoulder and studied the terrain through the scope. Foley, once outside of the landship cradled his assault rifle in his arms.

"See anything?"

"Nothing."

"Not too surprised."

The five stood on the landship and observed where the triplet parachute had finally dropped them.

"Drake, unclip us," the Sarge said pointing to the parachute. "Foley, you and Young roll the parachute. Quick. Fast. In a hurry," Sarge commanded.

Drake slung his assault rifle over his shoulder and moved to the four points on the landship's hull which held the platform the landship sat on.

Instantly, Drake unclipped the parachute from the four I-bolts and returned to scanning the terrain. Foley and Young dragged the parachute to the landship and rolled it neatly into a storage container.

All the while, Sarge was studying the terrain, his assault rifle against his shoulder sighting any targets which might be visible. The lieutenant rubbed the back of his neck. He adjusted his photochromatic goggles and sat on the turret which held the Ak-Ak gun. He did not speak but did a three-hundred-and-sixty-degree scan of the landing site.

"What you seeing?"

"Squat," Foley announced.

"What you seeing?"

"Sand. Lots and lots of it," Drake said. "It looks like we landed in the biggest kitty litter pan ever."

"Foley give me our coordinates," the First Lieutenant ordered.

"Right," Foley, scanning the horizon for something distinguishable. "Based on the Gargantuan mountain range which is two miles long and at least a mile high," Foley began, "We're about eighteen miles from the settlement if we go due east."

"Foley, LT wants our coordinates," Sarge snarled.

Drake looked back and smiled at the comedy of Foley under the watchful eyes of the First Lieutenant and the Sarge. "Poor sap," Drake grinned to himself. He was about to return his eye to the scope when he noticed a bright blueish purple crystal the size of his pinky by his foot. He picked it up and examined it. "Souvenir," Drake thought and slipped the ice cream cone shaped crystal into his utilities cargo pants thigh pocket.

"Yeah, yeah," Foley said scanning the horizon with his range finding binoculars, looking for landmarks. "There's the mouth of the mountain range." As he studied the terrain he said, "The way I see it, LT, we are just two clicks from the mouth of the Gargantuan mountain range and if we head south from the mouth of it, we will be at the settlement in under two hours, give or take." The private added, "If the naming of the mountain range is debatable and still up for grabs, I vote for Foley's Milky Way mountain range or Foley's Starburst mountain range to be considered."

Sarge chuckled. The First Lieutenant smiled. "I'll take that under advisement," the First Lieutenant laughed.

Looking to Drake the First Lieutenant narrowed his dark eyes. "This sand going to be a problem?"

"Naw, we got filters LT," Drake announced.

The lieutenant nodded and, after stretching, returned to the interior of the landship without a word. Sarge stood with the assault rifle at the ready. Foley and Drake stood looking at the alien terrain they found themselves on.

Young stood on the fender of the landship and toed the desert soil which had gathered there. The medic, in desert MARPAT utilities, bent down and looked at the fine gravel and picked up a small crystal. Young studied the small purple crystal in his hand.

"What you got there Young?" Sarge asked.

"It appears to be tanzanite," Young replied.

"Tanzanite?"

"What? Thought there was no more tanzanite," Drake said. "Thought that there wasn't no more of that anywhere," he said, removing his eye from the scope of his rifle.

"There ain't no more of that on any planet we've been on," Sarge smiled looking to Drake. "Think we're pretty safe here on this pile of sand," he said, tapping Drake on the shoulder. Drake lowered his rifle.

"That means that little gem is valuable, right?" Foley smiled.

"Might be valuable everywhere but here," Young said, looking out on the sand dunes and seeing specks of purple intermixed with the brown and gold of the fine sands. Young gripped the half inch piece of tanzanite and studied it only to flick it from between his fingertips and back toward the surface.

"So, you sure that's tanzanite?"

"Not 100% sure," Young smiled. "I'm not a geologist."

"But you think it's tanzanite," Foley badgered.

"Yes, I think it's tanzanite," Young smiled.

Foley shook his head. "Cheese and crackers," he said. The private looked out onto the terrain for other gems. "That can't be the only piece of tanzanite, can it?"

Drake smirked. He stood up and cracked his neck.

"Can you believe it, man?" Foley grinned.

"Interesting," Young said studying the ground.

"What's interesting?"

"It's diamond dust or diamonds or whatnot," Young attempted pointing at the fine fragments. Based on the sunlight the glints which glistened as if there were diamonds in the fine powder.

"What?"

"You know, this place just got really interesting," Foley grinned broadly, picking up a purple gem among the granules that might have been two-carats and examining it in his gloved hand.

"Ain't no way that's diamond dust," Sarge said.

"That's diamond dust," Foley drooled.

Drake shook his head, no.

"This sand is filled with diamonds," Young said.

"Get your fur-lined hat out of here," Drake said, with a shake of his head.

"Seriously," Sarge said over his shoulder.

"Seriously," Foley repeated.

Drake and Foley looked at each other.

"We 'bout to be rich, rich," Foley smiled broadly.

Foley and Drake laughed. Sarge only sulked. Young flicked the small piece of tanzanite toward the dunes that they had landed on.

"Put it back in your pants, Foley. We didn't come to Rigo-C to turn into some freaking treasure hunters. We aren't soldiers of fortune. We are Galactic Force Space Marines with a mission. We have a job to do. And we're going to get it done," Sarge said.

"Yeah, yeah, we all know in war times and in times of peacekeeping soldiers come upon things that may have some value. We do not encourage looting of any kind. We do understand that a soldier, in the Galactic Forces, is only human. So, we all understand they may have a trinket or souvenir to remember their stay at unusual locations. That is acceptable. That is not frowned on by the higher ups in any way," the Sarge concluded.

The Sarge's words were a balm for Drake. They quieted any thought of the Galactic Force being just a front for a mercenary outfit of some kind going through the galaxy and looting goods and resources from still undiscovered planetary bodies.

"Okay, now that is out of the way," Foley said, with a smile, "What are you going to do with your gabillion credits?"

Drake chuckled. Young nodded approvingly. Sarge shook his head.

"We ain't mercenaries," Sarge gnarled.

"I know that," Foley said. "We do this for the greater good."

"Yeah, yeah and I want to be a superhero," chuckled Drake.

"Naw, I'm serious," Foley restarted. "I know we ain't mercs."

"Yeah, we ain't low-life mercs and ain't lowly space pirates either."

"Space pirates are the worse," Foley spat.

"I have to disagree with you on that one," Sarge stated.

"What? You think a merc is worse?"

"By leaps and bounds," Sarge nodded.

"How?"

"Space pirate is not necessarily in it for the money," Sarge pointed out. "They may have always wanted to be astronauts or space explorers. They had no intention of being a headache for others."

"Bull," Foley spat. "Space pirates launched with the intention of becoming rich, just like the mercenaries that were hired to protect them." He was sifting through the sand on the landship looking for diamonds and precious gems.

"Mercs are hired guns. They work for whoever will pay the most. They have no allegiance. No loyalty. They sell out for cash and creds," Young said. "Talk to one of the space pirates and you won't hear them say they would give up exploring if someone paid them."

"Space pirates are the same as mercs!" Foley fumed. He looked at a promising crystal and slipped it in his utilities cargo pocket.

"Relax, Foley," Sarge spoke roughly. "Look at the two moons and take a few deep breaths."

Foley shook his head at the Sarge's advice and looked back down at the dust which covered the landship. He bent down and blew the sand away to reveal a handful of diamonds and dropped them into his utilities thigh storage pocket where he stored his personals.

"Foley, get on task," Drake joked. "We didn't come to Rigo-C to turn into some freaking treasure hunters. We have a job to do," Drake smiled, imitating Corporal Payne's nasally tone. "Remember we can only take one souvenir for every planet we visit."

Foley smiled, mischievously. Drake looked at his teammate and shook his head. Young, the medic, straightened up and shielded his eyes to the sun overhead. Drake shielded his eyes and looked up into the bright blue sky and saw the two dark squares gently descending from an incredible height.

"Can you believe that we are here?" Young giggled. "We're like some real Robinson Crusoes, or something."

"Who the hell is Robinson Crusoe," Drake asked.

"Don't you read, Drake?"

"Of course, I read," Drake frowned. "Don't you take showers?" he added angrily.

"Calm down, Drake," Sarge barked. "Robinson Crusoe is a book about a guy that gets shipwrecked on a deserted island. He nearly loses his mind but finds a native who helps him survive. I think he calls him: Friday."

"Friday?" Drake laughed. "Why?"

"I can't remember," Sarge grinned.

"I think that's easy to figure. I mean, everyone likes Fridays," Foley joked.

"Okay, now that I got the skinny on your Robinson Crusoe thing," Drake said skeptically. "How is this like Robinson Crusoe?"

Young smiled one of those pie-eating smiles which made his normally broad smile almost look like it could reach his ears. "Well, this is the desert. We are on it. So, it's our island. That's all I got."

"Where's the palm trees, Robinson Crusoe?"

Foley and Drake laughed. Sarge just watched and remained silent. The laughter ended.

"How much longer are we waiting, Sarge?"

"Maybe another ten," the Sarge replied.

Drake nodded at Foley. Sarge, holding his assault rifle kneeled on the landship and examined the grit. He reached down and picked up a rock and grinned.

"What you pick up, Sarge?"

"Maybe, an engagement ring for the future Missus Sarge?" Foley laughed.

"Sarge, you got yourself a lady back on the *Sentinel* that we don't know about?"

"Can that," Sarge said gruffly.

The three on the landship looked at each other silently.

"Just joking around, Sarge," Foley avowed. "We didn't mean no harm."

Sarge nodded.

The three marines quieted. Drake aimed his assault rifle toward the landships slowly descending and followed the direction they were headed through the scope. Foley slipped his binoculars into the shatterproof case on his hip.

"Sarge, how long you been in the corps?"

"Eight years," Sarge responded to Drake. He was still holding the diamond Foley had joked about in his gloved hand. He stared at Drake skeptically. "Why?"

"Curious, I suppose," Drake said.

"You know, I think about being a part of the Space Corps and what it means," Foley said, suddenly serious. "I mean I'm not sure how long I want to do this. I mean, I'm sixteen... if I return to *The Arc*, what am I going to do?"

"*The Wanderer* is closer," Young abruptly pointed out.

"What?! I don't care. The point I'm making is, what is waiting for me there?"

"You ain't having fun out here?" Drake lowered his rifle and sat it down beside him. He studied Foley for a moment. "We all have questions, I think. But most of them are about what I'm going to do when I return to the *Sentinel*. All the other stuff is just noise."

Sarge twisted his lips on his dark face and frowned. He narrowed his eyes and studied the three marines on the hull of the landship. He stood up and inhaled reaching behind his back. He displayed a bronze disc the size of an old-fashioned dollar coin. He lifted the coin in the air and announced, "Coin check."

"What?"

"You heard the man," Young smiled tapping his left breast pocket and fishing out his challenge coin. He was the first to hoist the bronze coin into the air.

Drake tapped his left thigh and reached into his field pocket and lifting his own challenge coin into the air.

Foley tapped his breast pocket and fished out his challenge coin. He was the last one to lift the coin into the air.

All four marines had their challenge coins in the air.

Sarge was the first to put his challenge coin away. He studied the three marines with their coins in the air. He tapped the shoulders of Young and Drake. They replaced their challenge coins.

"What did you do to get that coin?"

"I got it for quelling a space prison riot on Mars," Foley granted. He smiled. "I got stabbed with a shiv."

"Remember we went to retrieve those prisoners who had space rage? Those guys on Mars were crazy dangerous," Drake added.

Sarge frowned at Drake. Drake went silent.

"You remember *why* you were given it?"

"Yeah," Foley nodded. "You said that I was calm under fire."

"Right, remember what the coin says on the front?"

Foley nodded. The coin was still in the air.

"Recite it," Sarge commanded.

"The task ahead of you is never as great as the power behind you," Foley stated.

"Remember that," Sarge said. "If you aren't sure, remember that you signed up to support your brothers."

Foley looked up and into the Sarge's eyes. The two marines did not blink.

"Lower your coin and tighten your act up. You owe us each a drink when we make the settlement or return to *Indomitable*. Your choice."

"Our choice," Drake burped.

Foley lowered his challenge coin and replaced it in his breast pocket. Drake reached out and tapped Foley on the shoulder.

"Hell, man, I mean, I been in the corps for nearly four years. I can't go back. I mean, what would I do if did go back?" Drake smiled at the thought.

"Once you sign up for the Force you should realize that life ain't ever going to end with you and your girl sitting and watching your rug rats running around and calling you daddy."

"This life ain't for everyone," Sarge confessed.

"This life ain't for anyone," Drake repeated and chuckled. "We are on the ass end of the galaxy and about to chase some four-armed mole people away from a settlement." Drake shook his head and blew air out of his mouth like he was a trumpet player. "The Galactic Force way of life."

"Ooh Rah," Sarge grunted.

"Ooh Rah," the three marines sounded.

The four on the landship's hull fell silent.

"You know that we are the first marines on this rock," Foley finally said.

"Yeah, there is that," Drake yielded.

"We the first marines to find diamonds in the sand, too," Foley pointed out.

"Yeah, that's true," Drake said, standing up again and sighting the slowly descending landships in the distance.

"Ain't that a song?"

"What? Shut up," Foley snickered, but the smile fell from his face, turning serious. "It's kind of amazing, if you think about it. We are the *first marines* on Rigo-C," Foley finally said. Drake and Young did not speak. They looked at Foley and Sarge and then around the powdery terrain that seemed to go on forever, for as far as the eye could see.

They were on a planet they had only heard of in a mission report. At first, with a cursory look, it might be any desert anywhere, but then looking down on the grainy soil Drake knew what Foley said was right. There were diamonds in the chalky ground. *Diamonds.* Drake toyed with the idea of just grabbing a bag of powdery ground and going to the *Sentinel* and cashing in and never having to work again.

The thought was so comical, Drake laughed for no apparent reason. He shook his head at his own foolish thoughts. He couldn't bag a handful of diamonds and high tail it to the *Sentinel*. There were too many obstacles in his way.

Drake had to simply appreciate that in history books he would be mentioned as the tenth man on the planet and one of the pioneers who liberated a dozen scientists from hostile natives. The marine smiled at the thought.

He was a pioneer helping to liberate scientists and settle a wild and untamed planet. Absently he wondered absently wondered if he would receive a plaque? It seemed only fitting.

Drake and the marines were on the far side of the galaxy in the Kuiper Belt where no planet had ever been discovered before. The gravity of the moment washed over Drake again and for an instant he could not think.

Young reached down and picked up a baseball-sized stone and looked it over before deciding to test his strength. He leaned back and threw the rock into the air as high as he could. The rock disappeared from Young's hand and went hurtling into the sky above and then raced toward the gritty ground below. Young smiled at his handiwork.

Sarge leaned against the gun turret and looked out toward the direction of the slowly descending landships just coming into view. Foley and Drake, however, watched as the baseball sized stone rose into the air like a bullet and reached its zenith. Young had sent it easily twenty yards into the air. As soon as the stone bounced on the loose sand there was a rumbling and a jolt which shook the landship and everyone in and on it. The tremor moved like a wave. The roll began in an unknown spot and continued moving through the grainy terrain like an invisible alligator hiding underneath the Alpha fireteam.

Instantly, Foley, Drake and Sarge grabbed for the hand holds on the top of the landship. Drake and Young were not fast enough or coordinated enough to reach the hand holds or ride the bucking landship as it rose and fell like it was moving sideways up and over a high curb.

The Sarge grabbed the hand hold and kicked his leg out to brace against the sudden bucking of the landship. He scowled and gritted his teeth, in the moment. Sarge seemed to move through liquid. His was suddenly moving in slow motion. His dark eyes thinned as he held onto the hand hold for dear life.

Foley had slipped and fallen. Spread out like a star, Foley's foot hit one of the handholds and quite fluidly the private spun and grabbed for the piece of metal. He clung to a foothold which stopped him from slipping off the landship. Foley found the hand hold and rescued himself from falling to the ground. He locked both his hands around the hand hold and dangled off the landship's roof.

The Alpha fireteam medic was jolted and though he tried to grab a hand hold, he tilted and lost his footing flipping off the landship. He tried to spin and imagine where he might land. The space medic only had his med pack strapped to his chest, another on his back and his service weapon strapped to his right thigh. Young flipped over and realized quickly he would not be able to land on his feet. At the last second, Young battle rolled and threw out his legs to stop his forward momentum. He jumped to his feet and found himself nearly twenty feet away from the landship. He looked around vigilantly, bent his knees to prepare for the next possible tremor. No tremor followed and Young searched the space between himself and the landship and only saw golden brown sand for as far as he could see.

The medic did not see Drake who had been beside him when the tumbler hit. Drake was close to Young when the tremor rolled through. At least, that was what Young thought as he surrendered to the inevitable flip, fall and recovery.

Drake had been standing on the roof of the landship watching a purple stone on the grained terrain when the tremor hit.

It was a violent jolt. It felt like something had crashed into the landship at full speed. He had gone head over heels as he flipped off the landship, seeing the screaming eagle symbol, the landship, Sarge, Foley and then the golden-brown granular soil of the slope of dunes the landship sat on. He hit the floury sandhill and tried to battle roll, but the powder-covered ground was harder than he imagined. It was like battle rolling on a concrete street covered in a thin layer of sand.

The mechanic bounced. He rolled. Flipped. Spun. The sky was above him, then to the left and then the right. Next thing he knew, the fine sand ground was above him. Grained floor replaced the sky and then he was losing his breath. It was all he could do to try to relax and let his body stop rolling.

Drake seemed to pick up speed and, for a moment, felt as if his fall would never end. The coarse ground slid beneath him. For an instant, Drake felt the lumpy terrain harden beneath him, as if he were battle rolling on steel for a few feet. Drake rolled from the hard to the soft ground and thankfully, unexpectedly, the particulate floor rose and aided in slowing the nearly unconscious marine's tumbling. Drake came to a stop as his body came to rest at a low point in the sandy ground. It was an unnerving feeling. He lay on the gritty floor, completely exhausted.

Instinctually, after finally coming to a stop, Drake attempted to sit up or reach for his face but his body, his arms and legs seemed, in that instant, to have no strength. All around Drake there was darkness. The world, the sky, the sand, the landship and everyone on it, moments before, were all gone. He believed his eyes were open, but he saw nothing. He tried to touch but felt nothing. All his senses, except one, had simultaneously shut down. He could hear his breathing but little else.

He knew he was breathing because if he was not, he was dead. Drake tried to register any other sound but there was little to grasp onto at that moment.

Drake tried to look left and right but the only thing which greeted him was an inky darkness. He tried to peer through the darkness but there was nothing before him. Drake could not look down. His head rested in the loose sand. He looked up but was surprised that the blue sky above was not there. Well, the sky he imagined was not there. All around him was an absolute blackness.

He tried to open and close his eyes, but other than hearing his breathing nothing registered. Drake knew he was breathing. He tried to feel his chest going up and down, but other than his rhythmic breathing there was nothing.

So, blind and unable to move Drake continued to fight against the invisible grip which took the strength away from all his muscles. He wanted to scream.

How long he lay there, Drake was not sure. The first sensation he registered was the warmth in the small of his back. The warmth was not like a fire but a slow warming of his lower back. The warmth radiated out and seemed to ignite other subtle feelings. The next significant feeling Drake felt was the ground beneath him rising and falling.

The slight lifting and gentle lowering of something invisible was distressing. Drake closed his dark eyes and tried to think. He was a marine. He was a *Galactic Force* marine. He was well-trained. He was one of the best trained soldiers in the galaxy. Drake only had to rely on his training. Laying still, controlling his breathing, he thought back to all the things his sergeant drilled into him and the others at boot camp.

Chapter 7.

Drake imagined he had somersaulted off the landship. He had **not** seen it. Others had.

His assault rifle had pinwheeled in the air. Drake flipped in the air and as he spun trying to stop himself from falling face first, he also tried to prepare himself for the inevitable impact ten feet below. The assault rifle speared the sand first, and a few seconds after, Drake bounced in the dusty sand and rolled and bounced. He kept bouncing and tried to tuck and roll.

The fine floor sloped downward and Drake knew the granular terrain he was headed for was the richest powdery floor in the galaxy. The chalky floor was encrusted in diamonds and precious gems. In the fall and crash, the gritty residue was in every open orifice, his safety goggles and helmet were torn off.

Drake recalled he had loosened his helmet's strap when he realized the squad wasn't departing until the two other landships landed. He had placed his goggles on the front lip of his helmet after the coin challenge.

Without helmet and goggles Drake came to rest at the foot of a sand dune. Covered in powdered sand Drake felt his right arm fall limply across his chest as he stopped and laid on his back. He could feel the grit of sand in his nose, ears and around his eyes.

He knew he could not have gone too far, but immediately, he felt heavy and tired. He felt as if gravity had increased a hundredfold on his chest, legs and arms. The pressure on him and on his appendages from above, made it impossible to move. He tried, but to no avail. He could not move, he could not open his eyes or call out.

A sound scratched at the edges of Drake's hearing. To the left and right he could hear the shifting of granules and feel something in his ears. He instinctually tried to shake whatever was slowly making its way into his ear canals, but he could do nothing to protest the invasion. He was an unwilling and unmoving victim.

The noise sounded again in his ears. It was grating and jangling in both of his ears, unsynchronized and both high and low pitched and though muffled, as if under something. Drake winced from the dissonance. He tried to determine where the sound emanated from, and at the same time felt something indescribable move over his face, nose and mouth.

Drake tried to twist his head and shake the invader in his ear that felt like a cat's tongue, dry and bristled. He wanted to gag as the desert sand and whatever was in the powdery land moved into his ear canals. The gritty, granular invasion was complete and utter, and Drake was incapable of stopping it. So, he gave in. He stopped struggling.

He breathed and the sticky, syrupy heat of Rigo-C greeted Drake. The breath evaporated in the hot, heady honeyed scents which were blended with the slight burnt hickory wood smell. In the darkness which enveloped him were all these distinct aromas around the marine. The mawkish powdery land was warm.

The marine tried to recall what had happened to him. He remembered he had been on the landship. Young had found a ball-sized stone and thrown it into the air. When it returned to the sand there was a shake of the sand and Drake had gone tumbling.

The coarse, molasses scented terrain held Drake in its embrace. The marine tried to move again but no matter how he tried he could not feel his body. Well, Drake could not move his body. It was as if his body was a cushioned and immobile casing and his consciousness was trapped inside. The casing was cushioned and immobile.

For an instant, Drake wondered whether he had blacked out, but he couldn't have. His last memory was... a somersault then darkness and warmth. The inkiness was complete. There was no light anywhere.

Drake recalled being knocked unconscious, and in that unconsciousness, being woken again and seeing specks of light in the darkness. Yet, in the darkness and warmth which enveloped Drake on Rigo-C there was nothing but complete blackness. There was no light to separate the darkness.

Drake heard the sound again, it was slight, abstract and alien. In the darkness, there was something trying to enter Drake's mind. The darkness uttered things Drake did not understand.

The grating, jangling noise sounded again but he still did not understand it.

Drake tried to understand the abstract and alien sounds. There was a wall between Drake and the unknown sound. Drake looked up and down the wall for a crack or entrance into the wall. There was nothing in the darkness. The wall seemed to go on forever.

The sound whispered to Drake. It called to him, but there was no way to decipher it. The sounds were clicks and clacks, high pitched noise which sounded more like birds made of glass and steel, twittering and trilling at a pitch just on the highest end of human hearing. The sound was painful to his ears. He winced in the casing of his body every time the sound rang against his ear drums.

The wall which separated ignorance from understanding appeared again and Drake realized there was no real, literal wall. But there was a wall in his mind. The foreign sounds, if they were nothing but sounds were lost on him. For a moment, as the strange utterance sounded again, the marine thought, there might be something familiar about it.

For the third time the sound hit his ears, reverberating through his body and around his mind.

The third time the sound rang out and the thing in his ears seemed to find a small anomaly in the wall of understanding and the high and low pitched, bone jarring wincings lessened. In its fading toward silence Drake noticed there was a small, perfumed doorway in his mind. The wincings, painful and nerve wracking, eased just a little and then and only at the end of the utterance there was an unlocking of the small aromatic door in the wall. The door did not swing wide open. It was ajar and in the sliver of an opening there issued a sweet-scented air that was heady if not intoxicating. Drake drew in in the sweetly perfumed air which washed out of the thin sliver of understanding and for the first time an understanding of the phantom sound grew in his mind.

The sound was too loud, at first. Then, it was too soft. Drake waited as the sound recalibrated and found a volume the marine could tolerate and understand. It was the ethereal sound of wind against tree leaves at first. Then the sound morphed into the sound of soothing raindrops on chimes. It, the sound, finally came to be a soft voice which seemed firm but friendly.

Breathe, Starfish. Breathe. The land holds you, Starfish. The land protects. The small sharp ones cannot have you, Starfish, unless the land gives you back. The land protects. The land is the many and the few, the big and the tiny. It is the protector of the protectors, the guardian of the guardians and the watcher of the watchers. The land has been for as long as there was. The land is. The land was. The land will be. The land has grown, Starfish. The land has retreated. The land is all around. There is nothing without the land.

Drake heard or felt this utterance in the darkness but was not sure where or when the voice was. The voice seemed to be in his head and all around him. He tried to look left and right, and up and down but only saw the utter blackness.

The land is. The land is.... We are harmony. We live and know, and this is ours and we are nothing but us.

The coarse honeysuckle scented coarse dust did not feel like anything Drake knew. Yet, it knew Drake. He tried to move, and the sweet-smelling coarse ground held him in its embrace. Drake tried to look down his nose and for the first time saw light and shadows. He could not see or feel his hands. He lay in an awkward way. His head rested on the scented sand, yet his body from his elbows to his boots were under the redolent sand. He tried to free himself.

The land, this thing, which held Drake in its grip did not twist or turn or apply pressure. It simply held Drake. There was no malice, anger, fear or trepidation in the thing holding him. It was as if Drake was an egg in the hand of a gigantic unseen thing, but not a thing. Whatever it was, Drake knew it was a living and breathing entity which was beyond Drake's understanding.

Out of the sky came the tiny prickly things. The land was welcoming. The land is always welcoming.

There was a pause. It felt as if there was a coldness at Drake's feet. The cold did not move from his feet. It swirled around his feet and made it uncomfortable, but not so uncomfortable that he felt pain.

We did not harm the tiny burry things. Tiny burry things came and tried the land. The tiny burry things thought to harm the ones that watch. But the land did not let them. We sent the watchers away. The land waited. The tiny burry things left the land. The land and the tiny and small, big and gigantic did not know the tiny burry things would return.

There was another pause. It seemed to last forever. The land inhaled but it did not breathe in the way a human would breathe. Drake felt a rise and fall or an elevation in the land and for an instant it seemed as if Drake was higher than he had been in the darkness.

We thought the tiny spiky things gone. Then, they returned. The tiny spiky things tried to scar the land. The many watched. The tiny spiky things tried to harm the many.

There was another cold pause. Drake could not move. He kept his breathing under control as he felt his body being poked and probed.

The land, Starfish, is the land. But now, Starfish, we have found you. We have sensed you. You, Starfish, shall help the land.

There was a pause. Instantly, in the marine's inner ear he heard scratching. Was there something in his ears? Was the land in his ears? The thought froze him.

In the darkness, for the first time, Drake noticed he was not breathing. Or, more specifically, he noticed that the normal functions of his body were absent. Being unable to open his eyes and see his surroundings did not disturb the marine. He did not rely solely on sight as a marine. He relied on his reflexes and his hearing more than anything else.

Even as he was unable to move, Drake found himself listening to the land all around him. The shifting sand gave Drake a bit of solace and he felt it loosen its grip. His arms moved, just a little. He could feel the weight of his legs. The noise was growing. He could hear bass drums in the distance. The sound was familiar, but Drake was not sure why.

Starfish, you are like the tiny prickly ones, but not like them...different. You can hear the land. The land hears you. So, you shall be our...vibris and firth.

The sound of the drums grew louder. Drake was still unable to move. He could only listen.

Beware, our protectors, Starfish. They watch over the land. When you walk back to your ship they will surface. They know your

78

path. They only protect. They will not harm you, Starfish. They will not attack the tiny burry things unless they attack them.

In the dark and distance, he heard a sound. The drumming was coming closer. A loud clack sounded like underground thunder. The drumming stretched and sounded far away again. Another loud crack jarred Drake.

Then, in the darkness, there was the sound of bells ringing. The bells rang and slowly faded. That was the last time Drake heard the disembodied voice for nearly three hours.

The bells jangled and the savory sand gave way, just a little beneath Drake.

"Drake!" Someone screamed. Hearing his name awakened his senses.

He opened his eyes and all his senses fully returned. He was buried in the sand. Drake snorted and blew flavorful sand from his nose and mouth. Ambrosian sand was all over the marine.

A rough gloved hand brushed the sweet-smelling sand from his face. He found himself looking up at the painted blue sky. There were no clouds.

Young was over him. The medic was on his knees and tried to pull Drake from the powdery ground. Drake looked at the medic in front of him, with his eyes big and determined. He was wearing his helmet and goggles, face focused. Young, up close and inches from Drake, seemed to have no pores. He pulled and dug, trying to lift Drake by his shoulders from beneath the chalky ground.

"You okay?" Young asked as he continued digging. "You took quite a tumble. It took us a few minutes to find you," Young told Drake. Foley was suddenly by Young helping dig Drake out of the silt. Foley and Young were pulling him up and out of the grainy terrain by his arms.

"A few minutes," Drake mouthed, spitting the sweet sand from his dry mouth, looking back over Foley's shoulder. They were nearly half a football field away from the landship.

Young and Foley finally unearthed Drake. The marine, once unearthed, climbed weakly to his feet. He opened and closed his eyes. He wiped at his face unsteadily. With Young on one side and Foley on the other, Drake stood propped up by his friends.

"Damn, man, were you and Young trying to swim in it?" Foley asked.

"Looked like he drowned more than swam," Young corrected.

"Yeah, I guess you're right," the gunner said.

Over Young's shoulder were two black squares of the two landships slowly descending by tri-parachute. They were the Beta and Nitro fireteams.

"How long I been in the sand?"

"Not long," Young said. "Maybe a minute or two?"

"Not much longer than that," Foley said.

The marine was suddenly confused. He had imagined he had fallen off the landship and hit the sand seconds ago. Drake thought he had been in the powdery sand much longer. The landships should have been on the ground in the marine's mind.

"You good?"

Drake nodded and took a few steps toward the landship when the next tremor jarred the Alpha fireteam.

"What happened?" His voice seemed hoarse.

"You don't remember?" Foley asked. He grabbed the arm of a still groggy Drake and placed it around his shoulder. Drake tried to speak. Aromatic sand streamed out of his ears.

"Hell, man, you and Young went cartwheeling off the landship. Young dove in the sand. You landed all the way over here. Young dug himself out and chased you down and found you like a dog looking for a bone."

Just then another tremor shook the gritty sand. The three marines braced and made sure that they did not fall on their butts. Foley had his assault rifle slung across his back. Young had a med pack in his hand and one on his back. On his thigh was his service weapon. Drake did not have his assault rifle, helmet or goggles. The small tremor subsided.

The three moved toward the landship. Drake felt gritty. He felt there was grit in his nose, ears and mouth. He reached up to brush his nose.

"Wait," Drake said. He looked to the left and the right. Drake looked across the horizon for the protectors. Not seeing anything substantial, Drake was bewildered. The voice which had held him had said they would appear on the way back to the landship.

"You, okay?"

"Yeah, just a little woozy," Drake said.

"Thought you had cashed it in. You were under the sand," Young mentioned as he and Foley moved Drake toward the landship.

Drake looked around and thought maybe he had simply blacked out. Maybe, he had hit his head and dreamed the whole weird voice. The more he thought about it, the more he was convinced he had just rung his bell too hard. That coupled with the heat of the planet, he thought, led him to hallucinate. People hallucinating heard voices in their heads, Drake rationalized.

"Man, no one said that we were gonna be on a shaker," Foley joked.

Drake was about to say something when the sandy surface of Rigo-C roiled. To the left of the marines, easily a football field away, appeared what was the first sign of the land protectors.

Foley pointed and yelled something but whatever it was had been silenced by the emergence of the bulbous head and humongous eyes which resembled the head of a thirty-foot tall space squid. To add to the squid image were the eight gigantic arms that pushed the cephalopod-like creature up and from the sand. The arms/legs issued forth from beneath the place where the squid-like head began. The top of the teardrop shaped head rose another twenty feet into the air.

The dreadnought space squid tilted back and rose up onto its four main legs displacing tons of gritty floor in so doing. Foley pointed toward the alien creature.

"What the figgety-figgety fig is that?"

"No, kidding, what the firetruck is that?" Young asked, narrowing his eyes and pointing. Drake shook more perfumed sand from his ears and had to crane his neck forward to be sure he saw what he thought he saw around the mountainous space squid. On the squid legs were smaller creatures that looked like darker, smaller versions of the elephantine squids. The smaller squids were man-sized, at least. Hundreds of the smaller dark squids scuttled around at the base of the leviathan squid and methodically climbed up the leg to the waist and hid. On the waist of the monstrous squid were what looked like hundreds of small, man-sized dark space squids.

"You think that's the mama squid?" Asked Foley with a grimace.

"Hope not," said Young. "I mean, I don't want to see the papa."

Drake laughed and tasted the bittersweet taste of tangy sand in his throat.

Another tremor shook the gritty floor beneath the feet of the marines just a few yards from the landship. A second astronomically large space squid stretched to its height and shook itself out of the arenaceous dune just fifty feet from the first. Hundreds of smaller space squids were dislodged and scrambled around the legs of the gigantic space squid. The smaller squids danced around the legs of the enormous squid trying to climb back onto it. The two bigger space squids were so unlike the smaller black squids. The monsters were dimpled, veined and generally the color of honey, ochre and the granulated terrain. Their arms and legs were a dark honey color.

The three marines continued toward the landship.

"Climb in," yelled Sarge as Foley and Young ushered Drake into the rear of the landship. Sarge locked the entry behind them.

"We're in," Sarge announced.

Payne accelerated the landship and the Alpha fireteam drove away from the space squids.

Foley buckled Drake in. Young did a quick concussion protocol check on Drake. He asked him the basic questions and checked Drake's pupils. At the end of the examination Young recommended Drake drink some water and do light work for the time being.

"What we doing, LT?" Asked Payne as the three marines settled in.

"What should we do?" Foley asked holding onto the ladder to the gun turret. "Should I chop those lobsters down with the .50 cal?"

There was silence. The First Lieutenant was monitoring the situation. He did not speak. He was thinking. The Sarge usually sure of himself sat and looked to the First Lieutenant.

"Sarge? LT?"

"Um, um," the First Lieutenant stuttered. "Based on the mission parameters," he trailed off.

Drake shook his head. He tried to remove the crumbly terrain which seemed to be everywhere. Drake wiped the grit from his ears.

"LT, don't harm them, unless they harm us," Drake offered. He shook his head. His throat was dry and scratchy. Drake tried to dislodge the cobwebs from his mind.

Payne and the First Lieutenant looked at Drake, curious. The Sarge shook his head and rubbed the back of his neck.

"What?" Foley looked at Drake curiously.

"Rule three. We don't harm them, unless they harm us," Drake repeated. He seemed exhausted. "We're visitors here."

Young was monitoring Drake.

"Can I have some water?"

Young gave Drake a biodegradable pouch of water. The First Lieutenant gave Drake a long look. He rubbed at the side of his hairless cheek. He looked at Payne and Sarge.

"Well, let's see what happens," the First Lieutenant announced. "Foley, man the .50 cal, just in case." Foley scrambled up the gun turret. "Okay, give them a wide berth," the First Lieutenant ordered. "Foley, watch the squids. Which way to the settlements?"

"South," Foley noted, manning the .50 caliber and watching the gigantic space squids which stood watching the landship's retreat.

"Okay, back this thing up. We need to wait for the two other landships. When they are down then we will head south toward the settlements," the First Lieutenant stated, seeming to get his second wind.

Payne reversed the landship up the gritty terrain to a vista point which allowed for a three-hundred-and-sixty-degree view of the landing site. East of the vista point was the mouth of Winchester mountain range. West of the vista point, the gravelly ground and desert stretched out for as far as the eye could see. To the north were the places where the two landships were gently landing just a football field's distance away.

When the two landships landed the first things the pilots did was jettison the tri-parachute. Pilots did not engage the engine until the landship was on the planet's surface. The Beta fireteam landship was the first to move after landing. The landship roared and rooster tailed the fine grain in its wake. Unlike Alpha fireteam, the marines did not exit the landship once they had landed. The landship magna-track tore across the rough terrain.

Nitro fireteam's landship shuddered to life. The landship tore across the sands following the Beta fireteam. The magna-track forced the loose ground into the air in the wake of the barreling landship.

"We have all landships down," Payne announced to the First Lieutenant. "I'm giving you all a beacon. As soon as you are near, we are heading to the settlement. Be aware, we have two king-sized problems that we are not messing with unless they mess with us. Confirm that," Payne the Alpha fireteam pilot told the pilots of the Nitro and Beta fireteams. He flipped a switch so everyone in the landship could hear the other pilots.

"We are down and rocking 'n rolling," Springer, the pilot of the Beta fireteam landship, roared. "Got your beacon. The distance is just about twohundred yards. We should be there in five minutes."

"Five minutes," Aricka King crowed. "Nitro team is down and moving. We will be at the beacon in three. We got scientists to liberate and power plants to dismantle," the pilot laughed.

"We will be there in three," yelled Springer.

"Last one there buys the team dinner," King sang.

"The teams are on their way, LT," Payne smiled.

"I heard," the First Lieutenant laughed. "When they are a minute out let's head south. We have to get to the settlement," the First Lieutenant announced.

Payne nodded to the First Lieutenant and shook his head at the race taking place on the landship monitor. Beta and Nitro were racing toward Alpha fireteams location. From Payne's point of view, it looked like Nitro was going to arrive first.

"Are you feeling better?"

Drake closed his eyes and rubbed the back of his head, feeling a small sore spot. Had he hit his head? There was only granular terrain all around him when Young and Foley pulled him to his feet.

84

"My head hurts, a little," Drake revealed.

"Yeah, you should be okay. Just need to give your noggin a little time," Young stated.

Payne engaged the landship.

"Okay, we are headed to the settlements," Payne announced. He spoke to the pilots. "We are moving. Catch us moving south."

The landship began the trek toward the settlements.

Almost immediately, Payne looked to the First Lieutenant for advice. "LT, what do we do about the Lookie Lews?"

Drake looked up.

"Circle around them. If they don't bother us then we don't bother them," ordered the First Lieutenant. "Foley be ready to spit death and fire if those space squids start to menace."

Payne, the driver of the landship for Alpha fireteam instantly swung right, and the two landships following behind the first followed without stop or pause.

Inside of the Alpha fireteam landship the five men roared at the sudden tilt and detour. The Alpha fireteam landship roared down the dune and descended and then attempted to drive up the edge of a created hill which one of the squids had created with a leg movement.

"This is some real Harryhausen stuff," announced Drake.

"Who the hell is Harry Hausen?"

Drake shook his head and sneezed out sand from his nose.

"This is crazy stuff," Foley agreed.

"It's an alien planet," Young pointed out. "What did you expect? Birds and deer? Flowers?"

"Shut up, Young," Drake said.

Sarge looked up and made his way to the front of the landship to speak with Payne and the First Lieutenant. The Sarge turned on Drake and studied him.

"So, Drake, how did you know that the squids wouldn't attack?"

The landship quieted.

"I don't know," Drake conceded. "It just seemed right."

Sarge listened to the private, skeptically. His dark eyes thinned, his permanent scowl deepening as he studied the private.

"Hey, command, the squids are moving."

With Foley's announcement the First Lieutenant and Sarge turned to the monitors. Payne was hearing the same report from the other landship pilots.

The landships rolled south. Alpha fireteam with their screaming eagle on the front and sides of the landship lead. Behind them was Nitro fireteam, piloted by the daredevil female marine Aricka King. Last, but not least, was Beta fireteam.

In the interior of the Nitro fireteam landship, Butcher flipped on the microphone. Suddenly everyone in the convoy could hear everything that was being said in the landship.

"I am so glad to have made it to the surface," Yvette Murray beamed. The rest of the convoy could hear the smile in her voice. She was recording everything on her small handheld camera and downloading and streaming it all simultaneously back to the *Indomitable*.

"You would be all giddy for a couple of forty-foot octopuses," Everett said with a shake of his head. "Me, I look out the porthole and think those things are bad juju." He gripped his assault rifle tightly. "Bad juju."

"Hell, man, this is nothing. We're on the frontier and being frontiersmen there ain't no such thing as juju, unless you talking about juju fruits," Valentine grinned adjusting his goggles.

The space squids moved and caused tremors in the wake of the landships.

"Hey, man of God, what your God got to say about those squid things following us?" Tyler asked looking out the landship porthole and watching the alien defenders moving slowly behind them.

Springer could only shake his head as he piloted and looked to the right at the hulking space squids.

"What? You ain't got nothing to say?"

"Leave him alone, Tyler," Williams grinned. "This is some life altering stuff here."

"It's not that," Springer grinned. "I mean, I know God is the God of all."

Tyler beamed.

"Even them?"

"Even them."

"Find that hard to believe."

"Why?" Springer smiled tranquilly. "Just because they don't look like us don't mean they aren't from God," the squad chaplain confessed. "We're all God's children."

"I ain't in that family," Tyler murmured.

At the lead of the convoy, in the Alpha fireteam landship Corporal Payne steered the magna-track landship across the continuously shifting sands of Rigo-C looking for the firmest portion of the desert and the straightest direction toward Echo Base, the ruins of a hurriedly constructed settlement.

The first mile was the slowest as Payne navigated based on telemetry and depth estimation mapping created by the On-Star driving command center. The command center was a watchful monitoring system which purported to have near true Artificial Intelligence. No one in the Galactic Force believed that but they did trust the On-Star command center.

The landship tilted and teetered as it found the firmness of the land below.

"According to the command center we have four miles of relatively firm and straight road to the settlement," Payne announced over his shoulder. He relayed the message to the other drivers. Sarge nodded. The First Lieutenant noted the corporal's words.

"What is going on?" Young asked, craning his neck and looking at the monitor. He could see the two radar blips of the supersize sand squids parallel to the landships. Drake did not say anything. He closed his eyes again and recalled the unusual conversation with the land.

"Man, oh, man, what have we gotten ourselves into?" Foley asked.

The landship convoy plowed on across the desert sands followed by the two gigantic sand squids. It was surreal.

Chapter 8

The estimated time of arrival at Echo Base was extended as the convoy weaved its way through the dunes and barrenness of Rigo-C. The On-Star navigation and sonar system, which Payne insisted the two other pilots engage, pointed out that the lumpy terrain was shallow in some places, sand covering an extremely hard base, but also pointed out deep underground caverns which had filled with the granules of the rhombus planet and could swallow a landship. Navigating the shifting sands and desert was more like driving across a gigantic chessboard where all the white squares were traps which could drop a landship hundreds or thousands of yards below the surface. Now, the pilots or drivers of the landships understood this as Payne ordered them all to implement the On-Star navigation and sonar system. If they were on foot the chalky floor would not be a problem. The crushed ground would not give way immediately to the slight weight of individuals on foot, but a two-ton magna-track landships would be swallowed up in seconds.

Sarge was the first to notice, in the Alpha fireteam landship, twenty minutes had come and gone. He tapped the First Lieutenant and in the cramped interior leaned over and said, louder than he intended, said, "What gives LT? According to my calculations we should have arrived at the settlement already."

"Is it me, or are things further than they should be?"

The LT, studying his monitors, nodded. He checked the three monitors again and said: "I think we need to stop and give everyone a minute to stretch their legs before we crest the ridge ahead. Based on the mapping we should be about," he paused to calculate the time.

"Ten minutes," Foley announced.

"Ten minutes out," repeated the First Lieutenant with a nod. Turning to their driver he said, "Payne, at the base of the ridge tell the landships to stop. We got a needed rest stop coming up. Pass that down the line. Tell the teams to stay close to the landships. One marine on the .50 caliber. One marine watching as they shake it. We are only giving them ten to shake and make it back before we hump it to the settlement."

"Ten minutes," Sarge chomped.

"Roger that," Payne noted passing the orders to the other pilots.

"LT, we are at the base," the corporal said. Payne disengaged the electrothermal engine.

The landships skidded to a halt. Alpha fireteam was in front. Nitro and Beta fireteams slid in beside them. The base of the slope seemed to rise for a mile.

"Tell them all we take ten to stretch and shake it then we're rolling," said the LT. "Sarge, ten minutes. Foley, get on the .50 Cal and watch those squids. If they do anything hostile let them know that we are the fricking Galactic Force marines."

"Roger that," Foley said from the gun turret. "Hey, Drake, hurry up and shake it and give me a break."

Drake nodded. His helmet rested comfortably on his head as he prepared to exit.

"You, okay?"

Sarge was the first out of the landship. He carried his assault rifle out of the vehicle. Young was next.

"Let's move!" Sarge bellowed. "We got ten minutes. Shake it and make it. Stretch and get your last tourist pictures because we're less than five from the base."

Young stopped at the exit and turned to examine Drake.

"You sure you're okay?"

Drake smiled awkwardly and nodded.

"Yeah, man, I'm good," Drake sighed feeling some grit in his ear. He tilted his head and rubbed at his nose as he exited the landship. Drake paused and looked down at the powdery terrain below his feet. The marine stepped out of the landship and as soon as his feet touched the gravelly floor he felt as if he was back underneath the loose sand, after he had been flipped off the landship.

Starfish returns to the land. Starfish, we have found you. We sensed you. You, Starfish, look and see the land. The land welcomes you. You shall help the land.

Drake looked around. Suddenly, he could see the smallest things in the honey-colored sand. In the direction the marines had come, in their wake, were dozens of bulbous creatures with no visible eyes and thick bodies which looked like they were an unnatural blend of honey-colored maggots with a circular mouth and six small legs ending in curly claws. Drake looked at the other marines and was surprised no one was sounding the alarm about the proximity of the bulbous creatures.

They cannot see what the land does not want them to see.

Drake looked back. To the right, just thirty yards from the landships, were what looked like hundreds of cosmic caterpillars, about half the size of the landship, with these disproportionately oversized heads. The creatures were segmented from head to tail and possessed eight incredibly small legs which defied physics. Their tails were divided into two ten-foot whips.

Drake spun around again and found himself stymied. The other marines, as they walked and moved, seemed unconcerned about the alien life all around them.

"How?" Drake asked under his breath.

The land protects. The land listens.

He studied Young and Sarge and watched as the marines walked toward the front of the landship. The two other landships were parked, Drake noted. He walked to the rear of the landship and smiled self-consciously seeing Tyler and Springer stretching. Everett was heading to a sand dune to shake it.

The land sees what you see. We know you Starfish.

The marine froze. He looked around again, still surprised that no one noticed the other creatures. Drake dug in his ear feeling something inside but finding nothing there but his finger.

We must trust you, Starfish.

"What up, Drake?" Tyler walked by Drake toward the direction the convoy had just come from.

"What up?" Drake said, distracted. He watched the giant of a mechanic walking toward the rear of the convoy.

Starfish, the tiny brambly ones named you. Christian. Drake. Starfish. Christian Drake. You are our Starfish.

"Chris? You, okay? Heard you were trying to do a belly flop or something, earlier," Valentine grinned.

"I'm fine," Drake said. He opened and closed his eyes and smiled broadly. He turned and pointed toward the front of the landship. Drake walked awkwardly away.

Starfish. The land is full of.... Wonder. Beauty. The land learns. "What's going on?" Drake asked no one in particular. He looked around from beside the landship and stopped short. He found himself face-to-face with the Sarge. The Sarge placed his hand on his service weapon and studied the private.

Kiss-Crisp-sun Lay ka? Strange. Starfish. Christian. Drake. It is a windsong? We know you. Look, and see the great and the small of the land. They are the land. We are the land. The land is all of us. "Drake, you, all right?"

Drake closed his eyes for a moment.

"Sarge, yeah I'm fine," Drake lied. "I'm supposed to relieve Foley."

"All right," Sarge said and turned and moved to the front of the landship.

Drake watched as the Sarge stopped at the fender and turned his attention to the gigantic space squids which looked to be about twenty yards away, not moving. Sarge stood with his foot on the magna-track of the landship as Drake climbed inside the landship.

We are all connected. The land reaches out to you. It is— As soon as both feet were in the landship the voice ceased. He waited a moment and hearing nothing smiled but felt surprisingly disconnected.

"Foley take your break," Drake said after entering the confines of the landship.

"Roger that," Foley chirped, descending from the gun turret. "The mega squids are posted to your two o'clock. Sarge said to watch them and mow them down if they do anything hostile."

"Roger that," Drake said as Foley bounced to the floor of the landship and pushed out the exit without another word.

Drake climbed into the gun turret and was greeted by the various buttons giving longitude, latitude, distance, altitude, ammunition and a host of information which was necessary for utilizing the .50 caliber cannon. Drake studied the gun turret's mechanism knowing that to fire the .50 caliber he had to flip and depress a series of buttons in the correct sequence, or nothing would happen. He shook the very thought out of his head. There was no need to even consider the idea.

The marine listened to the landship interior and paused. "Is there anyone in here?" Drake listened and heard nothing. "Can you hear me?" He looked around the gun turret and hoped to hear something but, again, heard silence in the landship.

Drake noted that the honey-colored sand seemed to shimmer. He magnified the view on the turret glass focusing on the shimmering sand and was surprised to see there were thousands of smaller sand squids moving around and beneath the leviathans. He was suddenly fascinated. The smaller creatures attempted to climb onto the legs of the large squids with varying degrees of success. The effort of the small sand squids climbing and falling and righting themselves and attempting to climb again was mesmerizing. He found that he could not stop smiling at the sight thirty yards away.

Drake saw the other aliens through the landship turrets. It was as if Drake were wearing X-ray glasses and could see things no one else could. It fascinated him. He looked out the viewfinder and saw the alien creatures that had not been caught on video. He wondered absently if they were dangerous. Dangerous or not Drake knew he was not going to press anything or flip anything which would unlock the wrath of the .50 caliber cannon. Turning his attention to the towering defenders, Drake found himself studying the slope which stood in front of them like a sand wave rising at a five percent angle.

"Maybe, I'm going crazy," Drake said. "That's it. There's a lot of stress in space travel," Drake rationalized in the gun turret. He looked down and noticed there were a handful of fine sand crystals on the shelf of the assault monitor. Drake brushed the fine crystals off the ledge and tried to focus. He closed his eyes in an attempt to calm himself. He tapped the screen on his monitor and there before him in one-third of the size was Young and the Sarge.

He swallowed. Drake blinked and placed his hand on the interior of the turret glass. The glass felt cold to the touch. While studying the veins on the back of his hand, he realized his hand was trembling on the glass. The thing which chilled Drake was not the coolness of the glass but the two ragged veins pulsating on the back of his hand. He pulled his hand away from the glass and in the action of removing his hand he noticed the faint outline of his handprint on the small window glass. Looking closer, he expected to see the sweat outline but not the thin sand outline which perfectly matched his handprint in sand.

He leaned closer to the glass and thought the thin sand outline had to be a trick of the light. He leaned ever closer and blew on the sand and watched part of it disperse. Drake blinked and felt something in the corner of his eye. The marine rubbed at it his eye and felt the build-up of sand.

"What the frack?"

Drake rubbed the sand in between his thumb and forefinger. He opened his hand and investigated his palm, curious. Small granules of sand rested there.

"Am I made of sand?"

Was he losing his mind? Had he already lost his mind? Drake felt his heartbeat speeding up. His chest felt tight. His breathing became shallow.

He turned the turret back to the direction the convoy had just come from and looked out at the horizon. The targeting mechanism highlighted a quick moving marine, tracking distance and range.

Foley stumbled back from the small sand dune and climbed into the landship. Drake climbed out of the turret and nodded to the returning marine.

"Everything, good?"

"Everything *was* good," Drake sneered. Drake stepped to the exit and Young, Payne and Sarge were standing there. The First Lieutenant appeared behind the three marines. Thwarted, Drake spun around and sat down in his assigned seat.

"Let's roll," the First Lieutenant announced. Young and Payne climbed into the landship.

"Button 'em up, we are rolling," Sarge announced outside the landship. Sarge was the last to climb into the landship. He locked the exit and sat down.

The corporal climbed behind the navigation console. The electrothermal landship engine engaged. The landship magna-track treads found grips and moved forward. As the convoy started up again, the two other landships fell in line behind the Alpha fireteam vehicle.

The view was surreal. There were the two great space squids moving beside the convoy. The space squids moved silently at a distance. The closer they were the more the sand and surface of the planet shook.

The three landships slowly made their ways up the sandy slope. Five minutes into the climb and suddenly there was a deafening sound that sounded like ancient helicopter blades whirring overhead. The sound forced everyone in the landships to cover their ears as the sound intensified.

In the landships of the Alpha and Beta fireteam the main monitor near the rear of the vehicle blinked on and everyone could see the conversation in the Nitro landship. There was technology in the landship which allowed everyone to speak.

"What the hell?" Yvette Murray screamed. She craned her neck to look out the porthole.

The sound roared continuously over the convoy.

"What is that?" Yvette Murray asked, pointing up toward the gray skies.

"Oh, hell! Not more weirdness," Butcher voiced. The muscular corporal leaned forward and looked out the porthole where Murray had positioned herself.

For the first time since the marines had landed on Rigo-C there was something in the air above them. Out of the sky appeared dozens of gigantic, winged creatures. They had dark triangular heads and looked a bit like insect heads, slim, dark bodies, bisected translucent wings and what looked like a gigantic scorpion's tail.

"This is like some Jurassic Park meets Space Invaders crap," Butcher said.

"I'm telling you," said Valentine looking out of the porthole near Everett.

"I thought there were only those Teddy bear-like things with the mole-like heads on the planet," Everett mentioned shouldering Valentine off his shoulder.

Murray grinned broadly. "Yeah, that isn't completely true," Murray said.

"What do you mean?"

"Well, there has to be a bunch of unknown extraterrestrials on Rigo-C," Murray began.

"ETs? You just said ETs are on Rigo-C," Everett chuckled.

Murray grinned. "Well, if you think about it, we are the ETs, here."

"So, what you thinking?"

Murray did not speak.

"You are the science officer," Valentine exhaled, turning back to Murray. "If you don't know, you know we don't know."

"Well, this is an entirely unfamiliar environment," Murray explained. "There is no way to know if we have seen all the native creatures here," Murray explained.

"How's that?"

"I mean, if you landed on Earth, back in the day, and say you landed in the Sahara you might think the whole planet was a desert, right?" Murray said. "If you landed in the Amazon you might never have been able to name all the animals and wildlife there. That is our problem presently. We know there are the hostile alien life forms the scientists ran into, but there is no way to gauge exactly how many more life forms there are on Rigo-C. There might be some that are even more hostile than the titans the scientist documented."

"We're screwed," Everett said, hanging his head.

"Grow a pair, Everett," King barked from the front of the landship. "We are here. We on mission. We do our job and get out of this freaky zoo in one piece."

"I just figured to dismantle the power plant and head back to the *Sentinel*," Everett said, under his breath with a shake of his head. "Now I gotta worry and being eaten by squids and scorpion wasps."

"Buck up, Everett," Butcher said, with a smile. "Things could be worse," Butcher said.

"How, Sarge?"

"We could be their food," Butcher laughed.

Valentine laughed at the Corporal's joke.

"You know that on Earth, before we evacuated, we had less information about the oceans than we did about space," Murray said to the fireteam. She paused. "The biologists said that they had identified only about eighty percent of the living creatures on Earth. We had hundreds of years and science to research and only identified eighty percent."

"So, what are we looking at?" Butcher asked.

"Can't say," Murray acceded. "I say that we don't do anything to stress the system. We need to be careful not to agitate this system more than necessary, that is," Murray elaborated.

"So, what's the worse-case scenario," Valentine asked.

Murray knitted her brow.

"How will we know that things have gone from crap to crap on fire?"

Murray just shrugged her shoulders.

"Come on, you're the science officer," Everett stated. "You have to have an idea of when this whole thing's goes from manageable to a trash fire. I mean, you saw the video of the mole head otter creatures. What is the worst-case scenario? How do we know that they aren't going to be our friends?"

"We are close to the top of the ridge," the First Lieutenant announced. "Need everyone to get in the game. Focus. Can this "frenemy" chatter. We have a job to do. Go radio silent," he announced.

The landships crested the ridge and began the short descent to the edge of the Echo settlement.

"Get ready to be the best the Galactic Force has produced," Sarge growled in every marine's ear.

Chapter 9.

The descent from the ridge toward the settlement was not long or steep. It took only a handful of minutes to descend the sandy slope and find the firmness of the surface again. At the foot of the descent the landships slowed and slid a little to the left and then the right as they maneuvered toward the settlement.

The ground became a little less sandy and more like a slightly bumpy road littered with potholes and ruts and the convoy found itself slowing. The navigators picked their way through the boulders that were the size of landships on the small end and shuttles on the big end. Some of the rocks leaned against each other like dominoes allowing the landships to move cautiously underneath their two steepled sides.

"Can we stop?" Rang in the ears of all the marines. "Can we stop, First Lieutenant? This is science officer Murray. I need to document this for our scientific logs."

"We are recording everything right now, Murray," the First Lieutenant advised. "Once we get to the settlement and suss out our mission, and we have downtime, I'll have one of the landships tool you around and let you document your heart out. Right now, we have to reach Echo settlement."

"But—"

"Radio silence," the First Lieutenant snapped, and the radio chatter went quiet.

A few minutes later, the landships stopped and the First Lieutenant and his squad climbed out of the landship to view the Echo settlement.

"Hold it together," the First Lieutenant announced to everyone in the squad. "We need to recon the settlement. Need to determine if any scientists are still in there. Rescue first. Engage second. Bring the scientists back. May have a dust off based on numbers."

"LT, how many scientists are we expecting?"

"There were eight at last count," the First Lieutenant declared. "Stop us one hundred yards from the site," he said.

"Roger that," Payne announced.

One hundred yards from the Echo settlement the three landships stopped.

"Everyone out," yelled the Sarge.

The marines exited the landships armed and ready for battle.

"Okay, now I have been to all the planets in the galaxy and I have never seen anything like this," Foley said, adjusting his helmet and looking at the horizon, tilting his head to the left slowly.

"How is this possible?" Butcher, the scarred corporal snapped.

In the distance, the Echo settlement stood against the honey-colored sand. Or what was left of the Echo settlement anyway. There were six ISS flags flapping in the northern entrance to the settlement. From one hundred yards, the marines could see the settlement was made up of a dozen prefabricated biodomes jig sawed together. Seven of the twelve prefabricated biodomes had been crushed. The extent of the destruction was surprising. The biodomes were made to be durable and tested to withstand incredible damage. Whatever had torn through the settlement had been extraordinarily strong. The marines couldn't help but acknowledge that their odds against whatever creature had done this were probably low.

"You think the mole things did this?" Tyler asked, looking through his binoculars.

"No, they were super strong, but they weren't superhumanly strong. The biodomes are tested against gale force winds. To be able to pop one of those biodomes you'd need a meteor or something with that kind of power," said Jenkins.

While Tyler and Jenkins tried to figure out the cause of the destruction, most were fascinated by the sight behind the Echo settlements and biodomes.

There were green rolling hills. Unlike the usual hills that gave way to the horizon, on Rigo-C, the hills folded, like a piece of paper, and despite the logical, natural, three-dimensional landscape the hills rose up at a right angle. The hills rising was not the unusual point of view, however. It was the eerie appearance of a flat sky. Exchanging glances amongst themselves, the marines had to wonder what happened if you climbed to the top of the hills?

"Well, the best I can explain is that Rigo-C is a completely strange place. The settlement, where things are based is in the corner of this square planet," Yvette Murray explained. Of all the members of the landing party, Murray was unarmed.

"Rhombus," Drake corrected.

"What?" Yvette Murray studied the private holding an assault rifle.

"Rhombus," Drake repeated. "The shape of Rigo-C is a rhombus, not square."

"Rhombus," Murray nodded. "So, the ISS settlement is up against Rigo-C's hills that look as if you climbed them you would go straight up the hill without realizing there is no gravity, or at least no gravity like we know it, like Jack in the Beanstalk. And just like in Jack in the Beanstalk, if you climbed to the top of the hills behind the settlement you would be in an entirely different place. In this case Rigo-D. A whole different terrain and environment, because of the whole four sides thing."

"What?"

"What do you mean, what?"

"I mean, what the French-fried potato do you know about this? I mean, you are just like all of us. This is your first time here," Foley said, frustration rising in his voice. "We're all first timers!"

Murray shook her head at Foley like one would at an insolent child.

"Can it," Sarge growled. "We have work to do." The Sarge assigned positions while the First Lieutenant and corporals determined the best approach to entering the settlement.

"Drake, you and Foley take point. Go out twenty and post up. Watch for any movement," Sarge ordered. Before Sarge had begun barking another word Drake grabbed his rifle and he and Foley took off running through the sand.

Starfish returns to the land.

Drake did not think. He just ran south. He ran, and the action alone allowed him peace. He loved running. He was a natural runner, like it was hardwired into his genes. When he ran all the world fell away. In the pumping of his arms and legs things just became clearer.

He found himself acutely aware of his own breathing as he ran, feeling the air being pulled in through his nostrils and filling his lungs. Simultaneously, Drake could hear his heartbeat as it banged in his ears and when he thought he might go deaf from the noise, the marine exhaled and was instantly felt refreshed.

Starfish is like the great ones in the hills of the land.

An alert on his helmet camera beeped. "Far forward point reached."

Drake skidded to a stop. He turned around and noted that the landships were out of sight. He checked his distance again and smiled smugly. Drake stood and allowed his heartrate to slow and his breathing to slow while he looked for cover.

Starfish, the land enjoys you. The land sensed you. You, Starfish, look and see the land. The land welcomes you. You, Starfish, shall help the land. The land likes this feeling in you, Starfish. You are... happy. The land does not know why. Why, Starfish?

He continued to scan the land around him for cover. "I just like—" Drake began only to stop.

He found an outcropping of rocks and used it to hide and survey the terrain. Slipping off his assault rifle, Drake took another deep breath and his heartrate and breathing were only slightly higher than before he had run. He was preparing to scan the settlement when Foley arrived.

"Man, who you think you are, Usain Bolt or something?" Foley said, placing his hands on his knees, out of breath. "You were supposed to wait on me."

Starfish, this tiny bristly one is not... happy.

Drake smiled at Foley. The marine had his hands on his knees and was trying to catch his breath. His rifle was at his feet.

This is private first-class Jonathan Foley. He is your... friend. Friend. The land knows this... feeling. The land listens.

"Sarge didn't say wait on Foley," Drake chuckled.

Foley shook his head and looked for a place to post up and watch the settlement, spying the same outcropping of rocks Drake had seen. He walked to the group of rocks, which looked like three knuckles in the sand, and sat down, tired. Drake scoffed and shook his head at Foley. Foley placed his rifle against one of the rocks and tried to catch his breath, taking his canteen from his backpack and took a sip of his water.

"Man, just saved you, like minutes ago," Foley reminded.

"You all sixteen and made of springs and attitude," Drake said, with a smile. "You was supposed to beat me, hands down." He allowed his smile to broaden. "Isn't that what you always telling me."

"That is what I say. You cheated. You started before me. You knew where you were going," Foley said, trying on a bunch of excuses hoping one would stick.

Drake scoffed. He turned and looked at the settlement in the distance, holding his assault rifle, and sighting down the rifle barrel. There was no movement from the settlement.

Foley threw a rock at Drake and Drake who just shook his head in response.

"You are childish," Drake said, with a scowl.

Foley flipped over onto his stomach and put his assault rifle to his shoulder. The two marines eyed the settlement which was only thirty yards away.

"Do you see anything?"

Drake did not answer immediately. He instead, looked at the settlement and for the first time noticed four outer space caterpillars, but unlike the ones he had seen on the other side of the ridge these were the size of the landship.

Starfish, the land knows you. The land hides the guardians from the tiny, barbed ones. The tiny, barbed ones do not see what the land holds.

"Why?"

The land is not for everyone, Starfish. The land is... living. That is what you think. The land lives. The land protects the small and the big. The land lives to protect.

"Did you say something?" Foley said across the expanse between them.

Drake looked at Foley guiltily, then coughed and cleared his throat.

"No, I didn't say anything, I mean... I don't see anything."

Foley nodded. He paused. "Are you talking to yourself?"

"No," Drake smirked. He looked away from Foley and sighted down the rifle, all business.

The land needs you, Starfish.

"Why?" He asked in a hushed voice.

Starfish, you understand the land. Not all the tiny prickly ones do.

"What does that mean?"

The land is not for everyone, Starfish.

"What does that mean? I mean, what do you mean that the land is not for everyone?"

The tiny prickly ones came here... uninvited. The land did not... ask the tiny prickly ones and their... prickly things to come here.

"What," Drake said, confused.

The land decides. The land sees. The land does not allow the tiny prickly ones to see.

"So, you make things," Drake said under his breath, watching Foley. He searched for the right word. As he did so, in the shadows of his mind Drake felt something. He could not identify what he felt but it was something unusual.

Invisible.

"Invisible," Drake said, under his breath.

The land protects.

"What now?"

Now, the land must protect.

"How?" Drake asked.

There was a beat.

"What are you doing now?"

The tiny thorny things must leave, Starfish. They are not welcome.

"But they, we, are here," Drake said under his breath.

The land will not welcome you, them, they. The land must protect the land.

"I know all that. But we won't stop," he paused and looked at Foley to make sure his voice was not too loud. Drake continued, in a whisper. "We are mean and well-trained. We will control the land."

Starfish, you are not like the others. They are mean and prickly. They are not welcome. They are bad and see the land as just...

102

something they can...claim. The land cannot be claimed. The land lives. It is not something to be bought or sold.

Drake listened and turned to look back at Foley. His fellow marine was sighting the settlement.

"Sit rep," chirped in the ears of the marines.

"Quiet here, no movement, just two jarheads on point watching nothing," Foley said.

Drake listened.

One hour after the call, Drake and Foley were relieved by the sharpshooter, Williams, and radio operator, Valentine.

Williams, the sniper, took Drake's position.

"Heard it's pretty quiet," Williams said. Drake stood up and looked back toward the settlement where the four gigantic deep space caterpillars were standing guard over the settlement.

"Yeah," Drake said, not sure what else to say.

Williams sighted through his scope and scanned the settlement from his position. Drake waited. He expected Williams to look at him and say something about the space caterpillars. The marine sniper looked at Drake and nodded.

"Anything else?"

"No, just watch and report," Drake said.

Foley shouldered his rifle and gestured to Drake and the two began walking back toward the landship camp. Drake nodded and could not believe that none of the other marines made mention of the giant caterpillars.

"What you thinking?" Foley asked as they slowly trudged toward the Galactic Force vehicles.

Drake did not answer immediately.

The land will expel the tiny, jagged ones, Starfish. It must. The land has no choice.

"I think that we are not the heroes in this story," Drake said.

"Why?"

"Just a feeling," Drake said.

Heroes, Starfish? Heroes. This is something the land does not know.

"Man, you have to get over that whole hero thing," Foley stated. "I mean, I know that we're supposed to be the few, the proud and the... whatever," Foley joked. "But we ain't always got a choice."

"It's always a choice," Drake countered. "A hero is supposed to protect the weak. A hero is supposed to protect those that have no protection."

The land is the hero here.

"Why you telling me this?" Foley asked.

"Just need perspective," Drake said, looking all around him and seeing the golden-brown sand which constituted the land.

Foley and Drake fell silent. The pair walked on arriving at the camp and the landships a few minutes later.

Sarge was sitting on the fender of the landship with his assault rifle on his lap. The Sarge watched Foley and Drake return to camp.

"Go get something to eat. Take a break. Shake it if you must. We are moving to the settlement soon," the Sarge declared.

Drake nodded.

The land is prepared, Starfish.

Foley nodded as well. Just a few steps from the Sarge, Foley turned to Drake again.

"How long you think we got?"

"Got for what?"

"You know, before going to the settlement."

"Maybe an hour or two?" Drake calculated.

Foley walked toward a small gathering of marines seated near an outcropping of rocks. Foley slowed and turned.

"Drake, what gives?"

"Think I'm going to stretch my legs before eating," Drake lied, brushing off the question. "Go on without me."

Foley shrugged his shoulders and continued. Drake watched Foley find a seat next to Tyler in the group of enlisted. Young sat wearing his medi-pack and helmet. Williams sat in the semi-circle next to Everett and King. Springer had his helmet off and at his feet.

Foley grabbed an MRE, Drake noticed out of the corner of his eye, and heard him ask, "What is this?"

"Your guess is as good as any," grinned Everett. He spooned some of the MRE into his wide mouth.

"Maybe it's horse?"

"No, it's probably rat," Tyler sneered. "I think that the *Sentinel* was overrun with 'em before we left."

"The belief is that it's Traveler's Stew," jested Aricka King. She was spooning the MRE into her pouty mouth.

Foley spooned the stew. It did not look appetizing. It had a consistency of soup and contained noodles and various square, brown globules of the mystery meat.

"Think I've scraped better off my boot," Tyler chuckled.

"You ain't eating?" Williams asked, but Drake did not hear the question. He was more interested in watching Murray crossing the camp than the conversation. He walked away, quietly following Murray at a distance.

Chapter 10.

Drake followed but from time to time looked back and thought absently that if he turned around and just walked to the enlisted and told them what was going on in his head, they would.... surely, they wouldn't listen to him. At the very least, they would think he was crazy. He shook the idea of the enlisted being any help. Perhaps, he could just walk past the enlisted and find Sarge. If Drake found the Sarge he might listen. Sarge would still be sitting on the fender of the landship guarding the front of the camp. Drake imagined telling the Sarge what was going on in his head. All he had to do was turn around.

Starfish, the land needs you.

With the voice in his head, he found the idea of turning around unpalatable and dismissed the idea of turning around. He would not stop, slow, or walk away from the directive given by the voice in his head. He walked toward the science officer.

Starfish, the land needs to listen to these prickly ones.

Drake looked around the small group and saw the First Lieutenant and the small *Indomitable* science officer standing near a rock formation which shaped like a three-rock pyramid. They were talking with each other.

Drake moved closer.

"I am here now," the elvish Yvette Murray pointed out. She was unarmed and not five-foot-tall. Standing beside the First Lieutenant she looked like she might be his kid sister, Drake thought absently. The First Lieutenant turned on the smaller woman and stared at her evenly. Drake understood immediately that they were having a heated conversation.

"Our mission is pretty clear," the First Lieutenant said through gritted teeth.

"It would be pretty stupid to try and complete a mission without consultation from a science officer, since this is actually a science mission you are on," Murray pivoted.

The First Lieutenant inhaled. "Proceed," the First Lieutenant relented.

"There are only a couple of ways to go about this, First Lieutenant."

"You are a science officer," the First Lieutenant noted. "But remember this mission is military. We clear?"

"Two ways," Murray stated. "Just hear me out." She paused and waited for a reaction from the First Lieutenant. When none came, she proceeded. "We are explorers. We are exploring planets we've never been to before. We can be on the planet and destroy its development, or we can be observers," Murray stated. "As observers, we are supposed to simply watch and do nothing else."

"We didn't come here to observe," the First Lieutenant bristled. "The scientists, the astronauts, who came before us did that." The First Lieutenant adjusted his helmet. "We came to complete a mission and nothing else. We don't have time for ethical hypotheticals. Hypotheticals are above our pay grade. We are given missions to complete. We don't weigh the consequences more than necessary."

"But this is a unique moment," Murray cried. "We are on an undisturbed planet. We need to do as little as possible to effect the aliens we encounter. I mean, we have already interfered with the normal and healthy development of an alien life and culture," Murray mentioned. "We need to step back. There are alien life forms here we could destroy without even knowing. Our presence could upset the entire development of this entire planet."

"Listen, I understand all that," the First Lieutenant stated. "I'm not a scientist. More importantly, we just don't have a choice. I can't, suddenly, grow a conscience and start questioning orders. That is not something that we, as marines, do."

"Perhaps, you need to," Murray said, crossing her arms in front of her.

The First Lieutenant opened and closed his mouth. The taller marine studied the science officer as if she were an alien life form. Yvette Murray looked at the First Lieutenant as if he were a surly child.

"We are visitors here," the science officer repeated. "If our first encounter with aliens is hostile and destructive, they would see us as our mortal enemies forever." Murray tilted her elvish head to the left. "We don't have to be the enemies. We don't have to be all crash and burn."

The First Lieutenant was growing tired of the science officer and her condescending tone.

"This ain't some stupid intergalactic road trip movie," the First Lieutenant said.

"I know, but we have responsibilities as explorers connected to exploration and discovery," Murray stated.

The land finds this one interesting, Starfish. Go to the bigger one. Listen to him. Answer his questions. Only answer his questions.

The science officer walked away from the First Lieutenant. At that moment, Drake stepped out of the shadows and into the view. The First Lieutenant looked at Drake.

"First Lieutenant," Drake said, saluting him. The First Lieutenant returned the salute.

"Drake, you got a minute?"

"Yes, sir," Drake said.

The First Lieutenant nodded, and Drake and he sat on two outcropping rock formations. The First Lieutenant checked his wrist monitor and tapped his breast pocket of his utilities then fished out a gel squeeze pack. He bit the end of the pack before squeezing the gel between his thin lips. Drake sat on the rock formation to the First Lieutenant's right.

At Drake's questioning look, the First Lieutenant said, "My CO swears by them, he says that they are better than the MREs. They are good eats but nothing to substitute for food supplements. They are good for extended energy bursts," the First Lieutenant said, folding the squeeze pack four times upon itself and slipping it into the leg pocket of his utilities.

Drake nodded. He had heard marines ate all sorts of meal plans. He preferred a plant-based diet, himself.

The First Lieutenant swallowed. He looked at Drake for a long moment before speaking.

"Are you, all right?"

Drake sat still on the rock and nodded.

"Why did you join the force?"

Drake was taken aback by the question. He studied the First Lieutenant for a second before answering.

"Wanted the adventure. Wanted to see different things. Wanted to protect the galaxy," he said.

The First Lieutenant nodded. He placed his finger on his lower lip. The First Lieutenant looked at Drake curiously and nodded slightly. He rubbed the back of his neck. "Okay," the thin leader changed his tone becoming serious. "I want to know how you knew that the exo-forms weren't going to attack," the First Lieutenant asked.

Drake did not speak.

"Let me ask it another way. What made you so sure?"

Drake shrugged his shoulders and scratched behind his ear. Still, he didn't answer.

"So, tell me how you knew," the First Lieutenant said, eyeing the private.

"I just...," Drake hesitated. "I just figured that they had the first opportunity to do something, and they didn't."

The First Lieutenant nodded. He did not speak immediately. He seemed to be grappling with something, internally.

Drake waited.

"You're a mechanic, right?" The First Lieutenant asked.

Drake nodded. He casually looked to the left and then the right noting the pair of pistol butts under his arms. The two-gun set-up was the hallmark of mechanics in the Galactic Force.

"I did some research," the First Lieutenant started. "You didn't study any exo-forms sciences prior to recruitment and boot camp," the thin officer stated, eyeing Drake evenly.

Drake did not speak. He just watched the man across from him.

"So, why would someone like you, with no experience in exo-forms or, for that matter, any bio-forms of any sort, have given such a confident suggestion on how to respond to them? How come you turned all Saint Thomas Aquinas on us?"

Drake grinned awkwardly. "Sorry, First Lieutenant, I don't know who Saint Thomas...whoever you said is," he admitted.

"Young said that you were buried in the sand," the First Lieutenant said, changing the subject.

Drake did not speak.

"Buried," the First Lieutenant repeated.

"I don't remember that part," Drake confessed.

"What do you remember?"

Drake instantly found himself back in the inky darkness. He had heard the undecipherable sounds. The cacophonous, high-pitched noises had hurt his ears, but he could not do anything to dampen the noise. He had no control of his body. It felt as if there was sand in every orifice. Something moved in his nose and ears.

This one, tiny and prickly, is not someone to trust, Starfish.

Instead, of relaying what he had felt, and the words of the voice in his head, Drake said, "Not much."

The First Lieutenant stood and took a couple of steps and when Drake blinked the squad leader was directly in front of him, dead in the eyes. Drake instantly climbed to his feet. The lieutenant studied the private.

"Any other insights?" The First Lieutenant asked.

Drake shook his head.

"That'll be all," the First Lieutenant declared.

Drake moved away from the lieutenant and toward the rear of the camp. He was only a few feet away when he heard the familiar voice in his head.

The land seeks the smallest one, Starfish.

Drake did not have to search very long. Yvette Murray sat in the non-com camp with Payne, Jenkins and Butcher. Drake stopped just out of the view of the quartet and looked for a place to hide.

There, Starfish, go there and the land will listen.

He moved to the left of the non-com camp and climbed over a small berm and watched. Drake sat and listened and thought. He investigated the still bright sky and the golden-brown sand. For a moment, his back was to the camp.

"How does this work?"

The land does not know, Starfish.

"I mean, you and me." Drake was talking low so no one could hear him. "When I am standing on the ground you and I are...." He searched for the right word.

Connected. Yes. The land and Starfish are connected.

"How come you are not connected to the others?"

The tiny prickly ones are not you, Starfish. They are different. Yet, this one, this small one, Yuri, is like you.

"How?" Drake asked. He shook his head. "I have a different question. Starfish? Why?"

The land heard you when we connected.

"Why did you need me there?" He pointed back where he had hidden to listen to Murray and the First Lieutenant.

There was silence.

Drake frowned. He was lying flat on the berm near the corporals' camp. He looked around to reassure himself he was alone. Drake looked in the direction where he left the First Lieutenant. The leader of the Lions of Apedemak squad was standing where Drake had left him, his hand on the service weapon.

Drake turned back toward the corporals' camp. All three corporals jumped to their feet. Something skittered by them.

Drake was confused.

The land is big and small, Starfish. It is up and down. It is the beginning, Starfish. It will be the end. The land hears it all. Though, at times, there seems to be too many to care about, Starfish. So, Starfish, the land protects but does not...control. The land gives the big and small...choice. Just now, a small one, a curious one, emerged and...scared the tiny prickly ones.

Drake shook his head, uncertain.

"What the hell was that?" Payne said, his hand on his service weapon.

Jenkins stood too. The corporal peered at the ground and smirked. Her hand was holding both of her service weapons, pointed toward the ground.

Murray stood in the middle of the camp with her hands extended toward Jenkins.

"Calm down," Murray said, calmly.

"Calm down?!" Corporal Butcher hissed. He was standing on a rock, looking down toward the sand and shaking his squarish head. Butcher looked up and back to the rear of the camp.

"Yes. Calm down. It is nothing to get all worked up about," Murray told Butcher. "We're on an alien planet. We are going to see all sorts of strange things," the science officer reminded all those around her.

"But... What the hell was that?" Payne asked again, scanning the campsite.

"Don't know," Butcher said with a shake of his head, as he came down from the rock he was standing on. "Just sit down and hold it together," he growled.

Jenkins sat back on the rock wearing her helmet and slowly holstered her pistols.

"Murray, what gives?"

"There are going to be different life forms here," Murray smiled uneasily.

"We know that," Butcher said with an eye roll. The scarred corporal was looking at the sand. He kept his hand on the butt of his service weapon.

"What the hell have we gotten ourselves into?" Jenkins spat looking back to the rear of the camp. Drake who was still watching the group, followed Jenkins' eyeline. There was nothing visible.

"Can't believe we are here, and those four-armed creatures aren't the biggest problem," Payne said. "I mean, we have to get the scientists back from those space teddy bears while worrying about the various life forms on the planet," Payne concluded. "No pressure."

The land needs you, Starfish.

Drake looked at the campsite where the corporals were gathered.

Butcher sat back down on the rock he had been sitting on earlier.

"You just going to sit there?" Payne asked. "I'm going to shake a leg," Payne said and spun on his heels and disappeared over the low sand dune.

Murray looked at Jenkins. "Any of you know what that was?"

112

Jenkins shook her head, no.

"I don't know it's scientific name or anything but I have to say, that is just one of many bio-forms on this planet," Murray said, amused.

"What?"

"Nothing," Murray grinned, shaking her head. "It was just another alien."

"No, explain it," Payne said returning to the camp.

"All I was trying to point out was that we just arrived here—" Murray began.

"Butcher, Payne," the First Lieutenant called. "I need you."

The two corporals jumped to their feet. Butcher was the first to move. Payne shoveled in a mouthful of the MRE and made a face. He looked around to spit out the distasteful food and, not finding a place, just swallowed.

"Bleh," Payne said, sticking out his tongue.

Butcher chuckled as he walked in the direction of the First Lieutenant. Murray and Jenkins giggled.

Payne rubbed at his tongue and looking at the two women with a scornful eye before following Butcher.

"That's first call," Jenkins said.

"First call?" Murray asked.

"Yeah, LT usually consults with Butcher, Sarge and Payne, since they have been enlisted the longest," Jenkins clarified.

Murray nodded. The science officer reflected briefly on what Jenkins said.

"I thought that we had gotten away from all that penis measuring and mansplaining long ago," Murray declared.

"Things don't change that drastically, Murray," Jenkins laughed.

"I have been a science officer in the Galactic Force for nearly half a decade and somethings do change. Somethings have changed," Murray corrected. "Our Galactic Force commander is a double X," Murray began. "Before we escaped to the stars, twelve presidents, had double X chromosomes."

"Things change, but not quickly," Jenkins conceded.

Silence fell between the two science officers. Jenkins checked her wrist monitor. "Think that there are other planets in the galaxy that are habitable?"

Murray snickered. "I mean, that's why we're out here. Right?"

"Yeah, but it's more likely we'll find a planet that has ice cream mountains and chocolate sprinkle raindrops than another habitable planet in our galaxy," Murray smiled.

Jenkins nodded. The corporal mindlessly reached down and picked up a diamond by her foot which was easily the size of her pinky.

"So, are you a reaver?" Murray smirked. "A picaroon?"

"A picaroon? What's that?" Jenkins did not like the sound of the word instantly. She felt insulted.

"A picaroon," Murray said, looking at Jenkins. "A rapscallion, scallywag or marooner," Murray explained, not certain if Jenkins knew the terms.

Jenkins looked at Murray as if she were explaining the time space continuum. She rubbed at her pointy chin.

"Can you break that college stuff down, a little?" Jenkins asked.

"A looter or bandit or corsair," Murray attempted. She tried to think of another term. "A marauder? A pirate?"

Jenkins darkened with the realization of Murray's implication and instantly knitted her brow in annoyance.

"I ain't no bandit. I'm a marine," she declared, examining at the diamond in her hand. She stood up and threw the stone onto the sand looking at Murray with anger in her eyes. "I'm a Galactic Force marine and proud of it!" Jenkins stormed. "We were having a reasonable conversation before you went all Karen and white righteous. I thought you and me, as the outsiders, had something in common. I suppose I was wrong." Jenkins turned and began to stalk off before stopping and turning around again. "I ain't trying to make no profit off this mission, college girl."

She stormed off toward the space squid pair just off to the west of the camp. They were unusually still.

Murray reached out and grabbed Jenkins by the wrist before she could get too far away. Jenkins spun on the smaller girl ready to fight. Murray jumped back then slowly opened her extended hand to Jenkins. She had the diamond Jenkins had thrown on the ground. She smiled her elvish smile.

"I think this would be pretty valuable anywhere," Murray said.

Jenkins whose hands were balled into fists, looked at the diamond then up at Murray. "Thought you thought I was a picaroon or pirate for—"

"Being human?" Murray laughed. "I didn't mean to insult you."

"You did," Jenkins steamed. The corporal exhaled, angrily. "I ain't no pirate. I ain't no science officer. Just because I read a couple of books is how I got that title." She shook her head.

Murray nodded. She closed her hand on the diamond. The science officer looked up at the sky.

"I was just thinking that once we leave and make our reports everyone will know that there are all sorts of riches here," Murray said. Shrugging her shoulders, she added, "I mean, if you are thinking about protecting your financial future...." she trailed off.

Jenkins evaluated Murray who smirked. There was a slight tension between the two. Murray studied her shoe tops. She opened her hand and studied the diamond in her palm. Jenkins was the first to break the silence.

"Protecting our financial future," Jenkins repeated. The corporal looked at the diamond in Murray's hand and reached out for it. The smaller, younger woman closed her hand around it. The bigger woman frowned.

"That's mine," Jenkins began.

"It used to be yours," Murray corrected. "Finders keepers," she noted. "One woman's trash is another woman's treasure."

Jenkins frowned at Murray who smirked again. The corporal turned and shook her head. She took a few steps away from the camp then spun on her heels and exhaled. "Think that before this op is over, I'll find a bigger diamond to protect my financial future."

"The likelihood is pretty high," Murray agreed.

"Why did you want to come down to the surface?" Jenkins asked, abruptly. "I mean, most of you lily space jockeys like to stay in orbit and not in space suits and helmets."

"This is a rare opportunity," Murray said.

"But the scientists have been here already," Jenkins countered.

"The scientists that came here landed and studied maybe point zero zero one percent of the terrain," Murray stated. "That's like landing in the *Indomitable* cargo hold and thinking that you have seen everything on the spaceship."

"So, you think that those are the biggest things on the planet?" Jenkins said, pointing to the stationary space squids in the distance.

"I doubt it," Murray admitted.

"So, you think we get to the settlement and you will find more aliens, once we get there," Jenkins asked.

Murray nodded.

"One hundred sixty-eight hours seems like an awfully long time all of a sudden," the corporal declared.

"Why do you say that?"

"Here we are, on this planet, and there are literally diamonds on the ground and gigantic monsters walking around, and things are...," she trailed off seemingly lost in her thoughts. Shaking her head, she came back to herself. "It just never goes well for the scientists," Jenkins noted. "That's why I never want to be a part of the landing party."

"What?"

"The landing parties. The guys that drop in and explore. It always ends up badly for the landing party," Jenkins explained.

"It never seems a good thing to be an explorer. I agree," Murray grinned. She nodded.

Jenkins was about to say something, only to pause.

"Technically, we are the landing party now," Murray pointed out.

"Yeah, ain't that right," Jenkins sneered and laughed reluctantly.

116

"Yeah, that's right," Murray chuckled and grinned like a Cheshire Cat.

From his plac in the shadows Drake smiled coyly at the joke.

The land does not know this...feeling.

"Hmmm," Drake grunted.

What is this...feeling. Light-heartedness?

Drake tried to quiet his mind. *It was funny. It was silly. It was...light, fun,* Drake thought. He knew the land was listening to his thoughts. It was in his head and though it had been there prior its presence suddenly seemed a bigger deal in this intimate, silly, personal moment. Drake was quiet as he realized there was no way to turn it off.

Starfish, you and the land are together. We are together. What you see, the land sees. What you hear the land hears.

I get it, Drake thought, bitterly.

Why are you upset, Starfish?

I don't want to be a slave to anyone.

A slave?

I don't want to be forced to do things I do not want to do, Drake clarified.

A slave.

Yes.

You are not a slave to the land, Starfish. We are together. You help the land.

Is that all?

Yes, Starfish. The others shall help the land as well.

Drake turned back to where Jenkins and Murray stood.

The two had quieted. Jenkins studied the white girl in front of her.

"What's wrong, Murray?"

Murray seemed to be struggling with some big idea.

"You close to the First Lieutenant?"

"Yeah, and?" Jenkins said. "What do you want?" She asked, narrowing her eyes.

"Need to convince the First Lieutenant not to go in guns blazing," Murray said. "We don't have to be the enemies on this planet. I mean, we landed here. We tried to take them prisoner," the science officer paused. "They have every right to imprison us, if you really think about it."

Jenkins looked at Murray curiously.

"All I am asking is if you could talk to the First Lieutenant and suggest not trying to blow away every alien he or the squad comes across? I would appreciate it."

"No cowboys and aliens?"

"Yeah, no "Brokeback Mountain" scenario," Murray chuckled.

Jenkins furrowed her brow, confused.

Chapter 11.

In the nothing, Starfish, the land awoke. From nothing, the land blinked and suddenly was. The land looked and saw nothing and tore through the darkness to see light and create something else. It, Starfish, had no beginning. It just was. Not one thing but nothing was around the land, at the time. The land did not like the nothing and welcomed the many smaller things. Though, the land at first, was nothing it became this...wondrous, magnificent thing. The land had sat small and changing inside of the nothingness, unformed. The land, in its beginning, knew that all that came after it would be a part of the land. But in the nothingness, there was no one else. So, the land tore out of the darkness and separated nothing from the heavens. The land was alone and called forth the amblers. He created the small, the not so small and the great. He nurtured the protectors. He created all on the land and above the land and those that move through the land. Nothing that is on the land is without the land's approval. The land, after it had done all that it could, slept. The land rested. What must have been a blink to the land was many...years to the small and great on us. They grew. They learned. They fought. They struggled. The great maws appeared. The ones above the land... multiplied. There was...dissension in the land. The amblers, always devoted, sought to stop the warring. The small, the soft and gentle, tried to negotiate peace with the not so small and great amblers.

The...crowns met. The crowns agreed to divide the land and live under a truce. To...seal that truce the...three crowns created a gift for the land: a guerdon for the land. The guerdon had one jetton from each of the seven ambler crowns. Those jettons, the guerdon, was a... representation of the love and devotion to the land. The jetton guerdon was placed in a great cavern and protected by the land.

The land protected the tiny and the great but there was a need for...balance. The great maws have a... purpose. They are the land balancers. The great maws keep the land safe. The great maws are wild and rarely listen. They crash and storm through the land unchecked and silent. Beware the great maws, Starfish. The land does not control them. None control them. The land knows the great maws. The great maws know the land. Yet, the great maws are...wild and...

primal. They live to control beneath the web of the land. The land allows. The land had to allow tiny and great to fall for the good of the land. Unlike the land the great and the small are only on the land for a moment. Each fallen tiny and great is remembered by the land in those jettons on the land. The land woke during the end of the truce and did nothing. The land had put all things in place. The amblers had done well. The land did not want to...interfere. The land heard many...sounds. The land saw through many... eyes. Nothing was too great or too small for the land to see or hear.

The jettons remind the land of its...duty. The land protects. The land remembers. The land holds onto those who tread, push through and... fly above. The land knows. The land began before...time, Starfish. The land is. The land has been. It has seen the small and the big appear. It has seen the tiny and great open their eyes.

The land learned of the many and their ways. The land has allowed the many to find the jettons and to make their homes in the land. The land has protected the many and not allowed them to be taken by the great maws swimming through the land.

The great maws, the leviathans, are mighty, Starfish. They are driven by a small brain. Their brain, Starfish, is the size of a jetton. Yet, they are one of the greatest things in the land.

The land has watched and learned. The land was fractured. The land was broken.

The small amblers, ever busy, discovered the mangled guerdon, but it was absent of the seven jettons. Each jetton was significant and unique for the great crown. The amblers fought and warred and warred and fought. It was all they thought about.

They searched and searched and found jettons. They sought to remake the crown for themselves. The land did not care. The search was meaningless, at first. They could not find a jetton. Then the loa appeared. In a fever dream, the loa directed the small ones and they uncovered the first two jettons.

Then, the tiny prickly ones came from the skies. The tiny prickly ones came uninvited. The tiny prickly ones saw the amblers as...animals. They saw the amblers as...monsters. But before the tiny prickly ones could see a season, they were gone back into the skies above.

The great protectors grew, and the land saw. The guardians, mighty and silent, sprang forth and the land welcomed them. Those that move high above the land are subject to the land. All rely on the land. The land feeds all. The land protects all. The land sees all.

The land has always been. The land protects all. The land must. The land and all that is in it must survive, Starfish. The land is more than...the mountains, the sand, the big and small, Starfish. The land, Starfish, is the light and the dark... the north, east, west and south. All above is still the land. All below is the land. All is the land. The land must survive. The land protects. The land protects.

The great maws broke into the cavern and destroyed the guerdon and the jettons. The amblers...accused each other of the...destruction and broke the truce. The warring might have gone on forever except the land awoke, and the tiny prickly ones arrived. The loa holds three jettons. She seeks the remainder.

"Wait," Drake said a little louder than he intended, yet still undetected on the other side of the dune. "You want me to find these jettons, whatever they are?"

The land asks for the jetton you possess now. The precious stone. When the guardian comes, give the jetton to the guardian.

"How do you know that I will not just keep the one I have?"

The land knows you, Starfish. The land sees what you see, Starfish. The land hears what you hear.

"But you didn't answer my question."

There was silence. The land *had* answered Drake's question.

"But, how?" Drake asked, his voice low. He wanted to know how all this happened.

You, Starfish, welcomed the land.

Drake repeated the words the land said in his head. *You, Starfish, welcomed the land.* How had he welcomed the land? Drake started to ask the land, but the voice seemed to know the question.

The land fell on you, Starfish. You and the other tiny prickly ones. Only you, Starfish, welcomed the land. You, Starfish, were the first to see the land's secrets.

121

Drake listened, confused. He did not know what the voice in his head was talking about. He recalled landing on the planet. He and Foley had climbed out of the landship and stood on the fender waiting for the other landships to float down from the sky. He had watched as Young climbed out of the landship and then the Sarge. Someone had said something and the Sarge had sighted the landships high in the sky and gotten bored. Drake had his rifle and had been looking at all there was to look at on the desert-like planet when things went wonky.

The land is surprised, Starfish. You do not recall the welcome? You finding the blueish purple gem? Then the white crystal you call: diamond? You still have the blueish purple crystal in your pocket?

Drake suddenly recalled everything the voice in his head said to him.

In the silence, Drake felt something shift beneath the sand. The shift was a brief undulation. Like something trying to surface from beneath his feet. He looked down at the sand and watched as a handful of sand crystals shifted away from his feet.

That...feeling, Starfish, is what the land seeks. The land does not have that...feeling. Now, beneath you moves a great maw. You felt it. The land felt it as well, thanks to you. You heard, Starfish. When you arrived, the land was aware.

"But I didn't know," Drake said feebly.

Starfish found the blueish purple crystal that we had sought for so long. You shall bring it to the land.

"But I am here on a mission," Drake attempted. "Isn't there someone else?"

The land is...the mission. The land hears what the tiny and the great hear. Those above the land we see but do not know. They saw the tiny prickly ones first. The protectors slept as the warmth and light lengthened and made the land...dry sand.

"I welcomed the land? When?"

There was this stillness. In the silence Drake felt something in his ear. He instinctually reached for it.

The land found you, Starfish. The land found you. We set upon you. So that you can hear and know.

122

"But," Drake began only to stop. As he removed his finger from his ear he noticed tiny bits of sand on his fingertip.

The land knows you, Starfish.

"So, you are connected to me through," he looked down and to the sand, letting the words fall away. "But I don't understand. How?"

Not how, Starfish. Now, Starfish. Now, the land knows you. The land needs you.

Drake looked back to the landships. When he was in the vehicle, the voice was not in his head. But why? The landship was on the sand. He was in the landship. Shouldn't the land still be connected to Drake?

Now, the land will use you. The land needs you and the tiny one to watch. There are more tiny prickly ones than before. The land must trusts you, Starfish.

Drake looked up and watched the two science officers in the camp.

Touch them, Starfish. The land will do everything else.

"You can't hurt them," Drake whispered.

The land protects, Starfish. The tiny prickly ones hurt.

Drake did not argue. There was no argument. The Galactic Force marines' mission was to serve and protect the interests of the Incorporated States of Sovereignty. They did not go out with the intent to hurt anyone, but anyone and everyone who stood in the way of the Galactic Force and the Incorporated States of Sovereignty— which had financed and created *The Arc, The Wanderer* and *Sentinel* and all its various and sundry endeavors— were mowed down in the process.

Skin-to-skin.

"Touch her?" Drake pointed to the petite science officer.

Skin-to-skin.

There was another long silence.

"Great."

Drake watched, not sure what he was going to do.

Go.

Drake stood just on the exterior of the conversation between the two science officers. He was nervous and unsure.

Starfish, go to the small one. Touch her.

"I can't just walk up to someone that I don't know and touch them," Drake stated. "I think that I have to introduce myself and then, maybe, touch her."

Starfish, touch her.

"I can't."

Trust the land.

"I am not ready."

Trust, Starfish.

Drake hesitated.

From somewhere inside, Drake felt himself step forward. He thought someone had pushed him. Looking back, he found no one.

Trust the land.

He took another step and then another. He walked forward and toward the two science officers. Murray turned, seeing the marine walking toward her and Jenkins.

Jenkins looked at Drake walking toward them.

"What do you want, private?" Jenkins asked as she placed her hand on her hip. "We are having a private conversation."

Drake closed his eyes and inhaled.

"Private," Jenkins said, narrowing her dark eyes. She instinctually put her hands out ready to fend off any attack.

Touch the feisty one first. Then touch the other, Starfish. Touch them both.

He hesitated. He tried to stop himself from moving forward but his body, seemed to be a marble rolling on a track downward, picking up speed without thought or apprehension. Drake reached out despite his misgivings and qualms and grabbed the hand of the marine mechanic turned corporal.

Jenkins opened her mouth and though she seemed angry no words or sound came out. The corporal's anger subsided immediately. She did not fight or struggle. She quieted and became attentive.

Quickly, Starfish. This one knows the land.

Drake stepped from the corporal to the unarmed science officer. The small woman blanched and started to raise her hands in protest. Drake stepped forward and reached out and gripped the *Indomitable's* science officer by the forearm. Yvette Murray recoiled

124

but Drake did not release the diminutive science officer though she initially struggled. Yvette Murray initially grimaced at Drake's touch, but when he touched her round cheek, as he had done to Jenkins, she quieted. The anger and panic were replaced with calm. It was eerie how quickly the change occurred. Drake marveled at the apparent muffling of the fight or flight stimulus in each woman's head.

"How," was all Drake could say.

The land knows this one, Starfish.

"What?"

The land welcomes you, Yuri.

Murray spun around and looked at Drake.

"What?"

The land welcomes you, Jenkins.

Jenkins turned around as well. She rubbed her ear. Jenkins did a hard stare at Drake.

Hurry, Starfish, move to the east.

Drake and the two women plodded east, away from the camp. They moved quickly and quietly from the sight of the others.

Drake sat down guiltily. He reached out and pulled Jenkins and Murray down to sit as well. The two women did not resist.

"Think that there's a voice in my head," Jenkins noted.

"Why can't I move my body?" Yvette Murray asked, a note of panic in her voice.

Drake raised a finger to his lips. The two women stopped

"Are there great maws here?"

The great maws travel through the land. During these times they are usually in the web of the land.

"Where is that?"

The place where the tiny prickly ones have attempted to claim.

Drake did not reply. The idea of some greater threat being near the settlement was disturbing to the marine. He wanted to turn around and go to the Sarge or First Lieutenant and tell them. He wanted to tell Foley, at least.

The land protects, Starfish. The land needs your...help.

"What do you need from me?"

125

The land needs you and the soft ones to go to the great...cave and bring back the jetton.

"The what?"

The great cave.

"Why me?"

The land cannot but the tiny one or the other or Starfish can.

Over his shoulder one of the space squids moved dislodging a dozen smaller space squids that plummeted to the sand only to scramble back up the ginormous's rubbery legs. From the dune where the trio sat emerged a spider-like creature the color of the sand. The head of the creature was beetle-like and covered with a dozen small glistening eyes. Three more of the spider-like creatures appeared beneath the first one and scrambled toward Drake and the two women.

The land needs you, Starfish, to bring the jetton.

"Okay," Murray mouthed. The small science officer from the *Indomitable* could not move. Her eyes flitted from left to right. She looked left and right. She mouthed again. "You're both hearing this right?"

Jenkins, sitting next to Drake, was immobile, like Murray, except for her eyes. She was able to move her, too, but could make no noise.

Drake climbed to his feet, then helped the two women to theirs. He turned toward the settlement.

The three walked on the outskirts of the camp. Drake looked out toward the horizon where the Echo settlement waited. Murray and Jenkins looked in the same direction.

The land needs your help. The small ambler saw a jetton in the cave of one of the great maws. The land wants you to return that jetton, Starfish. The great jetton, the main jetton, will unite the small and many and the big and small.

And that was all that Drake remembered until he opened his eyes and found himself standing staring at the landship as Payne and Butcher marched toward him.

"Listen up, marines, we are heading out," Butcher announced. "We need to clean up this campsite and be in the cans and ready to roll in twenty. Let's go," the corporal said to all who were nearby. The First Lieutenant appeared behind the two corporals and surveyed the campsite.

Drake felt his senses returning. It was as if his feelings were in a glass that was slowly being filled to the brim. As the glass was filled higher and higher, the returning feelings would overflow and become something else entirely. Thankfully, the marine found himself again. When he had fully come back to himself, the marine looked at Jenkins and Murray.

The two women stood as if frozen. Drake stepped toward them and they seemed to suddenly awaken. Both looked at each other, then at Drake, and back to the chaos of the marines breaking down the camp.

"This ain't no Sadie Hawkins dance, Drake," the Sarge growled. "Get yourself a bag and clean up and get in that landship."

Drake nodded. All the marines, including Drake and Jenkins, were in motion. Drake snapped out a biodegradable trash bag all the marines were required to carry and instantly began inspecting the campsite for any miscellaneous trash which might be traced back to the Galactic Force.

"Let's roll," shouted the Sarge.

Instantly, everyone was moving toward the landships.

Drake paused and the voice spoke.

Starfish, you and the others will help the land.

"How?"

The great maws. The jettons. The land knows you, Starfish. The land protects.

"Now what?"

Remember, Starfish, you welcomed the land. Remember, the land...requires you, Starfish. You shall protect the land. The land shall protect you.

Drake blinked. He placed a hand against the Alpha fireteam landship suddenly feeling heavy. He looked around and watched as Murray climbed into the Nitro fireteam vehicle. Jenkins had climbed into the Beta fireteam landship.

"Drake, let's go!" Sarge snarled.

Drake climbed into the Alpha fireteam landship and the connection was broken, like a video conference or ancient cellphone

127

call. For the first time, Drake heard a distinct and constant humming in his ear. He scratched at his ear, but the humming continued.

Chapter 12.

The short, bumpy landship ride to the settlement was ten minutes of tension. Ten minutes of imagining the worst. Ten minutes of preparing for every possibility. Everyone was helmeted, armed and on edge. Everyone was ready for anything.

On the jaunt from the campsite to the settlement, Murray managed to get on the monitors dedicated for general information. The science officer spoke from the Nitro landship navigated by Aricka King. Valentine chuckled. Everett could only shake his head.

"First Lieutenant, may I make a suggestion?"

"Murray, how in the world?" The Corporal shut his mouth. "Have you decided to lose your mind on this op?!" Butcher hollered.

"First Lieutenant, I am the science officer, and this is really a scientific mission. As a result, this mission should seek the advice of the science officer present. To cover your ass, you can always say I threatened Butcher and the mission."

Butcher studied the petite science officer. He was easily a foot taller and one hundred pounds heavier than Murray.

"When I am facing a military action, I will cede the decisions to you and be all ears. I just think if we go in guns blazing then we will be the bad guys written about in history," Murray suggested.

The First Lieutenant scowled.

"Well, unlike you, Murray, I have to answer to someone over me. The decisions you want me to make are above my pay grade. My command wants us in there to find the scientists and shut down the power plant."

"I understand that," Murray said over the intercom. "It just seems that we will get better results if we go a little slow here."

"There's nothing to shoot at," Jenkins offered from the Beta landship. "We are scanning and picking up nothing. There are no lifeforms present LT."

"When did this become a democracy?" The First Lieutenant growled. "Now, listen up. Corporal Payne, Jenkins and Butcher, get your houses in order. *I* am the commanding officer in the field. Murray is a guest. Butcher, if she commandeers the microphone again you have my permission to taser her or handcuff her or whatever you deem appropriate to shut her up. Am I clear?"

All the corporals agreed.

The First Lieutenant removed his helmet and brushed his hair back, looking around anxiously, thin lips twisting on his flat face. He replaced his helmet before speaking again.

"Let's go in nice and easy," the First Lieutenant advised the squad leaders. "If there is any hint of hijinks or shenanigans, gunners heat 'em up and chop 'em down," the First Lieutenant commanded. "We came down with fifteen and we're returning with fifteen plus the scientists."

"Roger that," snapped the Sarge with a small smile.

"Okay, I'm clocking this," the First Lieutenant said reluctantly. "We park. We deploy. We secure." The First Lieutenant paused then said, "Note, science officer, I'm not opposed to intimidation."

Drake smiled despite the seriousness of the First Lieutenant's words. The landships continued to bump across the short distance, just minutes away from the settlement. As the landships rose and fell on the uneven surface, Drake quietly wondered what Jenkins and the elvish science officer were thinking. Were they worried? Were they anxious?

The troubled marine had his concerns. Was he leading his team into a trap? Was the land really a protector? What were the crowns? The amblers? The great maws? How had he found the blueish jetton? Had he really welcomed the land?

He put his head in his hands and tried to stop thinking. Drake just wanted to get moving, to be busy, and stop his concerns. Yet, in that wish he was reminded of the land.

"Two minutes," Sarge called.

Drake shook the thoughts out of his mind as the landships crossed the undulating terrain to the Echo settlement.

"You feeling okay?" Young asked Drake, sitting beside him.

"Yeah, I'm fine," Drake smiled.

"You sure? You seem," Young paused, then added, "I don't know...not yourself."

"I'm myself. I mean, who else could I be?" Drake chuckled.

Young nodded and shrugged his shoulders and looked out the windscreen of the landship as Payne drove toward the three biodomes less than twenty yards ahead. The closer the landships got the better the picture of the destruction of the biodomes became. There were three biodomes on the northside of the settlement. Two of the three biodomes were broken and caved in. The biodome's structural fiberglass hexagons laid over a pole structure. The hexagons were triple layered and were connected like Lego pieces, Drake recalled.

"All right, team, based on the settlement layout we are going to enter on the northside of the settlement. I want Beta to take the eastern side of the settlement and secure the southeastern entryway. The settlement is damaged on the eastern side and we will buttress that section first. Jenkins once Beta team is in and secure, I need you to lock that section down. Nitro team you will park on the northside of the settlement at the only functioning entry. Setup a post there. Lock down the two entries to the eastern settlement. Alpha will control the southwest entry to the settlement all the way back to Nitro," the First Lieutenant outlined.

"Roger that," chirped everyone in the First Lieutenant's ears.

The first two landships tore past the northwestern entry. The Beta landship veered dramatically to the east and then back to the south toward the southeastern entry point.

"Focus your attention," the First Lieutenant reminded. "Nitro, secure the first biodome. Lock it down. That's our exit point." The First Lieutenant paused. "Butcher, after you lock down that exit walk the science officer down to me."

"Roger that," Butcher sneered.

The landship streaked by the biodome and a fiberglass hallway, past another two biodomes and finally slammed to a stop on what was the first long stretch of greenery the marines had seen since landing on Rigo-C.

"Alpha team is at the southwest biodome and about to evac," the First Lieutenant announced. "Beta team you should be on the southeastern side of the settlement. Lock down that position."

"Roger that," sounded in everyone's earbuds.

The First Lieutenant spun around and toward the interior of the landship. Drake assessed his First Lieutenant. He was a steely eyed man with a hooked nose who seemed be on the verge of punching someone or saying something profound.

"All right, team, we're moving in pairs," the First Lieutenant announced. The landships rear clamshell emergency exits were standing open. The fireteams exited armed to the teeth. First out of the landship was Foley, running point. He was always gung-ho, Drake mused. Next out was Drake himself. As he was about to exit the vehicle there in front of him, just ten feet above his head, was an immense green and red caterpillar-like thing watching him with four basketball sized black liquid eyes. Drake stopped before stepping out of the landship and into a surreal painting. The only thing missing was the hookah the caterpillar was supposed to be smoking.

"Come on, Drake!" Sarge snapped.

Drake stepped out of the landship and moved under the watchful gaze of the unmoving green and red Brobdingnagian creature. The marine, armed and licensed to kill, did nothing. The gigantic space caterpillar-like creature seemed to look at Drake and grin, but the marine knew that caterpillars could not grin.

"Move!" Young spat.

Drake moved as if his boots were filled with lead. Sarge pushed past Drake and shot him a sidelong glare. He closed his eyes and opened them, shaking his head to clear it of any thoughts of the caterpillar. He. Drake pushed past the Sarge to wind up shoulder-to-shoulder with Foley.

The land listens, Starfish. The land sees.

Foley, holding his assault rifle at the ready, entered the biodome. Drake held his assault rifle and followed Foley slightly to the left of him. Sarge was to the right and just behind Drake, with Payne behind Sarge and Young watching their backs.

The land trusts you. The guardians trust you as well. The one that watches you is the guardian Starfish will give the jetton.

Drake looked back at the titanic cosmic caterpillar that no one else seemed to see except Drake. The gigantic space creature was watching Drake and the team enter the biodome.

"Sshhhh," Drake said, under his breath. He looked left and then right and moved quickly and quietly.

Starfish, there is no one here. The guardians wait for dark. The amblers have taken the tiny prickly ones away.

Drake looked back through the Sarge, Payne and Young. The First Lieutenant stood at the landship holding his notebook computer and monitoring the squad's development. He turned back and continued to sweep the biodome, pretending to be scanning for hostiles; he knew the marines would find nothing in the biodome.

"Where is everybody?" Foley asked.

"No idea," Drake said, keeping quiet and hoping the land would respond to Foley's question.

"Quiet, and keep looking," Sarge snapped.

The squad moved through the hallways and into the main area of the biodome. They scanned the entire biodome in just twelve minutes. After the scanning, Foley returned to the main entry and setup the portable .50 caliber assault cannon.

The settlement had been made up of twelve interconnected biodomes which looked like human-sized hexagonal gerbil enclosures. The hexagonal biodomes were ten feet high tri-layered panels and constructed of sturdy, reinforced metallic poles which could withstand up to two hundred mile per hour winds. Each biodome was a cozy nine hundred and fifty square feet of hexagonal space.

"Clear, LT," Sarge announced as the First Lieutenant walked into the biodome. Jenkins radioed that the biodome that she was in charge of was secured and cleared as well. Williams was the first to take up the post with Springer. The two marines hunkered down, and Williams sat behind the portable .50 caliber gun.

Because there were only five biodomes still undamaged, the fireteams were able to secure the settlement in less than two hours. They sealed entries to the non-functioning biodomes and made repairs where feasible. In another two hours the settlement was back online. Drake had the privilege of working with Tyler and Everett in the main engine room of the settlement to get the generator, a simple but powerful nuclear reactor up and running.

"Okay, who is going to check the fuel rods?"

133

"I'm checking that the lines are all solid," announced Everett.

"I got the turbine," smiled Williams mischievously.

"Great," said Drake, realizing that he was suddenly in charge of the containment structure. "Okay, if you are on the lines then check the cooling tower, Everett," Drake told his fellow marine. "And you," he turned to Tyler, "can do the turbine and water pumps on the exterior."

"Roger that," Williams and Everett grinned.

Drake shook his head. No one really liked working the containment structure. It had been rumored that long exposure in the containment structure could give you cancer or brain damage. Drake did not believe it. There had been no support for the claim. The longest any mechanic stayed in the containment structure was maybe two hours and that hardly constituted long exposure.

What is this place, Starfish?

"The place for energy," Drake said, looking around and making sure no one was in the containment structure with him.

What is energy?

Drake thought to say something snarky but chose not to. He smirked and tried to think of a way to explain energy to a five-year-old.

"It is how we stay warm and safe," Drake decided.

It is the first thing that the tiny prickly ones made on the land.

Drake, unsure of how to respond, changed the subject. "Where are the scientists?"

The land has hidden them.

"Are they alive?"

Yes. None have been harmed.

"Where are they?" He asked again.

The land will send a guardian and it will take you to them.

"What?"

The land will send a guardian—

"They will search for you to punish you for kidnapping them."

Kidnapping? The tiny prickly ones are not kids. They do nap.

"Your taking the scientists is all the reason they need to come here and destroy all of you."

The land will protect.

134

"How? You don't seem to have a lot of technology. You don't have weapons. You aren't really advanced."

Yet, Starfish, the land can talk with you. The land has hidden more things than your technology can see. Our protectors have not harmed anyone, though they could have. The ones above the land know the land and protect the land. The land protects all. The land has much the tiny prickly ones do not know.

"I suppose you are right about that."

The nuclear reactor sat in the middle of the settlement, closest to where the Beta fireteam was situated. It was in a reinforced bunker which had pipes running from it. Entry to the bunker required punching in a code on a keypad. Drake always smiled at the arrogance of the scientists of the Galactic Force in the hundreds of years the Galactic Force had been in existence, the entry code had never been changed. Not once.

Drake punched in the same four numbers he punched in every time he had to go to check or do maintenance on any nuclear reactor on any planet with a Galactic Force presence and waited for the red light to switch to green. The lock opened and Drake entered the first building all first contact teams and scientists and scientists were instructed to build: the nuclear reactor containment structure.

Drake knew that without this innovation there was no space exploration. There was a need for energy. Without energy space exploration was just imagining.

Inside of the steam room where the heat was always at least eighty degrees Fahrenheit Drake noted the bunker was divided into four distinct areas. There were the fuel rods immersed in water in the reactor pressure tank. There was a water pump which was rhythmically churned along. There was a pressure tank which Drake rarely bothered with and a steam generator. All four of these distinct areas were connected by piping.

"Everything good in there?" Tyler called.

"Yeah, hot as hell, but that's to be expected," Drake announced. He checked the water pressure and made a slight adjustment to the water pump. The dials all were all in the green. "Everything looks good here. No anomalies. No nothing."

"Roger that," said the First Lieutenant. "Drake head to the southwest corner and relieve Foley."

"Roger that," said Drake.

"All right, wrenchers, heading to my day job," Drake smiled, tapping his earbud and heading back to the settlement.

Eight hours later and the first change in light occurred. Drake was a little surprised to find that night, if it was night on Rigo-C, was coming. He checked his wrist monitor and noted they had been in the settlement for thirteen hours. Foley was sitting in the mess room with his assault rifle talking to King when Drake walked in. Foley smiled and nodded and looked at Drake. King looked at Drake and smiled too.

"What y'all smiling at?" Drake asked, curious.

"We just catching up, is all," Foley said.

"Yeah, we don't usually get a lot of down time, you know," King said.

Drake looked at the two marines and smiled, with a nod. They were up to something.

"You ever wonder how we determine the time all the way out here? I mean, we're not on The Arc. We're not on the Sentinel or The Wanderer," Springer, the chaplain, said. "We haven't been on Earth in decades."

Murray walked into the small common area. She looked around the hexagonal space noting the five seated at one of the two tables. Murray sat just a seat away from Drake. There was an open seat and an open MRE between them. The science officer, after sitting, started to investigate the brownish MRE on the table.

"What are you talking about?" Murray questioned.

"Time," King stated.

"You understand the interstellar time continuum?" The chaplain asked Foley.

Murray returned to her newly discovered unidentified MRE.

"I mean, yes, but not like I used to when we were tested on it," Foley said. "That's been a while."

"Yeah, a long time ago," Drake laughed. "But the way I see it time doesn't change."

"What do you mean?"

136

"Well, our time here is based on Earth time," Drake said. He lifted his arm and showed off his wrist monitor. "We work in the twenty-four-hour military time we were taught on *The Arc* and then on the *Sentinel*."

"What is this?" Murray asked drawing everyone's attention to the MRE in front of her.

"Can't say," King smirked. The tattooed marine closed her mouth, thinking. "I mean, can't tell."

Jenkins entered the common area and made a beeline to the open seat next to Murray.

Drake shook his MRE and then opened it.

There was a pungent smell from the MRE. Everyone near Drake shook their heads.

The mechanic wearing his pearl handled pistols shoveled in the MRE. The MRE was not tasty. Drake looked around to spit out the distasteful MRE but found no place to do so and had to force the repulsive MRE down.

"That is awful," Drake said, sticking out his tongue and wiping it with a biodegradable paper napkin.

"Guys will eat just about anything," Jenkins grinned.

"Yeah, human dogs," Murray laughed, shaking her head.

Murray nodded at each other.

"Human dogs," Jenkins repeated.

Murray nodded and looked back at her own MRE.

"You got a dog?"

"Are you kidding?" Murray said, with a shake of her head. "Dogs are like space unicorns. Rare and incredibly expensive."

Jenkins smirked.

"You have a dog?"

"No," Jenkins stated. She paused, reflectively. "On *The Arc* there were a few dogs," Jenkins said. "They were *Arc* favorites."

Murray smiled broadly. She looked up and into the sky, longingly. "On *The Wanderer*, they had a few dogs, too, but most of them died. They couldn't get used to the no gravity thing and weren't able to reproduce. It was kind of sad."

"There were the little dogs I didn't really like," Jenkins confessed. "Not too into lap dogs. You know, purse dogs. But there were the bigger dogs that were owned by some steel billionaires who had made boatloads of cash before the launch."

"Billionaires," Murray said, narrowing her eyes.

"Yeah, billionaires created this whole thing," Jenkins gestured widely. Murray looked up and noted the corporal was gesturing toward the biodomes.

"Well, this whole thing began with billionaires and was taken over by adventurers and explorers," Murray attempted.

"Naw, that ain't true," said King. "The billionaires still run things. They still making all the decisions. They just let some adventurers feel like they're doing things, so no one pays attention to the people pulling the strings."

"Yeah, we're all working for some billionaire who sent these scientists out here," Foley said.

"Probably the same billionaire that approved the power plant to be put down and—," Everett said.

"And now wants to take it back and place it on some other rock," said Tyler with a scowl.

There was a lull in the conversation.

"We got one hundred and fifty-five hours and counting," said Foley with a smile.

Drake checked his wrist monitor and noted the time counting down in the right-hand corner of the screen. The wrist monitor held a treasure trove of data. On the first of seven screens there was time of day, messages, current heartrate, current weight, oxygen levels and blood type. On the second screen, accessed by swiping over the monitor his average heartrate, calorie expenditure, water intake and respiratory average. The third screen held the marine's medical records, psychological records, educational records and military records. The fourth of the seven screens held a dozen family pictures. Drake knew that there were three other screens on all the monitors, but he rarely accessed his banking records, or his career opportunities offered outside of the Galactic Force and the dreaded interstellar dating opportunities.

Drake looked past his wrist monitor to his feed and studied the thin fiberglass between him and the sand below.

The great and small are protected by the land. The great maws do not hear. The land is not always...peaceful. The land protects the big and small. The land seeks the last two...jettons. The land relies on you, Starfish.

Chapter 13.

"One hundred and thirty-four hours and counting," Everett announced as he placed the seventh remote motion sensor to the settlement exterior electronic fence. He adjusted the ten-foot pole with several sensors on its length. Drake and Everett had systematically placed the sensors as directed by the Sarge. There were flags placed by someone else to indicate where the sensors were to be located.

"One hundred and thirty-four hours? So, what does that break down to?" Drake asked on the far end of the settlement under the watchful eye of the interstellar caterpillar. It seemed to be watching him with a slight tilt to its bright red area which looked like its face and the black bulbous eyes which stared unblinking from its crowned head.

"Think that just breaks down to sitting here on this God forsaken rock for the next six days," Everett said.

Out of the corner of his eye, Drake watched the cosmic caterpillar watching him as he placed his last sensor.

"What are you looking at?"

The deep space caterpillar stared mutely down at him. The caterpillar, the size of the landship, was curled around the top of the exterior of the biodome. The creature was easily sixty feet long and at least five feet thick at the smallest point.

"How are you doing Drake?" Everett asked in Drake's ear.

"Just locked the last sensor in," Drake announced. He turned on the sensor and knew they would not activate until Sarge gave the green light.

"Okay, heading in," Everett finished.

"Two coming in," Foley sang from the Alpha entrance to the settlement as Payne, the corporal, stretched and stepped closer to the entry into the Alpha biodome. Drake smiled at Foley and Payne as he entered the biodome and tried to figure out what he had gotten himself into. Sarge stepped through the eastern hallway entry and studied Drake and Foley evenly.

"All the sensors in place?"

Drake nodded and he and Everett smiled at the completion of their work.

"Roger that," announced Everett proudly. He had rigged the exterior perimeter motion sensor fencing around the settlement. It was composed of eight main sensors which alerted everyone of any movement outside of the perimeter of the fencing. The sensors were highly sensitive but were calibrated so they did not go off if the wind blew or anything under five pounds meandered into the fencing.

Everett and Drake headed to the makeshift cafeteria.

At the head of the table where Drake sat was the oversized Tyler. He was leaning on the table with one heavy forearm and toeing the fiberglass flooring. Next to Tyler was the affable Everett.

Foley, sitting next to Drake, looked at the marine curiously.

"You okay, man?"

"Yeah, just tired," Drake lied.

There was a meeting in the main biodome where the teams massed and created the mess area. "We are cutting back security to one guard at each entry point. We will be rotating the watches every four hours. The schedule is posted on the wall. There will be an hour overlap with one of the corporals checking all posts regularly," the First Lieutenant announced. "We have to stay on our toes. This is not the *Sentinel*. Keep your eyes open and report anything that appears odd, or more odd than the carnival outside, to your superior."

The First Lieutenant looked to the Sarge.

"All right you magnificent beasts, we have a simple job. We are babysitting this settlement. Half of us at 0600 hours, half of us are going to try and track down the scientists. We will be triangulating them based on their ident tags." Sarge paused. He reached down and picked up his notebook computer. "According to the last recorded signal they are approximately one mile to the east."

Drake looked at Foley and Young and then at Jenkins and Murray. He was surprised that the scientists were so close to the settlement. If they could get the scientists, then they could take the power plant offline and be ready to return to the *Sentinel*.

"We will be taking volunteers for the excursion. Our plan is to locate the scientists, free them, bring them back to the settlement, and when the replacements arrive, jump back onto the *Indomitable* and jet out of this wacky four walled world," called Butcher. "I will be leading the mission tomorrow. Questions?"

The marines simply looked at each other. The mission seemed incredibly simple.

Foley reached out to Drake. Drake looked at the younger marine.

"You know the rule," Foley said. Drake nodded.

"The simpler the mission the harder it is to accomplish," the two marines said.

Valentine raised a hand. "Butcher, can I ask a question?"

The room got quiet.

"Other than the space squids do we have to worry about any other scaries?" Valentine smiled.

There was a bunch of nervous laughter.

Butcher gestured to Murray. The science officer stood up and smiled, awkwardly.

"Well, according to our brief excursion, I have noted several unidentified, previously undocumented alien life forms. So, in answer to your question, I have to believe we have yet to see the real scaries," Murray stated.

"What about the flying murder hornets from hell?" King asked.

"The sand rats?" Payne said with a shiver.

The First Lieutenant stood up and asked for silence.

"This is an alien planet," the First Lieutenant noted. "We are going to be facing aliens. Our job is just to hold the settlement for shelter. Our priority is to locate the scientists. Butcher will be heading the search tomorrow." He paused, in an attempt to quell his growing frustration. The First Lieutenant pursed his thin lips. "Drake, Everett, Tyler, how long is it going to take to take the power plant offline?"

The three looked at each other and back at the First Lieutenant.

"We'll need at least twelve hours," Tyler said.

"Jenkins will supervise that," the First Lieutenant said, noting the information in his notebook computer.

Butcher raised his hand. The First Lieutenant nodded.

"Don't need too many for tomorrow. Just going to run out, locate the scientists and bring them back. Easy search and rescue."

The First Lieutenant looked to Jenkins.

Jenkins reluctantly stood up. "I don't have much to add. We have a mission. We hold our posts. We protect the settlement. We get out of here. Simple." She shrugged and sat back down.

Sarge stood up and scanned the assembled marines.

"All right, you heard the man. We are still on the mission. Check the board. Get on your assignments. It's 1800 hours. Think that, based on the schedule. The next shift starts at 2000 hours," Sarge announced. "Get some food down your necks. Get some rest. We have one hundred and thirty plus to hold this place down, recover the scientists and put the power plant to sleep."

No one had any other questions.

Drake was just finishing his shift when he entered the mess area. There were three marines seated and geared up to search for the scientists. Drake retrieved his light breakfast and sat at the table with the three searchers. Springer was a part of the search team, Drake noted. There was no surprise the squad chaplain, besides being a spiritual leader, was a bit of an adrenalin junkie. Next to Springer sat Aricka King, the tattooed tough, who was always looking for a fight. Her tougher than anyone persona made her a perfect candidate for the search team. Young was seated at the end of the table wearing his medi-pack and helmet. Drake smiled at Young.

"You think you'll find the scientists today?"

"Butcher is all gung-ho. So, I have to give that a better than 50% chance of us finding someone," Springer answered in his quiet, calming voice.

"That's not how this works," King said. "We slog through the mud and the blood and the muck and we usually come up short."

"You are such a downer," Young smirked. "Really looking forward to listening to you bitch and moan for the whole march."

King shook her head and rolled her eyes at Young's comments.

"Let's roll," Butcher announced as he stood at the mess area exit with his assault rifle. On his back was a rucksack. He was dressed in his desert camouflage MARPAT utilities and all-terrain combat boots.

Young, Springer and King climbed to their feet. Young and Springer were wearing sidearms. Springer, carrying his helmet, had a red cross on his shoulder and on his back. King was the last to climb to her feet. She wore her helmet. She had her sidearm and was carrying her assault rifle.

"Good luck," Drake said.

Aricka King turned and smiled at Drake.

"Later, skater," she winked.

Drake smiled at the tattooed marine as she made her way to the exit and disappeared.

A handful of seconds later Payne appeared. He was dressed in his utilities and toting his sidearm. He had his assault rifle slung over his shoulder. Payne looked around the mess area and, seeing Drake, walked to him.

"Has search and rescue already left?" Payne asked Drake.

Drake nodded. Payne's shoulders slumped. He took a deep breath and shrugged his shoulders then turned and went to get something to eat. Drake looked at Payne and then to the opposite table. There was only Williams and Drake in the mess area. Williams was seated there with his breakfast in front of him. He studied Drake silently as he ate.

"Everything okay?" Drake asked seeing Williams watching him.

Williams smirked. He nodded but did not break his stare. Drake stood up and walked past Williams as he left the mess area.

Once in the hallway, Drake paused. He was tired but instead of heading to his bunk in the next biodome he took the short walk to the Alpha post to find Foley.

Foley sat behind the portable .50 caliber assault cannon.

"What are you doing here?"

"Good to see you too," Drake smiled.

"Oh, yeah, I forgot that we were suddenly watching each other's backs," Foley laughed.

"It's the marine way," Drake reminded him.

Drake studied the station notebook. It was synced with the First Lieutenant's notebook which was daisy chained, theoretically, back to the *Indomitable* and the *Sentinel* and whoever was in charge. Next to the mean looking assault cannon was the ammunition box which held at least five hundred caseless rounds of the deadly .50 caliber munition. Drake noted near Foley's combat boot was a strangely familiar plastic container of a brown, bubbly liquid.

"Didn't think that you liked Coke," Drake said.

"Don't," Foley smiled. "It's dreck. But it is one of the best stims produced."

"You need to make water or pinch a loaf?" Drake asked, looking out of the entryway and onto the window of greenery and space which led toward a vertical hill. "You know, before I go and sack out," Drake added.

Foley smiled. "No, I'm good."

After a beat Drake looked left and then right and said, "Well, have fun." He turned on his heel and headed to his bunk.

Foley waved. Drake walked to the biodome where the bunks were located. There were twelve bunks in the small room situated in three rows of four bunks. Already asleep and in their bunks were Jenkins, Murray and Valentine, who was snoring audibly.

When Drake walked into the bunk room he thought to go to Jenkins, but he did not. He found his bunk and sat on the edge for a few moments.

Drake sighed, grateful that he could get a few hours of sleep. He wanted to rest and recharge before the start of his next shift, but as he laid down on his bunk, he felt the pull of something else.

The tug was almost imperceptible but then it pulled a little more fervently. Drake lay in the darkness and from a faraway place came the sounds of drumming. The drumming reverberated through everything. A bell rang like it was being beaten by a thousand metallic raindrops. The noise was everywhere, and it gave way to the first sights. There was the muted brown and various gradients of the brown hue. In the muted colors was the dark black of straps and assault rifles. In a second, there were silhouettes of individuals moving across the sand. Four marines, silhouettes, walked across the sand. The leader was bigger and thicker than the others. The four climbed over a dune and paused.

The tiny prickly ones will not find anything, Starfish.

"Where are the scientists?" Drake asked in response to the voice in his head.

The land protects.

"They will find them. They have ways you don't understand," Drake continued in his head.

The land protects, Starfish.

"You don't understand these people," Drake tried. "They do not lose. They do not fail. We do not fail."

There was a sudden and absolute silence.

"Trust me," Drake pleaded in his head. "They will not stop until they have the scientists. Then they will not stop until they control the land."

The land cannot be controlled, Starfish.

"They will find a way," Drake concluded.

The land cannot be controlled, Starfish, the voice repeated.

He did not know what to say. Drake simply thought of all the lands humans had taken through violence, subterfuge, blackmail, political leverage and manifest destiny. The history books were filled with the conquests. It was no different in space.

"They will plow your protectors and guardians under like so much wheat or corn," Drake pleaded. He squirmed in his bunk, wrestling with an invisible and unconvinced voice in his head.

The land will not be controlled. The land cannot be...plowed under.

"You do not understand the nature of the men who have come to this place," Drake attempted, feeling the frustration rising in his mind.

The calmness of the voice in Drake's head was irritating. The calmness was beyond calmness. It was a smugness which made Drake twist and turn in his bed.

Drake sat up, stock still. The first face he saw was Murray, the elvish women with the almond eyes, broad smile and thin lips smirked at Drake. Beside Murray sat Jenkins on the bunk, watching Drake blinking and trying to figure out what he should do next.

"What are you two doing?" Drake was rubbing his eyes and trying to untangle the sheet twisted around him, when he stopped and looked at the two women on his bunk. Drake rubbed the back of his neck.

"We heard the conversation," Murray said.

"What? How?" Drake extricated his legs from the sheet and threw his legs over the edge of the bunk. He was still dressed in his utilities.

Murray looked at Jenkins. Jenkins rubbed at her square nose.

"Hell, man, neither one of us know why or how. We came because we thought...," Jenkins trailed off.

"We thought you might know what was going on," Murray said.

"Yeah. So now we're waiting for you to tell us how this is happening and what is going on," Jenkins said.

Drake looked at Jenkins and then at Murray. Jenkins looked at Murray and then Drake. Murray looked at Drake and then Jenkins.

Drake craned his neck, looking to see who else was in the bunk room.

"There's Valentine, but he's sound asleep," Murray said, reading Drake's mind. "Williams is the only other person who should be resting but no one knows where he is." The *Indomitable* science officer paused, thinking.

Drake smiled awkwardly.

"So, what is going on?"

Drake narrowed his eyes, a bit confused.

"Did you drug us?"

Drake smirked. "Why would I drug you?"

The two shrugged. Murray grinned without joy.

"You really don't know what is going on?"

Murray and Jenkins looked at Drake blankly.

"You don't remember me grabbing you at the camp before we got to the settlement?"

The two women looked at Drake as if he were speaking another language.

"Drake, how did all this start?"

Drake did not answer immediately. He climbed out of his bunk and the three sat in the corner of the quiet bunk room.

"I don't know where to begin," Drake said.

"Just start at the beginning and get to the part where we can hear your thoughts and something that calls itself the land," Jenkins said, emotionless.

He retold the whole story of his arrival, burial in the sand, the sand in his nose and ears, the voice in his head which no one seemed to hear but him, the protectors, the protectors seemingly following him, the land asking Drake to touch Murray and Jenkins— pointing out the land called Jenkins, "feisty." The invisible guardians. The land hiding the scientists. The land thinking it could beat the Galactic Force, the marines, humanity and manifest destiny.

"You know something," Jenkins said. "I think I would have preferred if I was just losing my mind."

Drake shook his head. "I think I drowned," Drake yielded.

"Drowned?"

Drake nodded.

"I don't think you were drowned," Murray corrected. "I think you were submerged or buried," the science officer said. "But you didn't drown."

"Buried," Jenkins laughed.

"Or baptized," Murray said. "Or something."

"I went down one way and came up another," Drake replied.

The guardians tell the land that tiny amblers have stopped listening. Be on the lookout, Starfish. They are...tricky.

"Tricky," Drake repeated.

They have stopped listening to the land. They are up to something.

"Wait," Murray remarked confused. "What are guardians?"

Drake looked out the biodome window and toward the outer space caterpillar to the northwest. He pointed toward the sixteen-foot-tall galaxy caterpillar curled around the inner biodome. Drake looked back at Murray and Jenkins and gestured back toward the window.

Murray and Jenkins looked out the window. For the first time they saw the gigantic empty space caterpillar. The two women did doubletakes.

"How come—," Jenkins began only to stop and point in the direction of the intergalactic caterpillar.

"Wait, why didn't we—," Murray continued and trailed off.

Drake nodded. Murray and Jenkins looked at each other.

"What the—," Jenkins uttered with a shake of her head. "No one else can see them?"

Drake nodded.

"How does it work?"

"I can't really explain," Drake said quietly. "The land has some magical properties, I guess," Drake tried.

"Magical properties?" Murray sneered, skeptically.

"Yeah, somehow only I could see them," Drake declared. "Now, for some reason, you can see them too."

"What other crazy stuff has happened since you drown—I mean, were buried?"

Drake gestured toward the pair of thirty-foot-tall protectors which were a mere one hundred yards away. "The land is connected to these protectors that we cannot see unless it wants us to see them."

"What? How?"

Drake did not speak. He shrugged his shoulders in answer.

"Wait," Murray asked. "Are there more of those things than the two that we see?"

"No," Drake declared. "At least, I don't think so."

Jenkins narrowed her eyes and looked left and right as if by squinting she might be able to see something no one else could.

Drake smiled at Jenkins' efforts.

"You know, you only just became a member of the club," Drake joked.

"Are they, *our* protectors?" Jenkins asked. She looked at the odd creatures.

"I thought that they were following the convoy," Murray responded.

"Are they following us?"

"Wait," Murray stated. She looked at the gigantic creatures moving slowly in the distance. "What?"

Murray looked at Drake. The marine looked sheepishly away only to find Jenkins was looking at him as well.

"Me," Drake nodded. "At first it was me. Now, it's us."

"You knew," Jenkins asked, curious.

"I wasn't certain, at first," Drake confessed. "Then I sort of figured it out."

"The land believes that it can fight us," Drake whispered.

"What?"

"The land took the scientists because they were not good for the land."

Jenkins shook her head, unbelieving.

"Okay," Jenkins replied rubbing at her eyes. "Let me get this straight. There is this voice that is somehow directing us to do things for it. We don't know what the hell the voice is. We don't know what the voice wants. We do know that it kidnapped the scientists and had its space monkeys destroy the settlement," Jenkins attempted. "Am I tracking this so far? Am I getting this right? Did I miss anything?"

"The land thinks that it can fight us," Drake repeated.

"The land thinks that it can fight the Galactic Force," Murray said in a deadpan voice.

Drake sat in his chair and shook his head, frustrated. It sounded ludicrous. Everything was so outlandish.

"Now, somehow, we're connected to this... disembodied voice that is... psychically connected to us and...," Jenkins trailed off. "What?"

Murray and Drake looked up at the corporal. Jenkins was frustrated. She was chewing at her lower lip, thinking. She checked her wrist monitor. Murray and Drake checked their wrist monitors as well.

"What is the plan here?"

Drake did not seem to understand.

"I mean, what does the voice want?"

"I don't know," Drake repeated. "I told you everything."

"So, what's next?"

Drake pursed his lips.

150

"I think we have to try and save this planet," Drake reported, knowing that what he said did not make any sense.

"Save this planet?" Jenkins smirked. "The three of us?"

Chapter 14.

Drake froze in mid action. **Jenkins had exhaled and, in that moment,** she crossed her arms in front of her and stopped packing the small room. The smallest of the three, Murray, had looked from Drake to Jenkins when she found herself unmoving. There was a handful of seconds the trio in the bunk room were held invisibly immobile.

Seconds passed. No more than a dozen, if that, slipped away from the trio. Anyone who would have walked in at that moment might have thought the three were playing some childish game.

The oldest and the smallest had not been alive for a quarter of a century. The junior to the eldest had barely seen one fifth of a century of life. The only male in the bunk room at the time was still half a dozen months from his twentieth birthday. The idea of the three staging some elaborate stunt was not far-fetched.

Murray was the first to be released from the invisible hold which had been upon her. Her mouth closed slowly. Then Drake nodded in response to a question asked earlier. Jenkins looked at her crossed arms and back at Murray and Drake.

The three looked at each other, confused. The trio winced at the same time. Drake put a hand to his ears and grit his teeth. Jenkins slapped her hands to her ears. She closed her eyes to inaudible pain, grimacing with the pain. Murray bent in half and twisted against the pain she felt, reaching out for something to support her, using the closest bunk.

She opened her eyes and noticed Valentine sleeping with one arm out of the bunk and his hand touching the floor. He snored on.

He sleeps, Yuri. But he tries to listen. Go now. The land calls.

When the pain subsided, Drake then Jenkins and Murray moved quickly and quietly from the bunk room. The three moved in a line down the short hallway.

"Where are you headed?" Williams asked as he appeared at the bottom of the northern hallway.

The three walked silently past the sniper. Drake seemed focused. Jenkins did not speak. Murray was nearly invisible as she walked past Williams. Williams, never the friendliest, shrugged off the lack of communication.

The three appeared at the Alpha fireteam post and paused. The trio stood behind Sarge. The Sarge was focused behind the .50 caliber assault cannon. Their muted appearance startled the sergeant.

"What the hell, man?" Sarge yipped. Before he could decide his next step, Drake slid around the Sarge and the .50 caliber assault cannon and out and into the morning.

"You weirdos creep me out," Sarge admitted.

There was no curfew. There were no prohibitions. Anyone could go outside of the settlement if they returned in a reasonable amount of time. So, though the trio had shown up unannounced the arrival was not a cause for alarm.

"Where you guys going?"

Drake was out of the settlement. Jenkins and Murray followed him, marching pass the Sarge and out of the settlement. None of the three who exited offered an answer.

The trio, once outside, and a safe distance from the biodomes blinked and seemed shocked to find themselves outside of the settlement's bunk room.

"How did we get here?" Jenkins proffered, her eyes wide.

Murray and Drake shook their heads.

"This is some strange sauce. Drake, what is going on?" Jenkins asked.

Drake shook his head.

"You have to know," the corporal said.

"I'm thinking we're puppets," Murray said.

"Puppets?" Drake said, confused.

Jenkins reached out her hand and wiggled her fingers.

"Come on, man. This is serious," Murray said.

Drake rubbed at the back of his neck again.

"Drake, answer my question."

Drake did not answer.

"You don't know," Murray said.

"You have to know!" Jenkins fumed.

"I only know that it controlled you and Jenkins," Drake countered. "And me."

"Controlled?" Jenkins repeated.

"Does that mean that it will release us when it is done with us?"

Drake pinched his lips not knowing what to say.

"Drake, you know. Don't you?"

Drake looked at Jenkins, uncertain.

"Do you?"

The marine shook his head, no.

"Are we this thing's thralls?" Murray asked. She looked sideways at Drake.

"Thrall?"

"You know, slave, puppet? Doing its will, whatever it wants us to, and not having any control of our own," the science officer explained.

"I don't think that we are thralls," Drake piped. "I don't think. The land said I was not a slave."

"Okay. Well since the land said you won't be a slave then we don't have to worry about that," Jenkins said, unconvinced.

"What does it want? You've got to know that," Murray said, her voice growing strident.

Drake did not answer.

"Where is it, the voice, located?"

Drake smirked. He gestured toward the sand dunes all around them. Drake shrugged his shoulders. He started and stopped. Drake turned and looked at the two women.

"It calls me: Starfish," Drake said, embarrassed.

"Think this thing might be a symbiote?" Murray said.

"What is that?" Drake asked.

Jenkins looked at Drake unbelievingly.

"A symbiosis is a relationship," Murray said with a small smile. "There's three types of symbiosis: mutualism, commensalism and parasitism." Murray paused and seeing Drake's confused look, added. "There's the good one, the not so bad one and the bad one." Murray took a breath and said, "I think whatever this is, it's worse."

154

Suddenly the space squids turned toward the east. They did not move from their spots on the horizon but for the first time they were not still and observant. The smaller leg climbing space squids all momentarily froze.

Without warning, there was a piercing noise in all three of their heads, bringing them to their collective knees. Instinctually, the trio knew that the noise was from the east.

The noise intensified. Drake compared the sound to that of the high-pitched tone of air being let out of a basketball combined with squeaky wheels, but at a million times the decibels.

Collectively, the three saw the scientists being taken from a cavern in the desert. The four marines led by Butcher were backing out of the cavern with their assault rifles and sidearms drawn. Springer was helping one of the injured scientists out. Young had another scientist. King and Butcher were screaming in the vision, but no one could hear what they were shouting. In the darkness of the cavern there was a single creature which burrowed deep into the shadows.

With the last scientist stepping out of the cavern the white-hot pain which lanced their brains subsided.

The three on the edge of the Echo settlement blinked and took their hands away from their ears. Drake had fallen to his knees. Murray was pressed against the biodome. Jenkins was seated on the sand as if she were resting.

"What was that?" Murray pushed further away from the biodomes and toward the dunes. She opened and closed her eyes and massaged her temple.

The marine mechanic pressed himself to his feet and shrugged his shoulders in answer.

"Welcome to my world," Drake managed, steadying himself.

Jenkins climbed to her feet, shakily. She looked like she had seen a ghost.

"What the big red firetruck was that?"

"This is definitely a bad relationship," Murray managed.

Drake nodded.

"So, the quicker we solve this problem the quicker we shake this relationship," Jenkins concluded.

"Hope that it's that easy," Murray said.

"What do you mean?"

"Most symbiotic relations don't separate voluntarily," Murray noted.

"Let's deal with that after we save the planet," Drake said.

"Yeah, that one seems the easiest," Jenkins said, her voice dripping with sarcasm.

Murray looked at Drake and Jenkins.

"What?"

"This is impossible," Jenkins exhaled.

Murray shook her head. She was logical and calculating. "Is there a sign or symptom that warns of the takeover?"

"Who you asking?"

Murray and Jenkins looked at Drake. Jenkins looked like she wanted to throttle him. Murray particularly looked at the marine as if he were a lost puppy.

"What?" Drake asked, defensively.

Jenkins studied Drake silently. The corporal shook her head, disappointed.

"You have to notice something," Murray said.

Drake looked blankly at the two women in front of him.

Jenkins shook her head. Murray crossed her arms in front of her chest. Drake tilted his head and twisted his lips, thinking.

"Think this is going to be up to us," Jenkins said.

Murray nodded.

"So, what do I do?"

"For now," Jenkins said seeming to regain her composure and brushing herself off. "Nothing."

"We'll figure this out."

Without another word the trio made their way back to the biodomes and re-entered the settlement.

"You three having a moment out of doors?" Sarge asked with a slight grin.

Jenkins smiled. Murray looked at the sergeant and continued walking. Drake entered awkwardly and followed Jenkins and Murray through the hallway.

Payne appeared in front of the mess area. "We need to prepare for the arrival of the scientists," he announced.

"Drake, need you with Sarge, Valentine and Tyler," Payne ordered. Before Drake could grouse Payne added, "That's coming from the top. Get your weapon and hard covering and muster by Beta post in ten."

With that, Payne walked away. He stopped short and gestured to Jenkins, turned back around and headed into the mess area.

Jenkins and Murray looked at Drake. He scratched his head and found himself in motion. Murray exhaled and smiled at the retreating Drake. Murray looked back at Jenkins who looked longingly at Murray. The corporal turned and found herself following Payne.

A few minutes later, Drake was on the edge of the settlement armed and waiting for Butcher and the scientists to return. Next to Drake was Tyler. Ahead of him, just ten feet out and to the east, stood Williams and Sarge.

"We have movement," Willams called looking through his scope. With the utterance of those words everyone went on alert.

Tyler held his assault rifle ready to fire. Drake held his assault rifle at the ready.

"You ready for this?" Tyler asked.

Drake nodded.

Over the dune to the east of the settlement trudged Butcher and the eight harried blue coverall wearing scientists. King was to the right of the two scientists near Butcher with her intimidating assault rifle. Young was in the middle of the caravan. At the rear was Springer.

"What up?" crowed Butcher in triumph. "Search and rescue goes out on a mission and search and rescue finishes what needs to be finished!"

Sarge and Williams smiled and guarded Butcher and the scientists as they walked past. The two marines were the front guard and tasked with making sure there were no sneak attacks. They had assault rifles and were scanning the horizon for any hostiles.

"Any trouble?"

"None," Butcher grinned. "Well, none after we fragged the outliers, smoked the baddies and fried a big bad," the scarred marine laughed and pushed past the first wave of guards toward the settlement.

Drake noted the eight scientists, five men and three women. He didn't know any of them.

"Is that everyone?"

Drake tried to remember how many scientists had created Echo settlement. Eight seemed familiar. There were eight scientists returning to the settlement. That seemed right.

The scientists moved lock step behind Butcher. Drake could only watch as the group made their way toward the settlement. Behind Springer back pedaled Sarge and Williams, covering the rear.

"We're good. Bring up the rear," Sarge stated. The two marines fell in line behind Sarge and Williams. They watched the dunes for any hostile activity.

The scientists, bedraggled, marched into the settlement and were immediately taken to one of the repaired biodomes where the bunks had been arranged for them to get some rest. The scientists biodome sat to the east of the bunk room the Galactic Force had taken over.

The rescued scientists were given a couple of hours to rest and recover after their arrival. The marines had prepared a small celebration for the scientist's safe return. Everyone gathered in the main mess hall for the scientist's celebration.

"Welcome back to civilization," the First Lieutenant grumbled. Beside the First Lieutenant stood Butcher, flanked by Jenkins and Payne. Young, Springer and King stood with big smiles on their faces. Valentine was filming all the festivities with three drone cameras.

The first scientist to speak was the commander, Lawrence Green. Drake looked at the ordinary man in the blue coveralls with his name stitched over his heart. He was a brown-haired man with a square jaw and watery blue eyes. Dressed in his blue coveralls Green looked a bit like a farmer. Around his neck was the ident tags all the scientists wore. The ident tags gave off a distinct signal which was used to locate those outside of the settlement.

"I... thank you... for... finding us. We can... never... thank you enough," Green admitted with a shake of his head. "Thank you."

The second scientist to speak was the assistant to the commander. Martha Haley Mason was a brown-eyed woman with a short pixie hairdo. She was a thick hipped and stood only sixty-four inches tall.

"I... thank... you all. I... thank you," the assistant said. Drake stood near the hallway entrance listening when he noticed Murray moving through the crowd. "Thank you...for your ...," Mason stumbled. She looked around at the assembled marines with a big smile on her face. "Thank you so much."

Sean Doty, the engineer, stood up. He was a putty faced man with gray hair and thin lips. Doty looked as if someone in his past had been a bullfrog and he was the conglomeration of a human, bullfrog and a pot-bellied pig, if that were possible. He wore glasses which only gave his bullfrog look more credibility especially as he spoke. "Thank you. Thank you."

Murray was moving through the small group, making her way toward Drake, who stood near the exit. Drake smiled at the small science officer as she approached.

Murray did not look amused or happy when she came close to Drake. She looked disturbed. Drake returned her look with one of concern. Murray pulled on his sleeve and gestured for him to follow her.

"What?"

"You don't notice anything unusual?"

"No," Drake answered.

"Listen to the scientists," Murray whispered. "They sound odd."

When Drake and Murray returned the last two scientists, William Geller and Andrea Prescott stepped forward and spoke.

Geller was an orange faced block of wood. He had a small mouth, protruding brow and big ears. He was nursing a pot belly and was out of shape, and an unattractive and grating man.

"I... thank all of you. Thank you."

Andrea Prescott stood up. She was a shorter, unattractive woman. She had shoulder length hair and an uneven complexion.

Prescott looked anxious and nervous. Unlike everyone else, she did not seem to be comfortable addressing the room.

"Thank... you. Thank... you. Thank... you."

Drake listened, and for the first time the words that were being said did not sync with what he was hearing. It was troubling.

Chapter 15.

After the intimate ceremony and safe retrieval of the scientists, Murray and Drake found themselves uncertain as to what to do once they had left the jerry-rigged biodome and hurried to the hallway which was closest to the Beta post. Before Murray could say a word to Drake, Jenkins walked up with a smile on her face.

Murray shook her head and instead of talking in the hallway she headed out of the settlement under the watchful eye of a bored and uninterested Tyler who was manning the .50 caliber assault cannon. Behind her followed Jenkins and Drake.

Tyler seemed apathetic about the gathering and the seeming need for privacy. The mechanic behind the assault cannon checked his wrist monitor. He adjusted his night vision goggles and rested his chin on the weaponry, bored.

"Where are you three on your way to?"

"Walk under the moons," Jenkins said.

Tyler nodded, more interested in a conversation.

"Well, it's pretty nice out," Tyler continued as the trio walked past him.

The three were out of the settlement before Tyler could say anymore. They walked away from the settlement and into the slowly growing dimness on Rigo-C. On the other side of the invisible fence Murray stopped.

"What's going on?"

"What do you mean?"

"You know exactly what I mean," Murray trembled with rage.

"Okay, okay," Jenkins said, raising her hands to calm Murray.

"When did this all go *Invasion of the Body Snatchers*?"

"Invasion of the —" Drake began.

"Shut up, Drake, this is big girl talk," Murray snapped.

Drake scowled.

"Murray, you need to watch your tone," Jenkins defended.

Murray leveled her almond eyes at Jenkins and studied her calmly. She seemed about to sneer or laugh. She did neither. Instead, the science officer nodded.

"Sorry, Drake," Murray said finally, looking at her feet. "I just get ahead of myself and can run a little hot when that happens." Murray looked up at Drake and continued. "I can be a little abrasive."

"A little?" Jenkins smiled, rolling her eyes.

"I don't care about that," Drake said deadpan. "What I care about is, what the frack is going on with the scientists?"

Murray clenched and unclenched her small hands. She took a moment to count to ten. Jenkins watched the science officer try to remain calm. She knew that would not last long.

"Those aren't the scientists," Murray finally said in very slow cadence.

Drake and Jenkins stared at the science officer.

Murray was in motion. She started north. She walked to the edge of the settlements invisible force field and continued on. Another hundred yards and Murray was standing on the lush, green carpet of what substituted for grass on the alien planet. Jenkins and Drake had followed reluctantly.

Standing on the green carpet which vaguely resembled blades of grass, Murray turned and looked at Jenkins and Drake. The science officer looked to the left and took in the swatch of greenery which ran for as far as she could see into the darkness of the Rigo-C night. There were hills on the swath. There were valleys there as well. Behind the greenery there were the hints of rocks and hills and mountains which rose upward toward what would anywhere else be the sky but on Rigo-C was a sheer cliff of rock rising into the night.

Murray stopped at the first rise of the greenery which seemed to go north for miles. She placed her hands on her hips and surveyed her surroundings. She looked up and down, agitated.

"What is the break down, Murray?" Jenkins asked just a few feet from her.

Murray slowly turned around. She seemed out of sorts and struggling with something. Drake arrived with Jenkins.

"We hear from the voice and then we don't hear from the voice," Murray began as calmly as possible. She pointed at Drake. "He recruits us. But for what reason?" Murray looked at Jenkins. "Now we're somehow tied to this madness."

Jenkins nodded.

Drake seemed confused.

Murray sat on the knoll, overwhelmed and exhausted. Jenkins knelt. Drake remained standing.

"So, the way I see it, the voice selects us, you and me, because it needs us." Murray looked at Jenkins, thinking. She cocked her head.

"What about me?"

Murray turned and looked at Drake condescendingly. "Yeah, it needed you too." The science officer glared at him for a moment, then continued, "But for some reason it decided to go all *Invasion of the Body Snatchers* and try this."

"It has to know that this is going to be found out," Jenkins said.

"What's going to be found out?" Drake asked.

Jenkins opened and closed her mouth. Murray looked at Drake and grimaced.

"What's going to be found out?" Drake asked Jenkins.

"The scientists that they brought in," Jenkins explained gently. "Aren't really the scientists."

Drake suddenly felt stupid.

"No," Drake finally said.

"Wait, you are the one that told us about the whole voice in your head," Jenkins pointed out.

"Yeah," Drake said.

Murray watched Drake and Jenkins talking. The science officer smiled. She turned on Drake and climbed to her feet. She reached out to him. "When was the last time that you heard from the voice?"

"I don't know," Drake admitted. "It's been a while."

Murray and Jenkins fell silent.

"What are you thinking?" Jenkins asked.

"I'm thinking that the voice in our heads had more plans than the one we knew of," Murray stated.

"How?"

"Drake said that the voice was magical," Murray concluded.

"Yeah, but nobody believes in magic," Jenkins said.

"Don't have to believe in oxygen but we breathe it every day," Murray pointed out.

"That's not magic," Jenkins said.

"It's not magic to you, now but go back two or three hundred years and anything that people couldn't see they didn't believe," Murray said. "To them there was magic."

Jenkins shook her head.

"So, what do we do now?"

The three looked at each other in silence.

"What are your ideas?"

"Well...," Drake began only to trail off before he could go any further. He smirked at the two women. "What you got?"

Jenkins twisted her lips, thinking.

"Okay, this is how I see it," Jenkins began. "We have to find the voice. We know the space squids appeared because of the voice. So, I say that we head to the space squids and they will lead us to the voice. They have to know something."

The *Indomitable* science officer paused. She puckered her lips, thinking. Murray detailed a hastily drawn up plan of action for the trio. They suddenly had responsibilities. They had goals. More importantly, they wanted to remove the voice from their heads.

"So, you think that it will work?"

"You know that there's no guarantees in anything," Jenkins declared.

"It's better than nothing," Drake chimed in.

"This is not better than nothing. This is something. This is a plan. But we have to move cautiously," Murray clarified.

The three fell silent. Yvette Murray climbed to her feet. Drake turned and looked up at the mountain face just a few miles away then noticed Murray and Jenkins were walking back toward the settlement. Drake trotted toward the women.

When he caught up with them, Jenkins cast Drake a sidelong look. Drake smiled awkwardly. Murray remained silent, thoughtful.

"So, you think this will work?"

Jenkins looked at Drake and smirked. "Hope so."

"Yeah, me too," Drake said. That was the last word until the three returned to the settlement and the biodomes.

Tyler watched the three return, but barely seemed to acknowledge the trio's passing. Murray led the others to the hallway. They stopped briefly in front of the mess area.

"Okay, phase one," Murray announced. She and Jenkins walked into the mess area.

Drake was tasked with watching the scientists for the first eight hours, noting any and all activity of the scientists. He was then to report anything he observed which seemed out of the ordinary to Murray or Jenkins.

The troubled mechanic walked to the Nitro post and the communication center, complete with audio and video, set up and manned by Valentine. There were surveillance cameras placed throughout the settlement to track movement of marines and to make sure that there were no intruders. On the perimeter of the settlement were eight operating cameras. On the exterior of the settlement aimed outward.

At the Nitro post sat Valentine, bored and with his back to Drake. Drake surveyed the setup of the monitors only three monitors up and running. One was focused on the exterior, cycling through images every few seconds based on movement. Drake imagined the cameras had recorded his and the science officers walk earlier. The second monitor was focused on the north to south interior hallways. The last monitor was recording movement in the interior east to west hallways. There, Drake found that the cameras showed three distinct views: the mess area, the bunk room and the repaired temporary bunk room for the rescued scientists.

Drake was trying to recall what he remembered of video recording when Valentine looked back and smiled, seeing him just standing in the communication center.

"What you doing over here? Slumming? Seeing how the real workers live?"

Drake smiled and walked away from the video monitors and toward Valentine. He dug his hands into his utilities pockets and moved slowly forward.

"Had some time off and couldn't sleep," Drake lied. "Thought I'd come and see what the world looked like from here."

"It's the same world just a different picture," Valentine admitted.

Drake surveyed the post, the portable .50 caliber assault cannon and its box of ammunition placed close at hand. Everett sat on a reinforced camp chair as he stared out into the darkness. Taped on the doorway was the various names scheduled to cover the post. Drake noted after Everett was King and after King was Butcher. The last on the list was Valentine. Everyone was on four hour rotating shifts.

"How long you been on?" Drake asked, trying to sound casual.

"Just an hour," Valentine sighed.

"You just began," Drake noted. "You need anything?"

"No, I'm good," Valentine smiled. "You figure that with the scientists back we should be out of here soon. Right?"

"No, man, you know how it is," Drake smiled looking back toward the hallway. "We are here until the end of the mission. Remember, we are supposed to take the power plant offline. We can't do that until we know when the Rescue team is in orbit." Drake said. "In all the time we've been in this space race have we ever been pulled early?"

"I know," Valentine laughed. "I was just hoping."

"Might as well hope that we get a pay bump from this op," Drake joked, then got serious. "Hey, did you hear they are reducing our pay?"

"Yeah," Valentine said, suddenly serious. "That ain't right. I'm still trying to figure out how I feel about it." Valentine paused. "I didn't sign up to do this for fun. I ain't that crazy," Valentine admitted.

"Well, enjoy your shift," Drake said pushing off the biodome wall and heading back down the hallway. Valentine nodded as Drake disappeared.

Drake headed back to the bunk area and checked his wrist monitor. He had six hours before his next shift. He figured all he had to do was figure a way to convince Valentine to allow him to monitor the hallway. Maybe, Drake thought, he could get Jenkins to step in and make their work a little easier.

When Drake walked into the bunk room with a smile on his face, he figured Murray and Jenkins would run to him and ask him what he had discovered. What he found was Payne, Foley, Young, Jenkins, Springer, Butcher and Murray sitting or lying in their bunks. Drake stood in the entry to the bunk room and eyed Murray propped on her elbow and quietly talking to Jenkins, who was seated on her bunk. The small science officer seemed intense. Jenkins looked exhausted. The mechanic stepped into the bunk room and the first person to notice him was Springer, the squad chaplain.

"We are all concerned with the idea of hurting these creatures that live on this land," Springer said. "We are not supposed to be the Philistines in this matter." Springer paused. "We find ourselves in a particularly unsettling situation. Many have come here for answers. Why have you come, my brother?"

"I just need a minute, padre," Drake smiled.

"Come join us," Springer said. "We are praying. Considering our path now that the scientists have been retrieved."

Drake smiled and shook his head pointing toward the far side of the bunk room. Drake lifted his index finger as he walked to his bunk quietly. Springer nodded. He took a breath and continued as Butcher and Springer lowered their heads.

"And when he came to himself, he said, How many hired servants of my father's have bread enough and to spare, and I perish with hunger? I will arise and go to my father, and will say unto him, Father, I have sinned against heaven, and before thee."

Jenkins blinked and looked at Drake. Murray sat up seeing Drake.

"What gives," Jenkins said.

Drake gestured to the corner of the biodome and walked to the isolated area. In the corner the trio talked.

"First, keep your voices down," Drake said looking over Jenkins' shoulder to see if anyone was paying attention. "I was watching the scientists, went to the communication center, and saw that there was a camera trained on the hallway. So, I figure we can monitor the scientists using the tech we already had."

Murray turned and looked back to see if anyone was eavesdropping. Jenkins looked at Drake skeptically.

"You came in here to tell us that there is a camera watching the hallway?"

Drake smiled.

"We don't want to rely on the camera, Drake," Jenkins said.

Drake frowned.

"Go back and watch the scientists. That's it. That's all," Jenkins concluded.

"But—," Drake attempted.

"No buts. Stick to the plan," Jenkins declared.

Drake turned to Murray.

Murray shook her head and crossed her arms in front of her.

Drake left the bunk room and walked dejectedly up the hallway to the entry of the hallway where the scientists were located. Drake looked up the hallway and to where Everett was positioned. He sat on the floor and watched the entryway.

Thirty minutes before the end of the first watch of the scientists Jenkins arrived. Drake climbed to his feet and stretched stiffly then rubbed at his eyes.

"Did you go inside?"

Drake looked at Jenkins, confused.

"Tell me, you went in there, at least once in the time you have been out here," Jenkins admonished.

Drake found himself shamed by the corporal. He wanted to point out he was not instructed to check on the scientists. Drake looked at Jenkins and chose not to say anything. Drake battled with himself.

"Okay," Drake said. "I ain't taking the blame for this one. I am a soldier. I do what I'm told. If I had been asked to check in on the scientists, I would have checked in. My responsibilities were simple and clear," Drake growled.

Jenkins listened.

"That is why I came to the bunk room earlier," Drake concluded.

Jenkins raised a hand. "Okay. I get it. Let's go inside and check on the scientists," Jenkins said.

Drake and Jenkins nodded at each other.

168

"Wait," Murray said as the two marines started to enter the hallway of the scientists.

Drake and Jenkins halted. They turned and looked at Murray who was suddenly rushing toward them.

The two marines stopped and waited.

"We have to go outside," Murray said under her breath as she drew closer. The science officer waved toward the two marines and retreated toward the Alpha post. The marines looked at each other and then Murray. Jenkins shrugged and began to follow Murray. Drake followed as well.

Murray exited the settlement and once again walked to the far side of invisible barriers. Jenkins and Drake followed along obediently. At the slight rise, where Murray had hatched the plan hours before Jenkins caught up to her.

"What gives?" Jenkins asked.

"Got a message from the voice a few minutes ago," Murray confided. Drake looked to Jenkins. Jenkins looked from Murray to Drake. Drake was shocked by the revelation.

"Wait, you got a message from the voice?"

Jenkins looked at Murray and then Drake. "I thought he was the conduit," Jenkins said pointing to Drake.

"Yeah," Drake agreed. Drake suddenly felt out of the loop.

"I don't know about that, but the voice gave me some instructions. It warned me. I thought that you had received the same message. I came looking for you because the voice said that the guardians would take us to see it."

"What?" Jenkins and Drake echoed.

"Yeah, I know," Murray said. "Again, thought that we were all getting the same message." Murray paused. "So, we're supposed to be guided by the guardians."

Drake and Jenkins turned and looked at the closest biodomes and noticed one of the gigantic caterpillars was moving toward the trio. Drake knew this caterpillar, because it was the one which had watched him first enter the settlement. He knew because of its distinctive coloring along its right side.

"I just don't know how come no one else sees them," Jenkins said as the interplanetary caterpillar approached.

"Magic," Drake said. Murray smiled at the marine's conclusion.

"How come they don't set off alarms?"

"Magic," Drake repeated. Murray giggled. Jenkins, though she tried not to, giggled as well.

The great cosmic caterpillar stopped a few feet from the three. Murray looked at Drake. Jenkins looked at Murray.

"Well, what do we do?"

"Think we climb on?"

"You first," Murray said.

"Of course, any other time and it's all girl power and ladies first," Drake said rolling his eyes. "Now, it's all Drake climb on the space worm first, just in case it bites you or bucks you off."

Drake walked up to the distinctive galactic caterpillar and reached out toward the unusual creature. The solar system caterpillar turned its gigantic greenish head with a red upside-down teardrop inside the green outline which held its four basketball sized eyes. Those four eyes watched unblinking as Drake hesitated. He raised his hands and the four eyes glistened and seemed to emote so much in the moment. The space caterpillar turned its head and Drake noticed the creature had a small goatee. He smiled and reached out and grabbed the soft skin of the creature. He hoisted himself onto its back and was surprised the caterpillar-like body only looked like a caterpillar. The creature was mostly muscle and more like what Drake thought a hairless thirty-foot-long snake bear would be like.

"Come on," Drake smiled behind the head of the galaxy caterpillar.

Murray and Jenkins moved haltingly forward. Murray was lifted by Drake to sit behind him. Jenkins climbed aboard the cosmic caterpillar. When all three passengers were on its back the caterpillar turned to look at its passengers.

"What now?" Jenkins asked.

Come to us, Starfish.

Drake smiled.

"The voice just spoke," Drake admitted.

"Yeah, I heard it too," Jenkins said.

Murray nodded.

The galaxy caterpillar began to move eastward, picking up speed as it moved. In moments the space caterpillar was moving effortlessly over the dunes and weaving its way toward an unknown destination.

Through the darkness the trio traveled. Then the cosmic caterpillar stopped. They had come to a group of sand dunes in the sameness of the desert at which point the caterpillar lowered its head.

Come to us.

Jenkins climbed off the ether space caterpillar first, followed by Murray. As Drake turned and was about to climb off the space caterpillar, the creature turned and looked at the marine. The four unblinking eyes studied him.

Give the guardian the jetton, Starfish.

Drake removed the bluish-purple gem from his pocket and slid off the infinite space caterpillar. The space caterpillar looked down at Drake. Drake handed the bluish-purple gem to the caterpillar. From the wrinkles of the cosmic caterpillar's body emerged two paddle-like appendages. The paddle-like appendages took the gem silently and hid it within its folds.

"Starfish," the great caterpillar with the distinctive mottling along its right side vocalized.

Drake nodded at the space caterpillar, which continued to watch him with its four unblinking eyes. Drake watched as the infinite space caterpillar lowered its gigantic head and looked out toward the horizon. Drake smiled, finding he was not scared or nervous, but grateful to be this close to such a powerful and gentle creature.

Drake turned from the caterpillar to see Murray walking north. Jenkins fell in step behind the science officer. Drake reached out to the cosmic caterpillar but did not touch it. He reluctantly turned and followed the science officer.

The three, led by Murray, walked north from the deep space caterpillar. She seemed to know where she was going, so Jenkins and Drake followed silently.

They walked to the foot of a dune, under the unblinking stare of the cosmic caterpillar, and they found themselves in front of a nearly hidden entrance. Murray stopped and dropped to her knees and crawled into the cave mouth. Jenkins followed. Drake fell to his knees and, he too, crawled into the two-foot-high entrance.

Drake crawled into the dark and did not hesitate or slow as Jenkins moved ahead of him on her hands and knees. The path went straight down for nearly ten minutes, after which it turned left. The path angled downward again and after a few more minutes opened into a vast, underground cavern.

The underground cavern was illuminated by some unseen light. Drake stood up beside Murray and Jenkins and noted that he was able to see in front of him and all around him. The cavern was easily the size of the cargo hold of the *Indomitable*. Around Murray and Jenkins, Drake was surprised to see a dozen space caterpillars and what was a creature which was four times the size of the giant space caterpillars looking at the three of them.

"The land," Drake mumbled.

"Starfish," the great infinite space caterpillar vocalized.

Chapter 16.

The three who heard the voice in their heads looked and could not initially put their thoughts into words their thoughts initially. For Drake, simply thought, "How did these gigantic creatures gather in this cavern?" Drake looked around the cave for exits. The green cosmic caterpillars, similar in size to the one which carried Drake and the others to the cave entrance, looked up with those four, unblinking, liquid black basketball eyes. Their bodies were greenish, and they had the caterpillar-like clawed legs which carried their incredible bulk. Like the other interplanetary space caterpillar, the head was green with a red hood inside the green exterior. Some of the smaller caterpillars had long white beards. The dozen smaller caterpillars sat on a ledge below Drake, Jenkins and Murray but above the largest galactic space caterpillar. The enormous galactic space caterpillar with a long white beard sat coiled like a rattlesnake on the floor of the cavern looking away from Drake.

The caterpillars could not and did not come through the small tunnel that the trio had, Drake knew. There had to be another entrance or exit for the gigantic cosmic caterpillars. Drake looked left and right and watched as Murray stepped forward. Jenkins sat on the ledge which did not seem to have a safe way down.

Before Murray, seeing Jenkins sit on the ledge sat down as well. Drake did the same.

"So, you talking?"

Murray, the science officer, nodded. As if hearing the questioning, the gigantic interplanetary space caterpillar which was four times bigger than the biggest outer space caterpillar Drake had ever seen slowly turned around and looked at Murray with its four-basketball sized black glossy eyes.

Before Murray could speak the image of a little girl talking to a caterpillar with smoking a hookah flashed in Drake's mind. The creature looking at Murray did not have a true face but with its long white beard it looked like Lewis Carroll's pipe smoking caterpillar called Absolem in some retellings.

Absolem? Lewis Carroll created a... story and in this... story there was something that resembled the land?

Drake shook his head, surprised, having been shaken from his memories. Drake looked to Jenkins, who looked back to him.

"Is the voice in your head?"

Jenkins shook her head, no.

"Do you have a name?" Murray, sitting on the edge of the subterranean cavern, asked.

The land is the land. It is everything below... all above. It is divided amongst the land's children. The land protects. The land protects the... parts of the vast spaces here on this... portion of the great vastness. The land prepares for the wet time. The dry sand commands most of the vastness here now. Soon the above will speak. The sounds will flood the land. We are the land. We have always been the land.

"Do you want to harm us?"

The land protects. The land does not harm.

"You told me that you would not make me into a slave, but you controlled me, us, earlier," Drake said out loud, frustrated.

The land chose to guide you, move you, for your protection. The land did not want to force you, but there... was no other way.

"We do not want to be forced to do things we have no choice in," Drake said, thinking of the history of oppression Jenkins and he had escaped when humans had escaped to the stars. "Give us a choice. If you trust us, let us decide."

The land did not speak. The gigantic space caterpillar swayed side to side like a cobra might, studying Drake and the two women sitting on the ledge.

"Wait, I have a question that has been bugging me for a while," Jenkins smiled awkwardly.

Absolem looked at the marine with its four unblinking eyes.

"I'm curious how you were able to stop us from informing others of your contact," Jenkins said.

Absolem nodded and silently informed all three of its ability to implement a governor in the three. The governor, a small thought implanted in the minds of those that the land encountered, would not allow the contacted to inform anyone of their uniqueness. The infinite space caterpillar went onto explain that another

174

consequence of the governor was the inability to act violently since contact.

Jenkins blinked and found herself looking into the four unblinking eyes of Absolem. The caterpillar moved back and away from the corporal.

The land does not control those that help the land. There is no need. You are the eyes and feet of the land.

"So, you are not going to control us?"

The giant cosmic caterpillar did not respond.

"Why are you hiding?"

The land does not hide. Nothing can hurt the land. Yet, Starfish made the land aware of your violent ways when seeing the... unusual. The land protects the tiny prickly ones from the... anger of the land.

"How come no one can see you or your guardians?"

The land protects. The land does not allow the tiny prickly ones' full sight.

The three were instantly educated by Absolem of the amblers' illusionist abilities. The voice also pointed out that the amblers, long before the tiny prickly ones arrived, were able to create illusions, images of anything, any size and make most believe the counterfeit.

"Wait," Jenkins said. "Did Butcher really frag the... smaller caterpillars?"

Caterpillars? The land is unfamiliar with this thing. It is what you think the land and the land's council are?

The land paused. There was a stillness in the chamber. The quiet held.

The land listened to the tiny prickly ones above and knew their plans. The land gave them what they wanted. The amblers thought to attack the tiny prickly ones. The land...convinced the amblers not to attack but to go and see.

The three learned the image in their head they had seen was what Butcher and the search and rescue party had seen thanks to the land and the amblers loa.

"How?"

The land...bargained with the loa.

175

"What is a loa?"

The land is timeless. After the land came to be, the loa appeared. The land is... forever. The loa is not so. The loa is... powerful. The loa leads the amblers. The loa allowed the land to rest. In the land's rest the loa gained power. The loa knows things about the land, the land has forgotten.

"How?"

The continual give and take of the land and the amblers is timeless. They try to control the land. They have tried to control so much but failed so many times. The land allows them to try and fail. You, Starfish, Yuri and Ginkins are like the amblers. You do not want to be controlled. The amblers and the loa push against the land's control.

"Why did you send the fake scientists?"

The land did not send the amblers. The loa and the amblers came up with their plan. The land understood the plan. The amblers figured it would be better to be inside than on the outside to know when to do things.

"What things?"

Any things.

"So, what will happen when they are discovered," Jenkins asked.

Silence.

The land does not know...discovered.

"Found out? Figured out," Drake said, with a slight frown.

"When the tiny prickly ones realize the amblers aren't the scientists," Jenkins concluded with a smirk.

The amblers will leave. They have a plan.

"You think that the marines will allow that?"

The tiny prickly ones cannot stop the amblers.

"They cannot stop the amblers," Murray repeated. "That sounds ominous."

Silence.

"Are the amblers dangerous?"

Not as dangerous as the great maws.

"Will the amblers attack?"

Silence.

"Where are the great maws now?"

Starfish knows. The land does not know. The great maws do not always talk to the land. The land tries to talk with the great maws, but they do not always listen. They are the wildest things in the land.

"I thought you controlled everything, here," Murray said.

Here the land does not control but allows or does not allow. The land knows there is a balance that the tiny prickly one's fear more than certain death.

"Where are the real scientists?"

They are safe.

"Do you understand that you have kidnapped humans and replaced them with aliens?"

Silence.

"Do you understand that the Galactic Force will not stop until they find and rescue all the scientists?"

Reinforcements. The land understands. The land also understands that if the scientists leave then the tiny prickly ones will leave.

"The Galactic Force is not in the business of losing," Jenkins said.

"The men and women you are dealing with do not *believe* in losing."

The land will release the tiny prickly ones when the tiny prickly ones leave.

"We are leaving when we get the scientists and take the power plant offline."

The land knows that there are reinforcements on the way.

"Four days," Drake explained. He looked up to the cavern's roof. "Fourteen times the sun rises."

Silence.

There was a little activity on the periphery. Drake noticed that three of the smaller cosmic caterpillars pulled back and into the dimness. Two of the other caterpillars moved closer to Absolem. One of the smaller caterpillars brushed against the massive space caterpillar.

Absolem looked at the three humans before it.

The land wants the tiny prickly things to leave the land.

177

"But the Galactic Force does not surrender," Jenkins pointed out.

Starfish thinks differently. Yuri thinks differently. Only you, Ginkins thinks like the tiny prickly ones.

"Okay, listen Abso—land, you know us, you can hear our thoughts. So, you will know if I'm lying to you," Jenkins said, her words slow and measured. She realized what she was about to say could backfire or create a bridge to solve both problems.

Jenkins took a deep breath. Murray and Drake watched her, listening closely.

"Okay, the way I see it, we are at an impasse. You want us to leave the planet. We want to leave the planet. But we cannot leave the planet until we find and retrieve the scientists, the *real* scientists, unharmed. After we get the scientists, we will shut down the power plant and leave. There will be one more group to land and retrieve the power plant. They will pick it up and that's it, that's all."

"The Force is not going to be happy with you making them look silly."

Jenkins shushed Drake.

"All I am asking is that you give us the time to leave," Jenkins said. She quickly added, "Give us a few scientists to prove that you are willing to let us leave with our people."

Time? The land shall give the tiny prickly ones' time. The land will give you three of the tiny prickly ones. They will be returned to the base of the tiny prickly ones. The land will listen and wait. There are many great and small who want to silence all the tiny prickly ones. The land has tried to be the peacemaker.

"On the *Sentinel*," Drake said to Jenkins, "a peacemaker is a type of gun."

"You cannot fight with the Galactic Force," Jenkins tried.

"They do not fight fair," Drake stated.

"They would rather make this planet a smoking husk than fail," Jenkins added.

Silence.

Three more smaller intergalactic caterpillars abruptly moved, seeming agitated. Drake could not help but find the activity interesting. Murray and Jenkins noticed the movement as well.

"What is going on?" Murray asked.

The amblers have been discovered.

"What?" Murray said, shocked. "You just said they wouldn't be discovered. They are magical or something."

They attacked while you were talking to the land.

"Son of a gun," Drake hissed.

The guardians were watching the tiny prickly ones but were told to leave.

"What are we to do now?"

You are to go back. Be aware that the guardians have been pulled back.

"Why?"

The amblers brought their... loa and somehow, she has called the great maws.

"I thought the great maws were uncontrollable," Murray reminded.

The loas are powerful. There are half a dozen on the land. They are rarely seen. Now, the loa and the amblers are trying to silence the tiny prickly ones. The land must... negotiate.

"This was a setup," Jenkins declared. "You invited us out here to allow the amblers to attack the settlement."

Return to the tiny prickly ones, all of you. Tell them this is their future. The land, the amblers, the protectors and the great maws do not welcome them. Now, the amblers have stopped talking with the land.

"What does that mean?" As Murray asked her question, the smaller caterpillars faded into the darkness of the cavern.

Tell the tiny prickly ones the land listened. The tiny prickly ones that are...kidnapped will be returned as soon as the land learns that the tiny prickly ones are leaving the land.

"We have no control of the ones in charge."

When you control the uncontrollable the land will control the amblers.

"How do we do that?"

Silence.

The guardians are outside of the settlement. They remain hidden, watching the tiny prickly ones. The protectors are prepared to destroy every tiny prickly thing.

"This is not good."

"You just noticed that?"

"We cannot make the leaders do anything," Murray tried.

Go.

With that, Absolem turned and studied the handful of smaller caterpillars gathered before it. The humongous caterpillar did not turn around again.

Jenkins was the first to climb to her feet. "I think that we were used," the corporal stated.

Murray and Drake climbed to their feet. Jenkins looked at the two seriously.

"We are getting the short end of the stick, here," Jenkins fumed. "Just like always."

"It's the Galactic Force way," Drake said with a smile that did not reach his eyes.

"We don't have time for this," Murray said. "We have bigger issues right now than who got screwed the worst."

Jenkins shook her head, dejected.

"We need to get back," Drake uttered. He looked left and right.

"Do you know which way to go?"

Drake nodded and started moving toward the exit. Jenkins and Murray looked at one another then reluctantly followed.

"The thing about this is that we can still win if we can convince LT not to nuke the planet," Drake said.

"Yeah, that ain't likely. It's more likely we could convince the LT of leprechauns and unicorns than convincing him not to nuke this rock," Jenkins stated.

"Here we go," Drake smiled, gesturing to the small tunnel they had climbed through on their hands and knees earlier. "Should I be chivalrous?"

Murray smiled and entered the tunnel. Jenkins smiled and shook her head.

"You going next?"

Jenkins climbed into the tunnel on her hands and knees and made her way slowly upward. Drake was the last to enter. Before he climbed into the tunnel he looked back and noted the shadowy figure of the towering galactic space caterpillar in the brightly lit underground cavern.

In a few minutes the three explorers were on the desert floor. Murray and Jenkins were waiting for Drake when he climbed out of the tunnel.

"So, what do we do?"

"What are our choices?" Jenkins looked south toward the direction they had to walk. "I mean, we have to go back. The question is, what are we going to do when we get there?"

Drake listened as the two science officers debated.

The guardian space caterpillar that had been waiting outside looked at Drake as he approached. Drake slowed and raised his hands to the caterpillar.

"It's us," Drake said. The gigantic caterpillar nodded and turned to allow Drake and the others onto its back.

"We have to get in contact with LT," Jenkins noted.

"I think that if we can convince the LT that the scientists will be returned if we just leave this rock," Drake said. "We might be okay. Think that is reasonable?"

"Since when is the LT or the Galactic Force reasonable?"

The space caterpillar moved over the sand swiftly. Despite its small legs carrying the bulk of the caterpillar, it sped silently over the sand. In minutes, the caterpillar brought Drake, Jenkins and Murray to the edge of the settlement.

Drake noted the dozen caterpillars now on the outskirts of the settlement.

"Thank you," Drake said, patting the space caterpillar on the side gently.

The three crested a sand dune just a few hundred yards from the settlement. Above Drake and the others was a strange sight: two moons.

"You don't see that too often," Drake commented to no one in particular.

"You know that Drake and I are screwed," Jenkins confided to the *Indomitable* science officer.

"Why?"

"Our military careers are over, because of this" the corporal continued. "I mean, I don't know how we come out of this untouched." Jenkins paused, thinking. "The laws of armed conflict are drilled into us from boot camp."

"But you and Drake haven't done anything," Murray said confused.

"Absence of duty is still incorrect in the law of armed conflict," Jenkins clarified. "Thinking that we are AWOL, for one. Then there is desertion of duty, two. Probably the most egregious charge is fraternization with the enemy. All those are dismissible offenses."

"I think you are being too tough on yourself," Murray advised.

"We will see," Jenkins sounded as she began walking toward the settlement, Murray following closely behind.

The silent trio walked on, trudging through the sand and over the dunes. Suddenly Jenkins stopped. The corporal stood with her mouth open, staring blankly toward the settlement. Beside her, Murray had stopped just as suddenly. The small science officer blinked, mouth agape, as she stared in the direction of the settlement. Neither woman seemed able to speak. Drake noticed the sudden stop and followed the eyeline of the women. The settlement was gone.

"What is going on?" Murray stuttered.

"What happened?" Jenkins demanded.

"There's movement," Drake said, pointing toward where the Beta post had been.

"Let's get down there," Jenkins ordered, and she and Drake were in motion. Murray unarmed and unsure allowed the marines to lead.

Chapter 17.

The Echo settlement Murray, Drake and Jenkins had left was **gone.** The forty foot by fifty-foot settlement of twelve biodomes was nothing more than a bunch of broken and bent structure poles attached to triple layered panels scattered across the sands. In the center of the settlement, Drake noted and pointed out the small nuclear reactor which remained undamaged. There were marines running around, and as Drake drew closer to the settlement, he saw the first of two sink holes between the eastern and northern corners of the structure.

The first marine Drake ran into was Butcher. The scarred mountain of a man was swinging his assault rifle around in front of him looking for someone or something to shoot. Behind him was the tattooed wild child, Aricka King. King was battle ready, equipped with goggles, helmet, gloves, utilities, combat boots and assault rifle.

"What happened?!" Drake screamed, but Butcher shouldered past the private, aiming his rifle toward the dunes. Drake turned around in a panic. Instinctually, Drake thought Butcher had sighted the space caterpillar which had brought them to the edge of the settlement. "Butcher, what happened?" Drake repeated.

"Where's LT?" Jenkins said to Butcher.

"Where were you? Butcher asked.

"Went looking for the scientists," Jenkins said.

Butcher pushed past Jenkins.

King slid up next to Drake and shouldered the marine. Drake turned his attention away from Butcher and over to King.

"All hell broke loose about two or three hours ago," King explained. "There was this...thing that came up from underground and wrecked everything."

"Where's the LT?"

Aricka King frowned. "He's dead," King grimaced. "He was zapped a few hours ago."

Jenkins and Drake reeled at the news.

"What?"

"King! Need you!" Butcher barked. Aricka King pushed ahead and was gone behind the flapping triple layered material which had once been the biodome covering.

Just then, coming west to east, appeared Springer and Tyler. Tyler was helmeted and swung his rifle left and right. Springer had an assault rifle as well and was moving lock step with Tyler.

Jenkins stood in front of Tyler and Springer. When the two marines saw their corporal, they lowered their rifles.

"Sit rep," Jenkins demanded. Hearing Jenkins order, Drake moved closer to the corporal. Murray drew close, too, as Tyler spoke.

"Maybe four or five hours ago one of the posts alerted LT of some aliens just on the border of the settlement. LT arrived at the post and for some reason ordered Williams to shoot at the aliens playing on the other side of the invisible barrier. Williams complied. Williams shot two of the aliens. There was a mass exit of the settlement by the scientists. They ran to the side of the shot aliens like they were trying to help them," the marine reported.

Drake listened, trying to understand what had led to the death of the LT.

Jenkins looked at Springer. She raised a finger to Tyler and the marine fell silent.

"Springer, that running right with your recollections?"

Springer nodded.

Jenkins focused on Springer.

"Continue," Jenkins said to Springer.

"When the scientists hit the invisible barrier, we could see they weren't actually our scientists were not scientists but those mole-like aliens that had attacked the settlement before we arrived. LT locked down the settlement and doubled the guard as a result."

"Fast forward to the attack," Jenkins commanded.

"Well, here's the thing," Tyler began. "There were a couple of things that happened that were weird. Well, weirder than what I just said."

"Okay, continue," Jenkins said.

"The scientists took their hurt and injured away. An hour later there were hundreds of those mole-like things surrounding the settlement. LT was jittery. He knew he had kicked over a can of shiite.

Then there was the appearance of this weird, skinny mole-like alien that was wearing something around its neck. Never seen an alien wearing jewelry. Anyway, the alien wearing the necklace chirped and chipped and then all hell broke loose."

"The ground rumbled. The walls shook. We were sure the nuclear reactor was going offline," Springer cut in.

"Yeah, for an hour something came up from underground like a freight train or a... I don't really know how to describe it. Maybe it was a lizard but nothing I've ever seen before and hellbent on destroying everything in its path."

"How did LT die?"

"Don't know," Tyler said. "Think it happened during the attack."

"How long ago was the last attack?" Jenkins asked.

"Maybe twenty minutes," Springer said.

"Who's in charge, now?" Jenkins asked.

"Sarge," Tyler pointed out. "He told us to secure the perimeter."

"Roger that," Jenkins said and nodded, releasing Tyler and Springer.

"Fudge pops," Murray exhaled.

Drake stepped forward and looked past the Beta landship that sat tilted precariously on its side.

"What do we do?"

"Find Sarge. Report in. Check and see what he wants us to do," Jenkins said.

Drake and Jenkins walked cautiously westward parallel with the footprint of the Echo settlement, noticing that no part of the biodome was left standing. In the wake of the destruction was what looked like twisted sticks and broken pipes which had once held the triple layer material which created the biodomes and the hallway structures.

"Can you imagine how Sarge is going to rip us apart, once he sees us?" Jenkins sneered.

"Yeah, think it might be better to face one of those great maws," Drake said.

On the westside of the settlement stood Payne and Foley. Payne was holding his assault rifle against his leg. Foley held the butt aimed at the sand. The two stood in front of a camp tent which could easily house ten people. Foley was the first to see and alert Payne of the approach of Murray, Jenkins and Drake.

"Well, well, well," Valentine sneered. "Look who decided to show up to the party all late and whatnot."

Foley did not speak. He simply studied Jenkins and Drake and the science officer from the *Indomitable*.

"Where's Sarge?" Jenkins asked.

Valentine gestured to the tent. Jenkins walked inside the tent, followed closely by Murray. Drake stopped and smiled awkwardly.

"Where you been?"

Drake did not speak. He looked away and suddenly felt the urge to leave.

A few moments later, out of the tent strode Payne, Jenkins and Murray. Drake perked up.

"Easy tiger," advised Payne, trying not to smile too broadly.

Jenkins turned and spoke to Payne. Murray stepped between Drake and Foley and looked Drake directly in the eye.

"I think that Jenkins smoothed things over," Murray said to Drake, looking briefly over her shoulder at Foley.

"How?"

Williams came marching toward the tent with his assault rifle ready.

"Where were you?"

Drake turned and instantly stepped back, extending his arms to protect the smaller science officer of the *Indomitable* from Williams. Foley, noting the anger on Williams' face, stepped forward in line with Drake. Payne, noting Williams' aggressive behavior stepped forward.

"I think that you set this up!" Williams screamed, aiming his assault rifle at Drake. Foley reached out and redirected the assault rifle above Drake's head. Payne was suddenly arm locking the angry Williams and turning him around and away from Drake. Jenkins disarmed the marine before he could reach for his sidearm.

"How could a mechanic set up something like this?" Payne screamed. "Do you realize how *insane* you sound?"

"Drake wasn't even here," Jenkins reminded Williams.

Foley and Valentine had Williams in an arm bar hold, restraining the hot headed private.

"Calm down, Williams," Payne advised.

As the action eased, Drake looked back to the science officer. Murray was cowering behind Drake.

"You, okay?" Drake asked. Murray nodded, visibly shaken.

"Wa-what's his problem?" Murray asked.

"That is the problem with jacked up marines and big guns in a nutshell," Drake stated.

Valentine and Foley held onto Williams.

"Jenkins, secure the perimeter," Payne said. Jenkins nodded and walked away from front of the tent with Drake and Murray in tow. She did not speak but tipped her head and walked south toward the other end of the wrecked settlement.

Drake looked back, then asked, "What are we doing?"

Jenkins looked to the left and at Murray then to the right. She pursed her lips before speaking.

"You're under my recognizance for now," Jenkins mentioned looking at the private with the two-gun rig, like herself, and his assault rifle slung across his back.

"What does that mean?"

"It means that you screw up and we're both in deep doo doo," Jenkins grumbled. "At least, the Sarge bought the story of us doing a search for the scientists when the attack was going on. There was no way to deny or confirm or location. So, we're going to lay low until we can get these attacks under control."

Drake nodded. "Saved by red tape," the private said. He paused then narrowed his brown eyes at the corporal. "Wait, do you think that the only three people on the planet unable to be violent are all together by accident?"

"No but I think we're the only ones that might have a chance to survive this," Jenkins said.

"Yeah, I don't see this as accidental," Murray agreed.

Murray and Jenkins kept walking. Drake tried to imagine the next steps.

"Wait," Drake said abruptly, stopping near the Nitro landship that had slipped into a depression leaving the magna-tracked vehicle pointed at a forty-five-degree angle. "I thought you were supposed to convince those in charge that killing these aliens was not worth the bother."

Jenkins stopped and turned to Drake and looked at him evenly. The corporal with the hooked scar hidden beneath her asymmetric haircut nodded. She looked at Drake evenly.

"There's a lot going on right now, Drake," Jenkins pointed out. "We just lost the LT. There was an attack. The settlement is decimated. No one knows if the attacks are over." Jenkins paused. "I didn't want to pile on. Not right now." Jenkins scratched her chin. "I know that we have to convince the Sarge, but everyone seems a little stretched."

Drake nodded.

"Don't forget that Williams shot at least two of those otter mole things."

Jenkins glared at Murray. Drake looked from Murray to Jenkins and back to Murray who smiled.

"The thing I don't understand in all of this," Drake said, reflectively. "Are those things," Drake pointed to the space squids and the creatures which fell off and scrambled back onto the gigantic rubbery legs. Murray and Jenkins looked at each other then slowly turned to Drake.

The three camped out on the southern end of what was the entrance to the settlement. They sat and watched for any sign of trouble. After three hours, Jenkins needed to stretch her legs.

"I'm going to check in," Jenkins said. "It helps to smooth out problems."

She left Drake and Murray at the southern end of settlement looking at the sand dunes. Drake recalled that days before they had bounced across the sand from the landing site to the wrecked Echo settlement with hopes of finding the eight scientists, taking the power plant offline and returning to the Indomitable. A simple operation.

When Jenkins returned from the camp, she informed the pair that they were due for mandatory sack time. They all were. Three hours. The elvish science officer climbed to her feet and she and Drake headed to the camp that was now five tents around the power plant.

"Drake, is Absolem talking to you?" Jenkins asked, looking at the marine in front of her.

"Nope," Drake answered.

"What about you, Murray?"

"No, I haven't heard a peep since the cavern."

"How about you?"

"No, nothing," Jenkins admitted. She studied her partners for a moment, then spun on her heels and headed westward. Drake stopped. Murray followed.

"Where are we headed?"

"I figure we are more likely to have success if we negotiate with the amblers."

"Wait," Murray said, stopping.

"What?"

Drake stopped a step ahead of Murray.

Jenkins turned around seeing Drake and Murray had stopped a few feet behind her.

"I don't want to sound mean," Murray began, diplomatically. "But... are you crazy?"

Drake looked at Murray and nodded. "What she said."

The two looked at Jenkins, skeptically.

"The amblers are on a warpath," Jenkins stated. "They have somehow gotten control of the most destructive creatures on this planet. Based on what we heard, we know that this was just one of those great maws. Now, if Absolem has control or unleashes the rest it would be...," Jenkins trailed off, squeezing her lips together.

"You want to go and find the amblers and try and reason with them?"

Jenkins smiled. "I know how it sounds but it seems the only logical way to solve this problem."

Murray and Drake shook their heads.

"Hear me out," Jenkins said. "Absolem, picked the three of us for a reason. It picked you Drake for your openness and welcoming nature. It picked me for my feistiness. It picked Murray for her brains." Jenkins paused a moment before continuing. "So, the way I see it, if we work together, we can put a tent on this circus." Jenkins raised her hand to stop any interruptions. "Give me a minute to explain. If it doesn't make sense, then I'm open to suggestions. But, for now I'm offering this idea." Jenkins paused and took a deep breath. "If we can get the scientists back then maybe Sarge signs off on us leaving, like the original plan and calling it a day. But we can't have that conversation without the scientists. We know the amblers have the scientists. So, we have to get the amblers to give them back."

Drake listened to Jenkins' argument, looking for holes. There had to be holes in the plan. Drake knew, there were no truly perfect plans.

"Are you sure we are covered?" Drake asked, imploring. "I don't have any protection if this goes south."

"This is not going to go south," Jenkins said. "I'll send a message to Payne now. He'll cover for us. I'll tell him we have a strong inkling of where the scientists are and didn't have time to deliberate with anyone. It was a matter of life and death." She typed onto her wrist monitor the message and then sent it. "There, we're covered."

"I'm under your recognizance, right?" Drake asked.

"Right."

"Okay, I get the plan," said Murray. "But I have a couple of questions." The elvish science officer took a step forward and said, "No one knows where the amblers are. More importantly, there's just the three of us. We could walk all over the planet and never find the amblers. No one knows where they hide. How are we going to find them? If we find them, and I say if, how do you know that they will negotiate? Absolem told us that the amblers are not reliable."

"Okay, good questions," Jenkins smiled. In response, the corporal looked at Murray and pointed toward the space squids. Murray and Drake looked in their direction and noticed that the protectors were not shoulder to shoulder but parallel to each other.

The point of view gave the trio of Absolem the perspective the protectors were not moving.

"I think what we thought were the protectors weren't really protecting us," Jenkins said.

"They were protecting the amblers," Murray said softly, realization dawning.

"Damn," Drake said. "Absolem called them protectors. I just thought that they were protecting us."

Murray laughed.

"You okay," Jenkins asked.

Murray had tears in her eyes from her intense release of emotions. She raised a hand and tried to catch her breath. She took a few deep breaths before talking.

"I can't believe how simple things can be," Murray smiled.

Drake smiled at the science officer's realization. He smiled because he had never considered the monumental space squids as anything but alien bodyguards for himself, Jenkins and Murray. The protectors had given Drake an incredible sense of self-importance. He had selfishly thought himself significant on the alien planet. Drake had imagined that because he was unique and different, he had been selected, identified and singled out by the voice in his head. Drake had thought himself essential to the planet though he had only arrived. So, when the voice had told him that the protectors would arise Drake had not seen the protectors as anything other than what the term meant to the Galactic marines.

"I thought you said that I was the brains," Murray said.

"You are," Jenkins smiled. "But sometimes your brain can get in the way."

Drake laughed.

"So, what do you say?" Jenkins smiled. She added, "Absolem did give us the responsibility of saving the planet."

"We really don't have a better choice," Murray nodded.

Chapter 18.

The protectors, Drake thought absently, seemed further away than he first imagined. The hulking giants appeared to be just two hundred yards from the settlement.

They, Murray, Jenkins and Drake, had begun the journey to the protectors an hour ago, leaving the ruins of the Echo settlement and their fellow marines to fend for themselves. Drake looked back occasionally, but after the sixth or seventh sand dune his sight lines were obscured, so he concentrated on reaching the space squids.

"We should be there soon," Jenkins announced. The three walked and climbed over one sand dune after another, their time in the desert pushing close to two hours.

"You know, this would be a good time to have a space caterpillar show up and give us a ride to the protectors," Drake said as the trio walked toward the squids on the horizon.

"Pipe down, Drake," Jenkins said. "I would have thought out of all of us that it would have been the science officer grousing."

"Hey, I haven't said a word!" Murray pointed out.

"I know," Jenkins said. "I'm on your side."

Murray kept walking. Drake smirked.

The corporal cut Drake a long side glance. "Get over yourself, Drake."

Drake opened his mouth and closed it without launching the acid rebuke he had thought to fire at Jenkins. Drake sulked.

He was still trying to get over the sting of the realization that the voice in his head had not selected him as the ultimate chosen one. Drake was instead chosen to find the brains and the strategist the voice needed. He was not special. He was not gifted. He was not even important to the voice.

Drake's only usefulness was having stepped on the planet first. He had been picked because his landship had come down before the others and for no other reason the voice needed him. It was a hard pill to swallow.

Murray stopped to make sure they continued in as straight a path as possible. The Gargantuan mountain range, with its mile-high mountains, was south of them the entire hike. They never got closer than half a mile from the base of the mountain range. Jenkins mentally plotted the rest of the course. Drake trailed behind, no longer special, over the dunes and toward the protectors. After just under three hours the trio crested a dune and found themselves on a sandy plain. The plains were a short, even space which gave way to the rise where one of the two protectors stood waiting.

"We're nearly there," called Murray.

Jenkins and Murray stopped and looked at the sandy rise which looked like a broken but scalable cliff face. The two women seemed to be looking for the easiest route up the cliff face. Drake approached the pair and pushed past them as they were sightseeing.

"Easy, tiger," Jenkins said.

Drake looked back at the two women and then toward the seemingly endless trek to the protectors. The mechanic walked a couple more paces and stopped. Drake noticed something. The first bit of strangeness happened just a hundred yards from the sandhill where the closest protector stood.

Drake pointed toward the spots which appeared to darken the hill behind the protector's leg. From the crest of the hill came hundreds of dark forms which had previously been falling and climbing back onto the protector's gigantic form. The fast moving, dark creatures looked like smaller, menacing versions, of the protectors but with crab-like shells and legs.

The clicking and chittering that accompanied the human sized crabs was a little unnerving. Even without pincers and hidden in their dark shells, the diminutive space crabs, compared to the protectors, still were intimidating. As the four-foot-tall mini protectors moved in their sideways progression toward the trio, the noises coming from the hundreds upon hundreds of alien creatures grew louder.

"Get ready," Murray said. "The baby space crabs are coming."

Drake had his assault rifle slung across his back, but he knew Absolem had told them all there was a "governor," in their heads, that did not allow them to cause any violence on the planet. Drake looked down at his sidearm and the knife sheathed on the side of his boot and knew worse comes to worse he could only run.

"What do we do?" Drake asked, looking at Jenkins.

"There's no point running," Jenkins said flatly. "We have to go up there eventually." Clenching and unclenching her fists, planting her feet as firmly as possible, she braced for the inevitable crash of the space crabs against her.

Murray smiled weakly as she stood between Jenkins and Drake. "When I came down here, I expected to be a silent observer and maybe name a few things," she mused. "Now, I'm in the midst of... I don't know what."

"Yeah, I didn't wake up and think I was going to be a Galactic Force marine who couldn't do what Galactic Force marines do because of some cosmic governor in my head. I mean, I didn't come to this planet thinking that I wouldn't be able to pull the trigger on the only weapon that matters on an alien planet," Drake said with an edge of annoyance.

The smaller protectors darkened the sand in all directions. They swarmed around the three standing at the foot of the cliff.

"Got to believe that Absolem wouldn't let us figure this all out just to be eaten alive," Jenkins said.

The first wave of space crabs hit Jenkins and Murray. Before they could protest, they found themselves pushed and then moving slowly back up the cliff face.

"Let's hope so," Drake smiled as the first wave of smaller protector babies swarmed around the trio.

Drake watched as the two women were lifted easily off the sand and the dozens of small-scale crabs began to move. Upon closer inspection, Drake could see the baby space protectors did have a resemblance to the giants overhead. The babies hid in dark shells, but their big eyes and legs looked similar to the behemoths Drake had watched since his arrival on Rigo-C.

The movement of the baby protectors as they carried the women away made Murray and Jenkins look like they were surfing the dark waves of the four-foot-tall crabs.

"Cowabunga," Drake said with a shake of his head.

Drake braced as he felt himself gently lifted off his feet and moved toward the cliff face. The dark creatures chittered and squeaked as they moved sideways. Drake looked down and into the four shiny eyeballs of the space crabs. The marine was amazed at the gentleness of the crabs as they moved upward. They had somehow lifted him onto their shells and between four of them were easily able to move the astonished Galactic Force mechanic. Ahead of him Drake could see Murray rising to the top of the cliff face ahead of Jenkins.

The climb, with the assistance of the fun-size crabs, took just a few minutes. Drake was the last to rise behind Jenkins, who had been preceded by Murray. When Drake had finally crested the ridge Jenkins and Murray were waiting. The space crabs deposited Drake as gently as they had picked him up at the bottom of the cliff face.

The trio stood and the pint-sized space crabs circled the humans. Drake looked up and found himself beneath one of the legs of the gigantic space squid. The leg was easily ten or twenty feet wide at the smallest point. The crab-like barbed leg rose at least thirty feet to the bottom of the shell which was the bottom of the protector. But the sheer size of these creatures' close-up was not the thing that caught Drake's attention.

Drake was mesmerized by the continual rise and fall of the mini space squids in their crab shells. On the leg were hundreds of the itty-bitty space squids clambering up the leg and falling off, squealing as they fell and landed on their backs, only to flip back over and clamber back up the leg. The motion was continual though futile. For Drake, it was hypnotic.

Jenkins pulled at Drake and got his attention. Drake turned slowly away from the rising and falling of the small creatures connected to the protectors. He watched as all around him were the hundreds of micro squids chittering and clacking and squealing. He looked back toward Jenkins and saw the two women moving along the ridge and away from the mammoth protector and the petite squids. Drake took a step and the Minikin squids scuttled out of his way.

Gesturing, Jenkins looked back and smiled. Murray was walking north along the ridge and toward the second protector when she stopped.

Drake caught up with Jenkins and Murray at the edge of the rise. The trio looked down and there just a few feet below the protectors, was their first collective sighting of the smaller amblers.

"What now?"

Drake knew the answer. He hesitated.

"Is there an easier way down?"

Jenkins looked around and, finding no easy way down, knelt and rested on the seat of her utilities and slid down the embankment. Jenkins tried to control her descent. She reached out and grabbed hold of the side of the dune to slow her brief but speedy dive.

Upon landing on the ledge, the amblers which had been close, scrambled down the path and around a corner out of sight. Jenkins gestured for Murray and Drake and watched as the amblers moved quickly and easily along the thin ledge which seemed to run up and down the face of the dune for miles.

Murray and Drake slid down the side of the dune as well. Murray skidded down the side of the dune without reaching out to slow down and nearly pitched off the ledge. Thankfully, Jenkins was there. The corporal grabbed the smaller Murray and shook her head at the lack of grace displayed by the science officer.

Drake was the last to reach the path. The slide was not even twenty feet from the rise where the protector and mite squids stood and gathered, respectively.

The cautious Drake landed on the two-foot-wide ledge and nearly slipped off the same. His hands had not found any roots or handholds to slow the bigger marine down on his descent. When he finally felt his feet land on the ledge his momentum pitched him forward and dangerously close to the edge causing him to dance on the edge of the small footpath like an old-time tightrope walker. Drake reached out with his left hand searching for something to hold onto. Thankfully, he found a depression for his hand which the marine used to pull himself back from the edge.

For a handful of seconds Drake just leaned against the face of the dune. He took a deep breath and turned around, looking over the ledge. He noted the fall from the ledge might not kill anyone, but it was a precarious and not something you could walk away from without injury.

Drake understood why the amblers had located their hideout between the two protectors. The idea of someone climbing up from the valley floor between the protectors might be possible but not logical or easy. There were hundreds of boulders which made climbing from the valley floor extremely dangerous and nearly impossible.

The mechanic turned his attention to Jenkins and Murray. They were already moving.

"Come on," Jenkins said.

Drake looked left and right and saw Jenkins was following the smaller Murray. He turned and found that he, not the biggest marine, had to move sideways along the ledge to make sure he did not pitch off the two-foot-wide path. He moved cautiously and slowly forward.

As Drake moved carefully along the ledge, he noted there were pathways which climbed back to the rise above his head and down toward the floor of the sandy valley. He saw that the amblers had disappeared. That was not a good sign.

They were on the amblers' home field and the amblers had the advantage. Drake looked back every once in a while, he looked back to make sure no one was sneaking up on them. He had only edged down the ledge maybe fifty feet when he looked back and saw three medium sized amblers appear from unseen hiding holes on the pathway.

"Guys, we have company," Drake said. Jenkins, hearing Drake, looked back and was surprised to see the medium sized amblers following him. Jenkins turned back and was shocked when Murray was pulled into an invisible cavern ahead of her.

Jenkins stepped forward and before she could relay what she had seen happen to Murray an ambler reached out of the side of the dune and pulled Jenkins in through an unseen cave entry.

Drake stopped just long enough to look back at the medium sized amblers getting closer and reaching out for him. Drake continued forward thinking of what he should do, having seen Jenkins and Murray disappear ahead of him.

He looked back over his shoulder and knew he could not back up. So, Drake moved forward. He braced for the inevitable ambler ambush. It was unavoidable.

The marine gave himself two choices: he could fight the amblers or give in and find out the next step of the journey. He braced

197

for the capture. Drake moved forward, and out of the side of the dune, a hand grabbed Drake's wrist. The amblers hissed.

Drake instinctually pulled against the tug of the unknown hand—if it was a hand. The pull was strong and steady and after the shock of the pull Drake gave in as the amblers pulled the marine into the darkness. The peeping, similar to the sound of a cage filled with canaries, began immediately inside the dark, cramped cavern.

Several hands behind Drake pushed him through a short, dark corridor. The hands pushed and pulled Drake keeping him moving forward. The continual trilling, Drake decided, was the ambler's language Drake decided. Inside the cavern the chirruping only got louder.

The marine covered his ears as the hands pushed him forward still. Drake felt himself climb up a slight rise and then over something which felt like a bridge before seeing the first glimmer of light. Drake had instinctively counted the time from the ambush to the first rays of light beneath the earth above. It had taken just under a minute for the medium-sized amblers to push and pull him and into the recesses of the cavern.

His eyes adjusted slowly, and the luminescence allowed Drake to see hundreds and hundreds of amblers gathered. The amblers, at a glance, looked like long nosed otters with four arms. But upon closer inspection the otters were toothy and actually resembled long-nosed, mustached badgers.

In the round cavern, Drake found himself looking at hundreds of amblers, varying in size. He paused, inspecting what Absolem called the planetary illusionists and wondered to himself if what he was seeing was real? What if there were only twenty amblers in the subterranean cavern? Drake took a step back and felt a few hands push him forward.

The amblers who grabbed him and pushed him were real. Drake knew that much. Of course, he struggled with exactly how many amblers were in the cavern with him, Murray and Jenkins.

Thinking of Murray and Jenkins Drake silently panicked. He had been pushed and pulled through the dark and when his eyes adjusted to the dimness, he realized he had not actually seen either one of them.

"Murray? Jenkins? Are you all right?"

His eyes having become more adjusted to the darkness of the subterranean cavern, Drake recognized the design of the underground hall. He was on the edge of what looked like a gigantic clock. If the cavern was a clock, then Drake found himself at the twelve o'clock position.

"We're okay," Jenkins said to his left. Drake looked and found Jenkins standing at the two o'clock position. Drake was surprised to see that Jenkins was not alone. She was guarded by four medium sized amblers, physically holding her back. Jenkins pointed to the other side of the circle.

"We're okay," Murray echoed, with a tremulous smile, from the ten o'clock position of the underground clock. Like Jenkins, Murray had four medium sized amblers guarding her.

Drake too had four medium sized amblers surrounding him. The two on either side of Drake snarled and kept the mechanic at bay. One of the amblers behind Drake continued to poke him in the back with something. He looked back in annoyance and every time he did the ambler snarled or bared his impressive fangs.

"Drake, don't struggle," Jenkins called.

Drake was about to say something when he noticed several smaller amblers sitting on a chiseled block of stone guarded by four monstrous amblers. The gigantic amblers were easily seven feet tall and like the others, had nasty mouths filled with sharp fangs and teeth. They were beefier than the other amblers, physically strong. Their arms rippled with muscles, like a bodybuilder.

The giant space mustached badgers stood guarding a small, thin ancient ambler wearing a surprisingly ornate necklace. Near the small creature sitting on the block of stone were two or three small amblers.

"The loa," Drake said, and Jenkins and Murray nodded. The trio found themselves looking at the small wan creature wearing a talisman.

From the shadows of hundreds of smaller amblers came a procession of six amblers carrying two inert bodies. Drake did not move. He watched as the two dead amblers were placed in the center of the round cave in a slight depression in the cavern floor. The six amblers circled the still bodies.

Drake was watching the procession and found himself wondering again, Is this real? Drake thought that he could believe his eyes for most things, but the amblers had pulled the wool over the eyes of everyone when they came to the settlement as scientists. So, naturally, he was skeptical. The marine found himself unsure of what to make of his surroundings.

The loa stood, and with the motion there was an intense tweeting and warbling in the round cave. The amblers' facial expressions were enigmatic. But Drake believed they were mourning the loss of their fellow creatures. The ear-splitting chirping and chipping continued for a full minute.

The cavern began to quiet when the loa started moving away from the chiseled block of stone, followed by the smaller amblers and two of the gigantic ones. The loa's slow movement caused a lowering of cheeping, chirring and mourning.

The loa arrived at the depression and the six amblers opened their circle and allowing the ancient inside. Drake watched through the space provided as the loa placed a small pebble on the chest of each fallen ambler. The two small amblers following the loa placed stones at the head and foot of the dead. The loa paused. The two amblers following paused as well.

"What are they doing?"

"Praying? Reminiscing? Remembering?" Jenkins guessed.

The loa turned and walked toward Drake. It was no more than two feet tall, Drake noted. Like the rest of the amblers, the ancient loa looked like a hybrid of a star faced mole and an otter, if his memory of those two creatures served him correctly. He had seen an otter in documents of Earth animals from centuries ago. There were rumors of animals on *The Arc*, but they were just that, rumors.

"A mole is a small burrowing insectivorous mammal with dark velvety fur, a long muzzle, and small eyes," the loa uttered condescendingly. "An otter has a long, slim body and relatively short limbs." The loa looked around and paused when its eyes fell on Drake. "You begin with an insult to me and the Sandharians?"

"I meant no insult," Drake back pedaled. "We humans..."

Drake looked to Murray unsure what to say.

"Murray, I thought the loa looked like a mole and an otter," Drake said loudly. "The loa took it as an insult." Drake added, "I didn't mean anything by it. What do I do?"

"Tell the loa that we, as humans, look for things we can relate to when we are in unfamiliar situations," Murray stated. "It's our nature." Drake repeated the exact words Murray had said.

The loa moved toward Drake. "Your kind have come and tried to capture and enslave us. Your kind have stolen from our land. Your kind have... threatened and... killed two of our young."

"We are soldiers on a mission," Drake thought. He shook his head. "We follow orders." He knew it was not the correct thing to think. "Loa, can you speak with Murray?"

The loa moved closer. Her pace was turtle slow.

"Starfish, it calls you," the loa sneered as it slowed and looked at Drake. "It says you welcomed it. But I think that it sought you out."

"Drake, what is going on?"

Drake looked to Murray and then to Jenkins. "The loa is talking to me." Drake paused. "You can't understand her?"

"No, all I hear is the click and clack and chirping or whatever the sounds are that they are making," Murray said.

"How do you understand it?" Jenkins asked.

"I don't really know," the marine said, confused.

"You have come here for what, Starfish?"

"Ask her if she can hear our thoughts," Jenkins called over the warbling and chirruping.

"How can you read my mind?" Drake paused. "I thought only... the land could do that."

"All that exists here is connected. The great one, that you call... the land, no. You call the great one Absolem," the loa said to Drake. "It is connected to you. We are connected to him. Thus, we are connected to you."

"How do you know that we call the voice Absolem?" He thought. "Why are you not connected to the others?" Drake asked, gesturing to Jenkins and Murray.

"We chose not to listen to them," the loa chirped.

201

"But they know more than me," Drake said.

"I do not think so," the loa said.

"Well, they can explain things better than me."

The loa stood in front of Drake and cocked its head a little to the right.

"Why is she only talking to you," Jenkins asked.

"I don't know," Drake admitted. "I told her about you and Murray."

The loa and her two followers stood before Drake unconcerned with the others. The loa stood near Drake and crossed its lower two arms in front of its chest.

"We, the land, the great one, the Sandharians, this," the loa gestured with her upper arms to the cavern. "Omata, from the farthest points to the other, is all connected. We cherish our Omata."

Drake did not respond. Instead, he tried to think of how to ask the loa to surrender the scientists Murray and Jenkins believed the amblers had captured.

The loa paused and tilted her head to the left.

"Your Absolem has not told you the entire truth. It has held back. It chose not to tell you what you needed to know. Your Absolem has not made you aware of us. We are more powerful than what your... Absolem tells you. If you are connected to Absolem then we are connected to you. We know all you know, and things you have forgotten as well." The loa stepped a little closer. "Unlike your Absolem we have never slept. We have never hidden. We are always awake. Our...brains absorb and are aware."

The loa took another step forward. The closer the loa got, the more the marine could see of the ancient. The feeble looking creature, which would give a Teddy bear competition as the cutest creature, looked at Drake with a wrinkled Pug like, yet adorable face. Behind all those wrinkles and cuteness Drake sensed that the loa was dangerous.

It did not matter that the loa resembled a cute and adorable mole otter hybrid or that she was hundreds of years old. Behind the aged and decrepit act Drake believed was a hardness, a callousness and unsympathetic creature who did not see humans as equals or superiors.

202

"The Sandharian have been here for longer than any can recall," the loa said as it once again continued its slow trek to Drake's side. Beside the loa, assisting her as she moved, were two smaller Sandharians, and flanking them, two giant Sandharians. "In that time, we have learned many things that Absolem has forgotten. All the knowledge of the Sandharians is passed down from one loa to the next."

"What do you want from us?" Drake asked.

The loa raised her hands and the four creatures which followed stopped. The loa drew close to Drake.

The towering Sandharians seemed so unlike the small and medium sized Sandharians. If the brightest was similar to humans, then the medium sized humans were chimpanzees and the titanic Sandharians were like mountain gorillas.

"The Sandharians need nothing from you, Starfish. What we offer you and your two-legged, two-armed, flat faced species is a chance to leave and never come back here before we stop being... nice. We offer you the chance to leave before we remove your kind. We do not want your kind on Omata. We have to cleanse Omata and reassert balance here," the loa continued. "Balance is what we have been responsible for since Absolem fell asleep and woke again."

"But I thought Absolem helped keep the land safe," Drake thought.

The loa was within arm's reach. If Drake wanted, he could reach out and grab the ancient. Yet, Drake knew he was incapable of harming any creature on Rigo-C. Drake shook the thought from his head.

"Absolem, before it fell asleep, did protect Omata. But since Absolem has been awake it seems as if it no longer knows Omata. It has made many a misstep. But I am sure Absolem does not deem that important enough to tell you, Starfish. I am sure the all-powerful Absolem never suggested the Omata's great protector abandoned Omata. Absolem, decided to rest and allow Omata to survive unguarded? Unprotected? The Sandharians took up what Absolem had abandoned. It has been the responsibility of the Sandharians, ever since, to make sure Omata stays safe."

Drake did not attempt to contradict the loa. Absolem had said it protected the land. Absolem had also said the amblers had given it a crown and the great maws destroyed it. Suddenly, Drake did not know what was fact and what was fiction. "Absolem has told you of the crown. The great maws? All that is true, Starfish." The loa was close. The fur and otter look made Drake believe the loa might be soft to the touch. He shook the idea of petting the loa from his thoughts.

"Your kind are filled with doubts," the loa continued. "Even as I stand here, you are not sure what is true any longer. Your kind are incapable of understanding the power the Sandharians possess."

The loa stopped and studied the marine who seemed to be struggling with his thoughts. The loa had these intense glossy black eyes which seemed to radiate rage. Up close, the loa was the exact opposite of the adorable and cuddly badger-like otter hybrid. It exuded hate. The slow moving loa belayed the true strength of the ancient ambler.

"We will exact our revenge, because that is our right. There is one other that must fall before we will return to a balance."

"A balance?"

The loa touched Drake gently on the hand and with the touch Drake saw the two amblers playing on the other side of the electronic barrier and Williams being told by Shepherd to shoot two of them. Williams had leveled his assault rifle and fired once and then again. The two amblers had fallen. The amblers pretending to be the scientists ran to the side of their dying kin. The dream vision ended.

"Balance," the loa said.

"No, you cannot kill another marine," Drake said, trembling.

"What is going on?" Jenkins asked, concerned.

"Drake, talk to us," Murray said.

"The Sandharians hold balance above all," the loa advised. "Your marine, Willyums, is already marked to balance the...loss."

"They are going to kill Williams," Drake said, dejected.

The loa instantly filled Drake's mind with the sight of the settlement. Williams was walking on the perimeter of the settlement armed with his assault rifle. He walked past a broken structure, kicking some debris out of the way, when the ground opened up like

204

a trap door and one of the monstrous Sandharian pulled Williams beneath the sand. Williams did not scream or struggle or get a chance to pull the trigger on his rifle before the sand swallowed him completely.

Drake had seen death as a Galactic Force marine. Death was a part of the Galactic Force life. People lived. People died. But seeing Williams sucked underground by one of the giant Sandharians was chilling.

In his mind, Drake tried to deal with what he had seen. He would have preferred to see Williams cut down by gunfire or impaled with a building structure rather than seeing the marine pulled beneath the grainy floor, and not knowing if he was alive or dead. Drake closed his eyes and opened them to the loa. The thoughts flitted in his head had to be ten times worse than Williams' final end.

Drake did not love Williams. He could not say he loved anyone more than his family, whom he had not seen in years. But he did not hate him either. He had lukewarm feelings for many, including Williams. Williams was annoying and a bit of a hard ass, Drake thought, but so, was he, if he was being honest. Still, Williams was a marine. He deserved better. He was suddenly grappling with the fact that Williams had to die because the LT had made a bad call.

"Absolem chose well," the loa chirped. "You are not like the others."

"What does that mean?"

"Drake, remember why we're here," Jenkins shouted over to him.

Drake turned and looked at her.

"Drake, get us out of here," Jenkins said. "Remember why we came here."

Drake looked from the loa to the two women on either side of him being guarded by the Sandharians. Drake took a step forward and the guards barred his forward progress. The marine nodded.

"What happened to Williams?" Drake asked. Then he paused, remembering what Absolem had told him about the amblers. "Was that...wait. Did that really happen?"

The loa paused.

"Absolem told us you are illusionists," Drake said. "We can't trust you."

"Drake, what is going on?"

"I think the loa is playing with my mind."

"How?"

"The loa may have put images in my head, like they did with Butcher," Drake said, furrowing his brow.

The loa turned from Drake to the corporal. The loa studied Jenkins for a long moment.

"Tell your two armed, two legged companions that other Sandharians have no need to issue a hoax. Hoaxing is reserved for those who threaten the Sandharians. You do not threaten the Sandharians. Absolem is jealous and envious of the Sandharians talents. Absolem can hoax but not as big as the weakest Sandharian."

"Can all of you create hoaxes?"

The loa did not respond.

"The Sandharians honor balance," the loa announced. "Balance is what the Sandharians fight for."

Drake refocused. "Loa, we came all this way, figured out where you were, to stop all this," Drake thought.

"Stop this? You cannot stop this. The Sandharians must stop this," the loa chirped.

"You said you believe in balance," Drake reminded. "We can offer you balance, loa."

"There is nothing you can offer the Sandharians that can bring balance to us," the loa said.

"Absolem told us we were brought together because we had different strengths. Absolem believed Murray to be bright. Jenkins to be strong. And me, welcoming," Drake reminded. "The three of us represent balance."

"Coming together means nothing. None of that matters," the loa stated. "The Sandharians shall simply wipe your tiny prickly soldiers from our land."

"But the marines will not go quietly," Drake thought, trying to remain in control of his feelings.

"The Sandharians have no fear. We have tamed and befriended many in the land for just this situation," the loa explained.

The fleeting images of protectors, the flying beasts Drake saw when the marines first arrived, the rumbling ground caused by the great maws, hundreds of dangerous unknown creatures that resembled long nosed dinosaurs, feathered insectoid-like things with stingers. Yet, it was the frightful fanged spider-like creatures which disturbed Drake the most; he had not seen them since his arrival.

Drake shook away the images planted by the Ioa in his head. "Loa, you are smarter than me."

The Ioa was silent.

"I understand that you and the Sandharians could destroy us all. But the question is: why? Why would you want to destroy your world when there is another choice? If you want balance, then we can offer balance."

The Ioa listened.

"You cannot imagine the mindset of the warriors who will be unleashed if you demolish the marines... the prickly ones. That will only bring more of us," Drake pleaded.

The Ioa studied Drake evenly.

"If more of us come then they will come with more weapons, technology and forces," Drake stated. "I tried to explain this to Absolem as well. We, the prickly ones, do not believe in losing."

The Ioa nodded.

"Starfish, if we are pressed then we can call down the undeniable power of the land. The unseen powers which are under our control could destroy all that threaten our balance."

"Okay." Drake understood. "But we are here now, Ioa, to offer you a better choice," Drake thought.

The Ioa looked up at the marine, curious.

"Loa, we were sent here to find and rescue the scientists you and your Sandharians have hidden somewhere. If you give them back to us, unharmed, we should be able to convince the Sarge and the others who make decisions to just leave this planet to you and your kind," Drake attempted.

"The release of the tiny prickly ones is not possible," the Ioa chittered.

"Why?"

"Balance," the loa chirped as if the word explained everything.

"I do not understand."

"Here, with the Sandharians, everything is about balance. You know? Give and take? For the Sandharians it is the same way. Your marines killed two of our Sandharians. To balance our loss, the two who caused it were returned to Omata. Balance," the loa explained.

"What do you want in exchange for the scientists?" Drake asked. But before he had finished the thought, the marine mechanic thought he knew the answer.

Chapter 19.

"**W**e only have about two days and a handful of hours to find Absolem and convince the great one to give us the crystal and return it to the loa before the reinforcements arrive and everything goes nuclear," Drake outlined.

"Thanks for captioning our insanity," Jenkins joked.

They were climbing a dune and looking out over the horizon at easily another twenty or thirty more dunes to cross. Drake was sipping from his water bottle.

Murray shook her head as she checked her wrist monitor. "How long?" Murray asked.

"What?"

"How long... until the others arrive?" Murray asked.

Jenkins checked her wrist monitor. "Fifty-three hours." Jenkins looked at Murray and shook her head. The trio walked on.

At the crest of the sand dune Jenkins spoke. "Drake, I think you forgot we have to get that crystal to get the scientists and stop the destruction of all of us before the Sandharians decide to unleash all the baddies of the planet on us and start a real-world war," she said pausing and stretching her arms above her head.

"Yeah, this is like some ancient video game," Drake remarked.

"I don't understand," Murray said.

"You never played those old video games where there's a mission and there's a team and they have to get something, but they have to beat up a big boss to get it?"

"That is every game ever made," Murray smiled, awkwardly.

"Yeah, that's my point," Drake said smugly.

Murray shook her head. Jenkins chuckled. Drake simply put his water bottle away and continued down the sand dune.

The three trudged across the sandhills heading back to the cavern where they had crawled on hands and knees to their audience with Absolem.

"Do you know where we're going?" Drake asked.

"Well, the settlement is over there," Murray gestured in the general direction of the west.

Jenkins furrowed her brow. She spoke. "The protectors are due east and we traveled to Absolem's cave it was pretty straight east from the settlement."

"You sure?" Drake asked.

Murray shrugged her shoulders.

"Wait a minute," Jenkins said, stopping on the ridge of a dune they had been walking on for a few minutes. "When we went to the cave the galactic space caterpillar took us to, it was guided by Absolem." The science officer pursed her lips. "I don't want to sound pessimistic but we're going to have to be all sorts of lucky to find that cave."

"What's the problem?"

"If that's true, we are—" Murray started only to be interrupted by Jenkins.

"We are literally throwing a dart into the sand and hoping to hit a bullseye on something we have only seen once," Jenkins divulged.

Jenkins exhaled. Murray seemed suddenly unmotivated.

"What's going on?" Drake questioned.

"We are literally searching for a needle in a haystack," Jenkins stated, trying to be optimistic.

"But we've been to that needle in this haystack once before," Drake mentioned.

The science officer looked at Drake sheepishly. "I don't know," Murray said, tired and sweating.

"What's to know? I mean, the whole planet is depending on us to find Absolem, get a crystal, and return it to some freaky little witch creature to save the scientists and get us off the planet. How it works out doesn't matter. It just matters that it works out.," Drake said, narrowing his dark eyes. "I mean, we're all just pawns in this cosmic chess game. I'm okay with that."

"But—," Jenkins began.

"But what? But we're on a planet that is trying to kill us all? But we're trying to find something that up until a few days ago I had in my utilities?" Drake paused. "Things happen. It's not anyone's fault." Drake took a deep breath. "One of my favorite lines I've heard from some ancient video, is we can get busy living or get busy dying." Drake chuckled. "I choose living."

The two women listened. Murray nodded. Jenkins had begun looking at Drake eye-to-eye but by the end of his words the corporal had lowered her eyes and seemed a little uncomfortable.

"So, what do we do?" Murray chirped, cheering up slightly.

"What choice do we have?" Drake asked gesturing forward as he began to walk toward the next dune.

"How do we know we're going in the right direction?"

"We have to be going in the right direction," Drake assured.

"How do you know?"

Drake smirked. "Well, I think you forget the loa and everyone on this planet is psychically connected to Absolem in some way. One of us will feel him," Drake told his traveling companions.

Murray shook her head, frowning slightly.

"Or he will call out to us," Drake said.

Jenkins nodded as the trio crested a sandhill and found themselves able to see in every direction without impediment.

"Let's pause for a second," Jenkins said. Murray paused and took a knee. Drake stretched at the top of the sandhill. He felt the bulk of his equipment and shook his head. He unclipped his helmet and shrugged off his backpack. He attached the helmet to the backpack and slipped it back over his shoulders.

"Look," Murray pointed. The science officer pointed to the outlines of the dark shadow of the settlement. Murray squinted and tried to see people even though she knew nothing would stand out from this distance. Drake looked where Murray pointed. He looked back to the protector standing on the ridge behind them.

"By my estimates," Jenkins calculated. "We should be close."

"Close to what?"

"The cave," Jenkins pouted. The corporal sipped water from her water bottle. She handed it to Murray who took a small sip and handed it back to Jenkins.

"You think we can find a hidden cave?"

"Thought you were a scientist, Murray?" Drake snorted. "Ain't you the type that believes science solves all problems?" Jenkins smiled.

"What's that mean?"

Jenkins was about to speak when Drake interrupted.

"It means, we're closing in on a hidden cave despite you and Jenkins doubting we would ever get there," Drake said. Jenkins shook her head.

"No, I mean, based on the general math of things, we're in the general location," Jenkins said.

"What she means is you poo poo'd the whole 'we'll find the hidden cave because we're connected' thing and she's rubbing your nose in the idea of us finding the needle in the haystack."

"What? I didn't... poo poo the idea of finding the cave!" Murray said.

"Hey, can it," Jenkins said. "Thinking that if we are parallel with the settlement and the protectors, we should be pretty close."

"That's science," mouthed Drake to Murray.

Murray smiled.

Perhaps, Drake thought they were closer than they imagined.

The trio continued walking.

"This would be a good moment for one of the guardians to magically appear and take us to Absolem," Drake said as he climbed what felt like the thousandth sand dune since leaving the loa.

Drake looked back and smiled. They had walked for nearly an hour and the protector, though never small, had shrunk just a little in size as the trio moved closer to their goal.

"How will we know... we are close?"

Jenkins slowed at Murray's question. The corporal did not answer. She looked left and right scanning the terrain for any landmarks.

Drake smiled and pointed toward the plain where they had been days before. Drake immediately began to run down the side of the sandhill toward the plain. Murray and Jenkins followed cautiously.

At the bottom of the sand dune, Drake paused, recalling the space caterpillar had been waiting near an oddly square shaped spot between two smaller sand dunes. Drake instantly looked for his footprints, expectantly. Of course, he did not find his footprints. He searched for his or Jenkins or Murray's footprints expectantly in the powdery silt but found nothing.

By the time the two women climbed down the dune and reached the plain Drake, was searching for the entrance to the cave which led to Absolem.

"Are you sure this is the place?"

Drake stood up and pointed to the opening of the cavern.

"Well, I'll be," Murray smiled with a slight glint in her eye.

"We found it," Drake smiled broadly.

"Maybe things are finally going our way," Jenkins said.

Drake was about to say something when he noticed for the first time the shadows of the Sandharians massing at the base of the dunes. The marine slit his eyes and pointed behind the two women who were smiling ear-to-ear at having found the cavern entrance.

Jenkins spun around, her military training kicking in. She drew her pistols from beneath her arm pits and prepared for war. Drake flipped his assault rifle forward, pointing it forward and menacingly in the direction of the Sandharians. Murray was the last to turn around and Drake watched as the small science officer glimmered for an instant and suddenly transformed before Drake and Jenkins eyes into a Sandharian.

"Sonuva—"

"We knew you would lead us to Absolem. It only seemed reasonable to have one of our own in your midst," the Sandharian who had pretended to be Murray chittered.

"What is it saying?"

Drake relayed the message.

"The protector of the land, your Absolem, like all those here are...secretive. The Sandharians are...territorial." The illusionist four-armed, otter mole illusionist looked at Drake. "The Med-Sandharians that you saw in our cavern are indebted to us. We saved them long ago when they were... fighting with the Lar-Sandharians. The... giants, have come to be indebted to us, Starfish. We, the original Sandharians are the only ones who have the hoaxing ability. We used it against our enemies. The loa controls them and avoids fighting between the two. We, the Sandharians, all have... talismans. They do not. This distinguishes them from us. It is how we hold power."

Drake looked at Jenkins, "Blah, blah, blah, slavery. Blah, blah, blah, racism and tribal wars."

Jenkins looked at the twenty or so Sandharians who had followed them.

"What now?"

"In truth, the loa ordered us to follow you and kill the protector of the land," the Sandharian stated. "The loa does not believe in the protector any longer."

"What is it saying?"

Drake told Jenkins what the Sandharian had said while training his assault rifle on the diminutive Sandharian. He aimed his weapon toward the ground suddenly. Jenkins, seeing Drake lower his weapon, stepped back to the marine and looked at him curiously.

"What are you doing?"

"I am getting this bad feeling that this whole thing isn't about us or the scientists or the settlement or any of it," Drake declared. "This a power grab."

"What did the Murray otter mole say?"

"They came to kill Absolem."

Jenkins knitted her brow, confused. "Why?"

"Like I said, a power grab."

Jenkins held her pistols aimed at the twenty plus Sandharians.

"We know Absolem put a governor in your heads," the Murray mole otter said. "You cannot harm anything here."

Drake slung his assault rifle and crossed his arms across his chest, insolent.

"We can put the guns away," Drake told Jenkins. "They know we cannot harm them."

Jenkins cut a sidelong glance at Drake, who shrugged his shoulders, in response.

"Wait, Drake. These bastards have Murray."

Drake acknowledged that point and reversed course, emotionally. He had been despondent and unconcerned about the politics of Rigo-C and Absolem and the Sandharians, but with the mention of Murray, the science officer of the *Indomitable*, being held against her will by the Sandharians Drake was furious.

"Where is Murray?"

"The tiny one is safe," the Murray mole otter said.

Drake and Jenkins looked at one and other.

"What's the plan?"

"Well," Jenkins began, hesitantly.

"Well, if we get to Absolem first and warn him then maybe we get some kudos and it doesn't kill us," Drake reasoned. He turned and measured how far it was to the entrance of the hidden cave. Jenkins, seeing Drake looking toward the cavern entrance, considered the same distance.

Drake turned and began to run toward the hidden cave entrance. Jenkins followed suit.

Simultaneously, the ground rolled. Drake skidded and slid toward the cave entrance. He reached out toward it as the ground bucked and roiled. Scrambling against the movement of the ground, Drake dove into the nearly invisible entrance, clinging to the side. He felt Jenkins grab at his waist as the ground trembled once more, then eased.

"Go!" Jenkins screamed and with the order Drake crawled fully into the cave entrance. He moved on his hand and knees and then he stopped in the darkness.

Turn around, Starfish. Turn around, Ginkins. The land protects. The amblers have been...rebuked.

The two marines backed out of the cave and back onto the sand plain. Drake, covered in sand and dirt, climbed to his feet and found himself in front of five space caterpillars. The towering cosmic caterpillars studied Jenkins and Drake. Drake could only smile when he saw the familiar galaxy space caterpillar with the mottled color on its side that had taken him and the two women to Absolem days before.

"Starfish," the mottled colored outer space caterpillar mouthed.

The amblers have retreated. My council has located the scientists. They will be liberated soon. One of you will go to them. One of you will go to the Sandharians den and offer my answer to the loa.

Drake raised his hand. "I will go to the loa." Drake's face was stern. "I have unfinished business with that lying loa."

"You sure? Jenkins asked.

"I can't say that I'm sure, but I think that of the two of us it should be me that talks to the loa."

"Good luck," Jenkins said, climbing onto her cosmic caterpillar.

"Good luck to you," Drake said. Without another word the space caterpillar he sat on began moving south toward the Sandharians' den.

Chapter 20.

Drake and Murray had been deposited by the cosmic caterpillar at the edge of the destroyed settlement. The space caterpillar had disappeared into the sands as they climbed over the dunes. The two adventurers descended the sand dune and walked back toward the three landship guarded tents which now made-up Echo the new settlement. There were four tents set up for the military staff. As Murray and Drake approached the landship, a gun turret spun around and aimed the .50 caliber auto cannon at the pair.

Drake instinctually raised his hands in surrender.

"Private Christian Drake, Alpha fireteam, May 211243XY Arc1," the marine stated.

Murray raised her hands as well.

"Science officer Yvette Murray, *Indomitable*, June 031237XX Arc1," the *Indomitable* officer announced.

King popped up from the gun turret and looked at the two curiously.

"What up, King?"

"Holy potato chips! What *isn't* up is more like it. We just got the scientists back," King said hanging an arm over the turret's lip. "Jenkins walked them in about an hour ago, all Captain America style. She's a real hero. She found them, single-handedly, and walked them all back here by herself."

"By herself," Drake repeated with a smile.

"Jenkins told us about your mission, but you are in hot water," King said to Drake, as a matter of fact. "She is a hero but got slapped on the wrist for some non-com gobbledygook."

"Gobbledygook?" Drake lowered his head and twisted his lips, not sure of what that meant.

King tapped something inside the landship gun turret and studied Drake and recently released Murray.

"The Sarge wants to talk with the two of you," King admitted. "I'm supposed to tell him when you get back." Turning her attention to Drake. "You know the three of you've been AWOL for nearly forty-eight hours?"

"But we saved the world," Murray said, exasperated.

King looked annoyingly at the science officer. "I'm not talking to you. We have no power over you. The Sarge told us that if you showed up before we left, we were to take you with us. But if you didn't show up not to worry too much about it." King looked at Drake. "You are in deep doo doo."

"Yeah, I figured," Drake said.

"Drake?" Murray asked.

"This is how the military works. Follow rules or face the consequences."

"It's not right," Murray said, trying to understand Drake's acceptance.

Tyler and Payne met Drake and Murray at the landship. They were all business.

"What gives?" Drake asked Payne. "I thought I was covered by Jenkins?"

"Jenkins?" Payne sneered. "The sarge asked us to make sure you made it to his tent," Payne told him.

Drake nodded, trying to read the corporal who was walking him to see the Sarge. All he could tell was that the stiff Payne was stiffer as he walked him to the Sarge's tent.

"Payne, what is this all about?"

"Jenkins deserted her post. You went with her. She's a hero. We can't touch her, not now," Payne said through gritted teeth. "So, Sarge is going to make an example of you." He paused. "I think Jenkins deserves worse."

"But I didn't do anything wrong," Drake said in response.

Payne did not respond.

In the tent were Sarge, Butcher, Springer and Jenkins. Sarge was seated at a makeshift table. The two men were grinning when Drake and Murray walked in. Once Tyler and Payne appeared, Butcher and Springer stood up. Sarge remained seated. Jenkins was standing at ease in front of the Sarge. She turned and, seeing Murray and Drake, gave an anguished look.

Tyler and Payne came forward with Drake.

"That'll be all private," Sarge said to Tyler. The two-gun rigged private turned on his heels and walked out of the tent.

218

"Drake what am I to do with you?" Sarge asked. He grinned mirthlessly. "Just heard the fairytale from Jenkins," Sarge pursed his lips. "You know I don't believe in fairytales, but she did bring back the real scientists."

Drake looked back at Murray. Murray looked around awkwardly and stepped past Drake to stand next to Jenkins. The Sarge gestured for Murray to have a seat. The science officer shook her head and stood next to Jenkins and implored her to do something, wordlessly.

Standing next to his corporal, Drake noticed Payne and Butcher were standing, and each had their hand on their sidearm. That did not bode well. Springer leaned against the air scrubber sitting in the corner of the tent. This meeting was not a friendly how do you do conversation. Drake looked to Jenkins for guidance. Jenkins shook her head.

"So, private, where have you been for the last forty-eight hours?"

Drake opened his mouth. After a second, he closed it again. He could not tell the tale he and Jenkins had been on. It was unbelievable. Worse still, he was not sure whether Absolem's governor would stop him from saying anything about the protector of the land and the Sandharians and their plot to destroy everything that was not native to the planet.

Drake said nothing.

The land protects.

Drake looked from the Sarge to Jenkins and then Murray.

Murray stepped forward and spoke then, even though she had no authority. "When we came to the surface of this alien place, we were greeted by the sight of the gigantic space squids and knew we weren't on the *Indomitable* or the *Sentinel* any longer. Nevertheless, we tried to do our work. We have faced many unexpected issues on this alien planet. We have made decisions that we might not have made anywhere else. But it was essential to protect all. In the last ninety-six hours, we have been to the edge of the Gargantuan mountains and trekked across the sand dunes trying to return to the settlement, with hopes of leaving this place without disturbing the delicate alien lives and ecosystem," Murray told the Sarge.

Drake listened as Murray continued, speaking of freedom, liberty, science, discovery and all things connected to them. The petite science officer's speech was passionate and articulate but served no real purpose, Drake knew. The marine knew that after Murray with her science related arguments and veiled threats of taking this to a higher court, that Sarge was going to thank the science officer but ultimately ignore her words and do what was best for the squad.

"Thank you, science officer Murray," Sarge smiled dutifully. "Now, if you will excuse us, we have some military work to do that is not for your civilian ears." Sarge gestured for Murray to depart. Murray hesitated. There was an uncomfortable silence, but after a few moments the science officer reluctantly left the tent. Once Murray was gone the Sarge steepled his thick fingers in front of his face.

"First Seargeant," Jenkins attempted.

Sarge looked and Jenkins closed her mouth.

"Again, having an attack, two deaths and hostile aliens in the area would draw attention. But we have the potential of an exo-form with psychic powers too. *We* are under the microscope." He paused. The First Seargeant studied Jenkins and Drake. "I understand that you were doing what you were asked, but the problem with you private is *who* you were listening to."

Drake looked at Sarge confused.

"The force cannot punish the *Indomitable* staff or the Galactic Force darling that Jenkins has become, saving the eight. Suddenly, she's Teflon. I have reported her, but I don't see a lot of traction or action coming down on her head. But you don't have the protection of a double X non-com hero." Sarge gave Jenkins a side glance. "You, private though, are my problem," Sarge said, dropping the lighthearted tone. Butcher and Payne watched with mirthless smiles on their faces.

"We have to maintain order in the ranks. What kind of Galactic Force would we have if the enlisted just did what they wanted and weren't where they were supposed to be?" Sarge took a deep breath. "You, private, are the sacrificial lamb. You are going to be sacrificed for the good of the force."

Payne, Springer and Butcher watched.

"Private, you are remanded to your tent until further notice," Sarge growled, the smile he had put on for Murray dropping away. "You will be dealt with after the reinforcements arrive. If you had showed up earlier, I would have killed you myself. But I've changed my mind, thanks to the return of the scientists and a little peace," Sarge told him. The sarge placed his trembling hands on the top of the table and took a deep breath. "The power plant is about to go offline. So, I suggest that you bundle up. Until the reinforcements arrive, you are to remain in your tent."

"Sarge, I thought that you would consider the extenuating circumstances," Jenkins said, her eyes lowered.

The Sarge gave Jenkins a cold stare. "You don't want me to add insubordination to your current charges now do you, Jenkins?" Sarge paused. "I listened to your fairytale. I know you are going to be a headache for the *Sentinel*. They will want to give you an accommodation and throw you out in the same breath." The Sarge seemed to struggle for control. "I said I would give what you said some thought." The Sarge paused. "I have contacted my superiors about the extenuating circumstances, but again the issue of alien psychic control is the bigger issue."

Drake heard as he was escorted to his tent. Valentine was the first on guard duty. His tent was a smaller version of the camp tent he had just left. In a pinch it could hold four people. He had a desk, a notebook computer, a lantern and a cot in the corner.

Drake ate, watched a video of some anime that had not been new for centuries, and, when he got tired, fallen asleep, slipping into a dream.

In his dream, he relived the whole adventure of going to see the loa. Drake held onto the flecked colored cosmic caterpillar as he and two other cosmic caterpillars raced along the sands. The three interstellar caterpillars moved effortlessly, and Drake watched the terrain change as the sun began to rise. To the east were the seemingly endless rising dunes.

"I think that I will call you: Zook," Drake announced as he rode on the back of the dappled space caterpillar. He smiled and patted the neck of Zook as they sped across the sands.

The trip to the Sandharians had been nothing like the endless walk Murray, Jenkins and Drake had taken. The space caterpillars easily traversed the terrain. At the top of the ridge, the celestial caterpillar stopped. The three galaxy caterpillars edged their bulks along the foot paths and entered the caves of the Sandharians.

Drake held on and in a handful of seconds he and his mount found themselves in the grand subterranean round cavern. In the cavern were hundreds of Sandharians. Drake noted the Med-Sandharians and the Lar-Sandharians, feeling a pang of sorrow looking at the indebted Sandharians.

"You know that in my history slave ownership never ends well."

"Slave owners," the loa said with venom in the tone. "Are you judging the Sandharians?"

"I suppose I am," Drake said. He found himself disgusted by the loa and the Sandharians.

"This anger...passion... bitterness in you is interesting," the loa hissed. "Be careful, you will not be protected forever by your Absolem."

"You are using these creatures against their wills," Drake said. It was disappointing.

"Wrong?" the loa sneered. "The Sandharians are ancient and all we do is for the Sandharians."

The loa sat on the block of stone, flanked by half a dozen Sandharians. The small creature tipped its mole-like head and chirped and chittered. Drake knew the talisman wearing mole otter creature was sneering at him.

"You have seen Absolem," the loa said and Drake heard the poison in her voice.

"I bring a message from Absolem," Drake told her.

"You are Absolem's messenger?" The loa sneered.

Drake paused.

"What is the message, messenger?"

Drake clenched and unclenched his fists, trying to remember what Absolem wanted him to tell the loa. He took a deep breath before he stated what Absolem had told him to say.

"The protector protects," the loa said at the end of Absolem's message that had been relayed by Drake. There was still acid in the tone. "The choices at present are agreeable, messenger."

The loa slightly inclined her mole -like and from the hundreds of Sandharians emerged Murray.

"How do I know this is the real Murray?"

"The guardians know," the loa hissed. "They can sense hoaxing."

The Sandharians deposited Murray on the floor of the cavern. Drake backed up and helped her to her feet.

"What is the last thing you said that made you cry?" Drake asked.

Murray did not speak immediately. Drake studied the science officer carefully. He looked from the science officer to the cosmic caterpillar.

"I can't believe how simple things can be," Murray recalled and smiled tenderly.

Drake smiled, satisfied.

"Balance," the loa said having released Murray.

"Yes, right," Drake said, reaching into his utilities and fishing out the blueish-purple gem he had handed over to Absolem days before. "Absolem told us to give you this in exchange for Murray and the scientists."

The loa upon seeing the gem rose to her feet. Her half dozen minions climbed to their feet as well. Drake, for a moment, thought to smash the gem onto the cavern floor and crush it under his boot heel.

"This anger in you is surprising," the loa remarked, the condescension dripping off every word. "You are truly different than the others."

Drake swallowed and reined in his anger. When the mole otter creature arrived and reached up for the gem, it took all the power in him not to heave the stone into the darkness of the cave.

"The Sandharians accept this...token, jetton, appeasement from Absolem and call for peace between the protector of the land and the Sandharians," the loa decreed.

Drake, with Murray's arm draped across his shoulders, followed Zook and the two galactic caterpillars from the cavern. Moments later, on the back of Zook and speeding back to the settlement Drake held onto Murray and asked her what had happened.

"The Sandharians are masters of deception. They lie all the time, Drake," Murray said as they held onto Zook. "It is hard to determine whether what they say is true," the science officer began. She rambled a bit eventually explaining that somewhere in the transition from the pulling in and dragging through the tunnel to the cavern that she had been gagged and bound.

"This whole planet has the annoying ability to read our minds," Murray pointed out. "That alone could be the reason enough that we could not live here. Imagine if there was a creature that could read our minds at any time. It would be disastrous."

Drake and Murray rode on across the powdery terrain speeding up and cutting the distance between themselves and the Echo settlement.

There was a noise which woke Drake. He opened his eyes and found on the desk a biodegradable tray with a biodegradable pouch of water, dehydrated banana and an MRE had been left for him. Drake sat at the desk and ate. The food was as tasteless as all the MREs he had since joining the Galactic Force. After eating he composed his first of three letters to be sent to his niece.

The hours in the tent were endless. Drake wrote his three letters. He ate. He watched videos. He slept. He dreamed.

After one of many naps Drake woke and washed up. While he was brushing his teeth, he heard a disturbance outside of his tent. A few minutes later, there was a lot of activity in the camp and Drake poked his head out of the tent entrance and saw a tall square faced man with dark hair holding an assault rifle. Drake had never seen the man before.

"Hey, partner, what's going on?" Drake asked from inside the tent.

"The reinforcements are here," the stranger with the assault rifle said.

"Who are you?"

"I'm Alexander," the square faced stranger said. He turned and Drake could see through the netting he only had the assault rifle. He was dressed in the red coveralls of the scientists of the compound.

"Foods on its way," Alexander told him.

A few minutes later and in walked another stranger with his breakfast. She had shaped eyebrows and big ears that stuck out a little beneath her dark, straight shoulder length hair.

Drake watched the woman drop off his breakfast and leave without saying a word. He climbed from his cot and had a simple breakfast of scrambled eggs, potatoes and washed it down with stale coffee.

Drake napped and waited for the inevitable.

Before midday Valentine appeared with a handheld camera. Behind him came Payne and Young. They escorted him out of the tent and to the southern end of the Echo settlement. Young secretly put a hand on Drake's hand. Drake looked out of the corner of his eye and noticed the corporal struggling.

Drake recalled that when they had arrived six days ago there had been only five biodomes standing and that with a little effort he and the mechanics had been able to fix a sixth biodome for the fake scientists. Drake shook his head at the thought.

In six days, Drake had met Zook and Absolem. He had met a loa, been deceived, betrayed, lied to and rescued Murray from the clutches of the Sandharians. And what did he have to show for it now?

As he was marched from his tent to the front of the ruins of the settlement and seated on a camp chair beside Jenkins, Drake knew nothing he had done was going to matter. There was perception and there was reality.

Sarge and some of the Lions of Apedemak thought Drake had deserted not once but twice in the face of battle and been AWOL for three of the six days. There was undeniable evidence, Sarge pointed out that Drake was fraternizing with the enemy. An anonymous source had gone on record and stated that Drake began acting funny in the biodome and attempted to influence others in the squad.

Payne and Young walked Drake to what would have been the front of Echo settlement and there found Sarge, Butcher, Jenkins, King, Murray and two others he had never seen before.

Murray was guarded by Aricka King as the proceedings began. In attendance were: Sarge, Drake, Jenkins, Murray, Valentine, Butcher, Young, Springer, King and Payne.

Also present to oversee the proceedings were Wanda Seals and Hank Penn, the Lieutenant and First Corporal of the reinforcement team, Victorious. Seals was a wide hipped woman in her twenties with a curvaceous figure and an Afro, which she divided down her round head into two Afro puffs. Penn was a round shouldered boy of eighteen with buck teeth and a pock marked face oversaw the whole proceeding. Neither offered any input.

"Under the authority of General Matthew McDaniel and the high command of the Galactic Force today we execute a field court martial for private Christian Drake for his cowardly, disobedience and for recklessly endangering and thus jeopardizing the safety of the squad by initially allowing himself to be possessed and controlled by an exo-form," Sarge stated. He was reading from his notebook. "At the heart of this court martial is the brazen disregard of the chain of command. The Galactic Force is only as strong as its weakest link. The blood of marines is on your hands."

"Sarge, there is no definitive proof of Drake being influenced by any exo-form," Jenkins said.

The Sarge looked at Jenkins coolly and the corporal quieted.

Valentine was recording everything on a camera drone.

"I want to point out that it is a Galactic Force standard for all personnel to follow all orders given by a commanding officer unless the order is against the Force's Code of Honor. If such an order is given the private is required to report that order. All Galactic Force personnel are also to report any unusual mental or physical sensations on alien locations, that might jeopardize the mission and compromise the squad's success in so doing," the Sarge continued.

"This will not stand up on the *Sentinel*, once we return," Jenkins attempted.

226

"In the field, all commanding officers have been given authority to conduct flying court martials if they so deem it necessary. This field court martial is just a formality. Everyone in the squad understands that once Drake suspected he was being influenced by an alien entity of any kind his duty was to report it to our medic, Young. Yet, the marine shirked that duty. He instead conspired to help the exo-forms. He was in league with the exo-forms when we arrived at the settlement and, for all we know, was aware of the plot to kill LT and Williams."

Murray stood up and offered her opinion. "This planet is not worth all the work needed to control it. The alien life forms all seem to exhibit a form of psychic ability. They can read our minds as easily as you are reading that manual. They have all been shown to be extremely intelligent and manipulative."

Aricka King restrained the science officer.

"The only reason you are here now, science officer, is to answer my questions," the Sarge growled. "My only question, is he free of the alien influence?" Sarge asked Murray.

Jenkins looked to the *Indomitable* science officer. Drake looked to Murray as well.

"On this planet," Murray responded. "I doubt anyone who is susceptible to influence is ever going to be free of alien control."

Sarge listened, saying nothing, so Murray continued. "I also ask you to reconsider your thinking on this court martial."

Sarge eyed the science officer coldly.

Drake looked at those gathered. Young seemed to be battling something internally. The marines seemed conflicted. All except Sarge, Payne and Butcher.

"What are you going to do?" Jenkins asked. "I mean, this is not Nazi Germany or Finland. This is Rigo-C, and we are the Galactic Force. We cannot allow some kangaroo court to proceed."

"Jenkins, you are here merely as a formality," Sarge pointed out. He stared her down and the before speaking again. "The verdict is guilty. The punishment: has been determined by the *Sentinel* rulings of Interstellar Military Law. I am well within my rights as the commanding field officer to summarily execute deserters, but it has been suggested that if any corporal punishment be exercised today it be measured. So, I will offer a *measured* corporal punishment."

Butcher, the sadomasochist, stepped forward, holding a hand braided whip in his hand.

"Today, before we return to the *Indomitable*, private Christian Drake is to be lashed seven times here, on Rigo-C, and then put in hyper sleep until we arrive back at the *Sentinel*. There, he will face the *Sentinel* tribunal, and either be executed or drummed out of the force." Sarge declared, looking at Drake. "We are going easy on you. I could have had you executed for your cowardly act, but that decision will now be left to the *Sentinel*."

Drake barely moved when he heard the punishment handed down by the Sarge. Jenkins had blanched at the verdict; she closed her eyes and tried to control her emotions. When she opened her liquid brown eyes again tears fell.

Starfish. The land protects.

"This is barbaric!" Murray screamed, held in place by Aricka King. Murray looked from the Sarge and Butcher to the First Lieutenant from the Victorious. "Do something! This is so wrong!"

Wanda Seals looked at the Sarge and nodded.

Drake was dragged to the hastily constructed flogging area where Everett and Tyler had constructed of two structural poles from the settlement, having planted them deep in the sand Drake and tied to the makeshift cross by Foley and Springer.

After Springer, the chaplain, had secured Drake he stood there, praying.

"Lot of good your prayers are going to do me now," Drake hissed.

Butcher stood holding the braided whip, ready to administer the punishment.

Drake was stripped down to his waist.

The land protects Starfish.

He received his punishment lashes from the whip and by the sixth he passed out.

In the anguish Drake was soothed and protected by the land, Absolem. It flowed through him and around him as the lashes tore his flesh. As tears fell from his eyes and blood ran down his ripped flesh Drake felt Absolem reach out. He, Drake, and he Absolem became

228

one in that pain and the greater entity reached out to those around him. Instantly, in the darkness he saw all the Lions and the reinforcements. For the first time he saw tendrils extending out from him toward the others.

The tiny prickly ones will know the power of the land.

"No," Drake said to Absolem. "Do not enslave them."

The land, your Absolem, does not enslave, Starfish. I give them and you choice.

Drake had passed out by the sixth lash but, despite him being unconscious, Butcher delivered the last on his broken and unconscious body. Carefully, Drake was cut down from the whipping post and carried unconscious to the landship.

In the landship, Young put on a salve on Drake's wounds and bandaged his back. A weather balloon was inflated and held the three landships ready to be taken from the surface of Rigo-C. The shuttle systematically caught and reeled in the four landships and prepared to return to the *Indomitable*. When the transport broke the planet's atmosphere and returned to space, the shuttle returned easily to the *Indomitable*.

Goodbye Starfish was the last thing Drake remembered hearing on Rigo-C.

Chapter 21.

The blinking lights of the hyper sleep chamber were monitored by Martin, the *Indomitable's* medical officer and Athena, the AI system. The Nitro and Beta fireteams of the Lions of Apedemak had all been tucked into their hyper sleep chambers along with the disgraced Christian Drake who had been heavily drugged and unconscious upon arrival after a flogging on the planet.

The scientists were checked and put in the hyper sleep chambers.

Most of the fireteams, after putting away their personals in their lockers, were also put in sleep chambers.

Drake was one of the last to be put in a hyper sleep chamber.

Jenkins had scheduled to be the last member of the Lions of Apedemak to climb into the sleep tube. Sarge was already tucked away and sleeping. Foley climbed into the hyper sleep chamber and Jenkins gestured for Payne to enter.

Jenkins and Martin watched as Payne climbed into the sleep tube. Martin observed as Jenkins pressed several buttons which began the slow and gradual routine of the addition of somnubol to the sleep chamber to insure a long, uninterrupted sleep.

"Athena, private mode, please," Jenkins said. The Artificial Intelligence monitoring blinked off. It would give the room five minutes of privacy before checking back in, Jenkins knew.

"What are Drake's chances of a full recovery?"

"Almost one hundred percent," Martin smiled. "Given enough time, his body will heal nicely. He will carry those scars forever, though. They are a brand of shame handed down by the Interstellar Military Code."

Young nodded. She turned and saw that all of the Lions of Apedemak were in the hyper chambers. She looked around for something heavy and her eye fell upon a wrench. Swiftly, she picked it up, moved over to where Martin stood, and swung just hard enough to stun the medical officer. Martin crashed into one of the control panels of the hyper sleep chamber.

Shaking his head, Martin spun around and reached out for the corporal. Jenkins, who grabbed Martin and hit him again across his head. Martin fell to the floor of the chamber, unconscious. From the side of Martin's temple oozed a white milky liquid. Jenkins smiled. Martin was a synthetic. Synthetics were controversial. There were concerns of the possibilities of the rise of robots but, there were fail-safes in place in all manufactured synthetics to protect against any robotic revolution.

Jenkins quickly scanned the blinking lights and made sure Martin had not damaged anything when he crashed into the control panel.

"Is everyone all right down there?" said Athena, the artificial intelligence of the *Indomitable*.

"Yes, Athena," Jenkins answered. "Martin and I had a disagreement. It has been resolved amicably."

"Are you sure? Martin seems to be offline."

"I am sure. I asked Martin to power down for an hour to give me time to calculate an equation he and I were considering. I asked for ten minutes to allow Martin the opportunity to recharge as well."

"Ten minutes?"

"Yes, Athena," Jenkins responded. "Just ten minutes."

"Very well. I will check back in at the appointed time to see what the conclusion is," Athena stated.

"Very good," Young said.

Still holding the heavy wrench, Jenkins looked at the unconscious Martin and smiled. She laughed. She set the wrench on a worktable and walked purposefully to the third control panel in the hyper sleep chamber. With three swift actions, Jenkins masked her next steps from Athena.

Jenkins flipped the first of fifteen switches which would liberate those in the sleep tubes. The medic watched the process and repeated those actions four more times.

Valentine opened his eyes and Jenkins slid the hyper sleep chamber lid open. Murray was already up and dressed. On her hip was a service weapon.

"I'm not sure if I'm supposed to be happy to see you or sad," Valentine frowned.

Jenkins reached out and helped Valentine out of the hyper sleep chamber.

Valentine once out of the hyper sleep chamber was handed his utilities and combat boots.

"We have work to do," Drake said, climbing out of his own hyper sleep chamber.

Standing beside Young and Jenkins was Everett. Murray shouldered her way forward from behind the four marines.

"Ooh Rah," Valentine swore.

"Ooh Rah," said Everett adjusting his two-gun rig.

"Yeah," Drake said. "Once we do this all the rules, we know, are out the window."

"All of them?" Young asked.

"Well, most of them," Drake smirked.

"So, we doing this?"

Drake nodded.

"I guess the next step is unavoidable," Everett grimaced.

The six slowly moved from the hyper sleep chamber and toward the bridge.

"I figure there has to be some good that comes from all this," Murray conceded.

"Well, if we believe in all the stuff they taught us in boot camp, then this was inevitable," Drake said. He had his two-gun rig in place.

Jenkins adjusted her gun belt and prepared for what was about to happen.

"Yeah, we are supposed to be the good guys and gals of the galaxy," Everett remarked.

Murray smiled her elvish smile. She looked at Everett's words.

"We ain't supposed to be the jackasses that ream planets because we can," Drake reminded.

"Yep," Valentine spat, his sidearm on his hip.

"But if we do this, we will automatically become the a-holes that took on Galactic Force," Young noted. "The rebels," the medic concluded.

Everyone fell silent.

"Well, we'll be better than the landing party," Murray said. "Right?"

Jenkins and Everett laughed. Drake shook his head.

Drake paused and studied the assembled. "No one is being forced to do this. We all know what is at stake. If you want to back out, then now is the time. Things are about to get real, real." He trusted the men and women who were with him were ready for this, but still, he paused and waited, giving everyone a chance to change their minds. No one moved.

"Okay, now that we've convinced ourselves again, we have to do the hard work," Jenkins announced, pulling her pistol from under her left arm.

"Poop in a pot, yeah," Valentine grinned.

"No one gets killed," Everett advised.

"Right now," Jenkins barked.

"There's going to be tons of killing coming," Drake answered. "We aren't going to tweak the nose of a titan and not expect stuff to go bad immediately."

"We don't have to do that, yet," Murray said.

Drake paused, feeling like the most unlikely of leaders. He smiled and when he did the dull pain on his back strengthened his resolve. "Remember I was whipped on Rigo-C. I was whipped because I helped stop the mutual destruction of a planet. We are not killers. But we are not doormats either. We are taking the B Class spaceship, and that is going to be violent." Drake paused. He studied the six faces looking at him. "We are focused and motivated. Most of the people we will come against are just going through the motions and won't be ready to fight. We have that going for us. So, let's attack this problem full on and let the chips fall where they may."

The six stepped onto the bridge and immediately spread out around the circular command center of the ship. Everyone, including Murray, had a weapon.

Ballmer, the security officer, was the first to react, but before he could do anything, he found the medic of the newly formed mutineers standing with a service weapon in his face.

"Sit down," Young demanded. The security officer sat and Young disarmed him.

Captain Alfred Page turned around seeing a bit of commotion to his right and was surprised to see Young with a pistol trained on his security officer. Page stood only to find himself face-to-face with the scarred corporal smiling. Page, tall and angular, stood in the middle of the bridge of the *Indomitable* and studied the assembled at the helm of the A Class-1947. Page scowled.

Lisa Milton, the communications officer, stood and sneered seeing Murray holding a gun on the bridge. "So, this is what it comes down to?" Milton laughed. "You've gone native?"

"At some point, this was inevitable," said Murray as she studied the assistant to the captain. She gestured and beckoned Milton away from her console.

Charlie Markham, the clean shaven, blonde haired, pompadour wearing, eighteen-year-old health officer on duty was the only casualty in the taking of the bridge. For some reason, the long-faced teen had reached out toward Valentine and tried to take his sidearm. For his attempt, Markham was knocked unconscious and left with a busted lip and bloody nose.

Drake studied the navigator, Owen Pryor, who was frozen with his hands just inches from his console. Pryor was being monitored by Jenkins. Drake and Valentine walked up to the captain's console. Valentine grabbed Page and dragged the commander from the bridge and led him to the security console where Everett was waiting.

"Okay, what's our timeframe?"

"Just need Page to authorize command to you and we are one hundred percent in charge," Everett noted.

Page frowned.

"Alfred, you know us, we are not above torturing you to get you to authorize the change," Jenkins announced. "Once you hand it off, we'll drop you off on the closest satellite and be on our way," Jenkins smiled mischievously.

It took Captain Alfred Page less than five minutes to authorize the *Indomitable* to Christian Drake and his unintentional space pirates.

"Take the five to the brig. No physical harm." Drake smiled. He looked at Alfred Page. "Thank you for your understanding."

Six mutineers had taken over the three story *Indomitable*.

"What next?"

Drake stood in front of the captain's chair. Murray was seated at the console of the captain's assistant. Young was now the health officer. Valentine had taken the navigator's position, with Everett and Jenkins as security officers.

"Well, you were right," Jenkins stated. "They were more than willing to submit "

"I thought it would be harder," Murray laughed waving her pistol in the air.

"It will get harder. But right now," Drake pointed out reflectively, "this is the easy part. Again, most of the people we will come against are just going through the motions." He paused. "That won't last long."

"So, we need to figure out where to go first before the *Sentinel* and the Galactic Force send in the big guns."

"Valentine, let's head for the non-planet Pluto," Drake smirked. "It seems the perfect place for a bunch of mutineers."

"Why?"

"Because it isn't a planet anymore?" Murray laughed. "Just like all of us. We aren't what we used to be anymore." The laughter faded from her face.

"We're no longer killers working for the faceless... colonizers," Jenkins said with a smile.

"Instead, protecting the unprotected," Drake said.

Everyone quieted down. There were lots of smiles. The assembled looked to Drake.

"We have a short window to celebrate," Drake smiled and gestured to Murray who tapped a few buttons and suddenly the *Indomitable* bridge and interior was bathed in the sounds of Prince's funky party anthem "Hot Thing."

Hot thing, barely twenty one Hot thing, looking for big fun Hot thing, what's your fantasy? Hot thing, do you want to play with me?

"You think we have time for this right now?" Jenkins frowned.

"When we have a win, we should celebrate," Drake chuckled. Murray was swaying to the music. Everett and Young were dancing.

Drake smirked and swayed to the music. He started to dance. "If we can't celebrate then why do it?"

> Hot thing, maybe you should give your folks a call
> Hot thing, tell them you're going to the Crystal Ball
> Hot thing, tell them you're coming home late
> If you're coming home at all

As the song played Drake smiled wider and wider. The *Indomitable* was slowly moving away from Rigo-C and back toward the Milky Way.

Jenkins smiled at Drake. "You are surprising."

"You have no idea," Drake laughed.